T0354348

The *Night* HAWK

The Night HAWK

ROBERT W. CALLIS

iUniverse

THE NIGHT HAWK

Copyright © 2017 Robert W. Callis.

All rights reserved. No part of this book may be used or reproduced by
any means, graphic, electronic, or mechanical, including photocopying,
recording, taping or by any information storage retrieval system
without the written permission of the author except in the case of
brief quotations embodied in critical articles and reviews.

This is a work of fiction. All of the characters, names, incidents,
organizations, and dialogue in this novel are either the products
of the author's imagination or are used fictitiously.

iUniverse books may be ordered through booksellers or by contacting:

iUniverse
1663 Liberty Drive
Bloomington, IN 47403
www.iuniverse.com
1-800-Authors (1-800-288-4677)

Because of the dynamic nature of the Internet, any web addresses or
links contained in this book may have changed since publication and
may no longer be valid. The views expressed in this work are solely those
of the author and do not necessarily reflect the views of the publisher,
and the publisher hereby disclaims any responsibility for them.

Any people depicted in stock imagery provided by Thinkstock are
models, and such images are being used for illustrative purposes only.
Certain stock imagery © Thinkstock.

ISBN: 978-1-5320-2257-9 (sc)
ISBN: 978-1-5320-2258-6 (e)

Library of Congress Control Number: 2017906275

Print information available on the last page.

iUniverse rev. date: 04/20/2017

DEDICATION

This book is dedicated to my long-time good friend, J. Roger Mann. Roger was my college roommate and the inspiration for several of the characters who have appeared in my books. No one was a harder worker or a better friend. Rest in peace, Roger.

PROLOGUE

One of America's greatest western artists was Charles M. Russell. In his lifetime, he created more than four thousand works of art including paintings, drawings, and sculptures. As a boy, Russell had been so troublesome his parents sent him from their home in St. Louis Missouri, to his uncle, who ran a sheep ranch in Montana. Russell hated the sheep ranch and took up with a hunter and trapper and spent two years living up in the mountains, learning hunting and trapping. It was during this time he began to draw the scenes of nature he saw before him.

Russell began work on a large cattle ranch as a horse wrangler and gradually worked his way up to the positon of night herder. These cowboys rode guard on the large cattle herds at night, keeping the cattle safe and quiet. They referred to themselves as "night hawks." After a year living with the Blood Indians, Russell moved to Great Falls, Montana. There he tried his hand at making a living as an artist.

Russell never forgot his old friends and kept in touch with letters. His letters were often adorned with water color paintings of scenes of western life. Today those letters are considered works of art. An original Russell letter with water color illustrations will bring north of one hundred thousand dollars in most art auctions. This is the story of one of those letters.

PROLOGUE

CHAPTER ONE

Kit eased his way down the old metal staircase, trying to make as little noise as possible. When he reached the main floor of the old bank building that was now his home, he made his way to the coffee maker. Kit was in the process of renovating the old bank building into a combination of home and office. He poured water into the coffee maker, added coffee from a tin and hit the power on button to start the brewing process.

While Kit waited for the coffee to brew, he looked around the main floor of his new home. It had been almost two months since his father had made him a gift of the old bank building. Kit and Swifty, along with several other local men had transformed the second floor into a large apartment. The apartment was almost done, but there was still a lot of work to do with the rest of the building.

Kit had decided to leave the small teller line alone for the time being. Swifty had pointed out it would make one hell of a bar, so Kit had spared it for the time being. The old bank president's office had been transformed and now boasted high tech phone and wireless services along with monitoring devices for all the entrances to the building. They still had to finish the rest of the first floor, and Kit needed to finish installing an indoor shooting range in the basement. The old drive-in was to be enclosed and converted to a large garage and storage area.

Kit glanced over at the teller line. Upon the wall behind the line was the sign his father had made for him. It was a large wooden sign painted green with white letters. The letters spelled out, "Rocky Mountain Searchers, Kemmerer, Wyoming."

Kit had the same name painted on the glass of the large double doors that made up the entrance to the building. The coffee maker beeped to let Kit know the coffee was ready. He filled a large coffee cup and added creamer and sugar. After stirring the coffee, Kit took his cup and headed for his office.

As he walked into the walnut paneled office, Kit could not help but smile. Kit had salvaged the large, old walnut desk from the bank's original furnishings, along with the ornate leather office chair behind it, but he did not care for the other furnishings. Kit was waiting for furniture he had ordered in Salt Lake City. In front of the desk were two metal folding chairs Swifty had rescued from the dumpster. The chairs were fine except for a few dents and scratches.

Kit checked his messages on his iPad and made notes on which ones he needed to answer. Then Kit checked his phone messages. There were not many, as he had been spending almost every day for two months working in the building and had rarely left town.

Yesterday, Kit had made a rare trip to Salt Lake City. Shirley Townsend, the nurse he had first met when he had been wounded, had managed to swing a long week-end from her job as a nurse at the Boulder Community Hospital in Boulder, Colorado. He had driven to Salt Lake City the previous afternoon to pick her up at the Salt Lake City airport. She had arrived at seven-thirty that evening, and they had stopped in the city to have dinner before returning to Kemmerer. By the time they got back to Kit's place it was almost midnight, and they were both tired and were immediately asleep.

Kit was trying to be quiet and let Shirley get some well-deserved sleep. He had finished listening to his messages and was in the middle of taking a drink of his hot coffee when Swifty burst into his office.

Swifty was Kit's best friend. The former Delta Force veteran was a cowboy through and through. He was tall and rangy like Kit, but his brown eyes sparkled with mischief and his curly brown hair seemed to have a mind of its own. Swifty was a man who liked a good time and was afraid of nothing. Kit and Swifty trusted each other to a level that few men achieve. They made a good, if contrasting pair of friends.

"Well, where the hell is she?" asked Swifty in a loud voice. Kit immediately put his finger to his lips to let Swifty know to keep quiet.

"What the hell is the finger and lips business? I haven't seen this broad since she was patching you up in the Wind River Mountains where that polecat tried to waste you."

"Keep it down, you moron. She's still asleep upstairs," replied Kit.

"Oops, my bad," said Swifty as he then burst out laughing.

"What's so funny?" said Kit.

"She ain't been here ten hours, and already she's in charge, you wuss," said a still chuckling Swifty. Kit's face got red, and then he relaxed. This was just Swifty being Swifty.

"Are you ready to get some work done, Swifty? It looks to me like very little happened after I left yesterday afternoon," said Kit.

"Me and the electrician finished the wiring on the first floor and the plumber got the main floor bathroom done. It's ready to tile and paint," retorted Swifty.

"I heard you tell me what the electrician and the plumber did, but just what was your part in those projects?" asked Kit.

"Well, hell, Kit, somebody has to supervise when you're not around," said Swifty with a sly smile.

"You said the main floor bathroom was ready to tile and paint. Why are you still standing in front of me?" asked Kit.

"I'm gonna have me a cup of that coffee, Mr. Slave Driver, and then I'll get to work on the bathroom," said Swifty as he retreated from Kit's office and quickly returned with a fresh cup of coffee.

Swifty sat on one of the metal folding chairs. "I know you're a cheapskate, Andrews, but when are you gonna replace these lousy chairs. They ain't fit for man nor beast," said Swifty.

Before Kit could reply to Swifty's implied insult, the phone on Kit's desk rang.

Kit picked up the phone and held up one finger to try to silence Swifty while he answered the call. Swifty just smiled and sat back on his folding chair and waited for Kit to end the call.

Kit had no sooner ended the call and placed the receiver back on the phone cradle when Swifty asked, "Who the hell was that?"

Kit looked at his old friend with a face that bordered on disgust. "Not that it's any of your business, that was Alice Cleary, Woody Harrison's assistant. She said some lady was in and wanted to know where to find me. Alice called to see if it was all right to send her over here."

"Probably one of your old girl friends, lookin' to collect on some promise you made her in a moment of weakness," said Swifty with a big grin on his face.

"You said you still had work to do. Why are you still sitting in my office?" asked Kit.

"I can take a hint, Mr. Big Shot. I'm off to perform my magic on the main floor bathroom."

With his smart-ass remark hanging in the air, Swifty rose from his chair and slid out the office door in what seemed like one continuous motion.

Kit just shook his head at his old friend's antics and took another drink of his coffee. Then he pulled out his construction file on the building and studied his checklist. The list was five pages long and items checked off to date ended a fourth of the way down the second page. "There is still a great deal of work left to do," thought Kit.

CHAPTER TWO

Kit's thought process was interrupted by the sound of the front door of the building being opened and closed. He looked up from his desk and out the large glass window separating his office from the main floor of the building. What he saw caused his stomach to constrict and his breath to almost come to a halt.

Standing in the middle of the entry way to the building was none other than Mustang Kelly. When Kit first met her, she was running her late father's garage in Kemmerer. She had taken his old Chevrolet Cavalier in trade for the 1949 GMC ¾ ton pickup when he first came to Kemmerer. He still owned the truck. Kit and Tang Kelly had become friends and then very close friends. Tang had sold the garage and gone back to her old job as assistant curator at the Field Museum in Chicago.

Kit quickly rose to his feet and moved to the door of his office. "Is that you, Tang?" said Kit, knowing full well that it was, but being stumped for what else to say.

Mustang "Tang" Kelly was dressed in grey slacks with a green silk blouse. Her blouse drew attention to her flashing green eyes and her bright red hair. Ms. Kelly was a very attractive woman, and she dressed like she knew it.

Part of the reason for her return to Chicago was her ability to pay off her deceased father's debts thanks to a generous loan made to her by Kit. She had made regular payments to Kit, and now the loan was paid in full.

"My, my," said Tang. "Look who has gone and bought himself an old bank building."

"It was a gift from my father," said Kit in a somewhat strained voice as he tried to recover from the shock of seeing Tang standing in front of him.

"I know that," said Tang. "I'm just pulling your chain, tenderfoot."

Not getting any response from a suddenly wooden Kit, Tang said, "Well, do I get a hug or at least a handshake, Mr. Andrews?"

Kit came out of his momentary confusion and stepped forward and hugged Tang. She looked good, she felt good, and she smelled good.

"That's better, greenhorn. I see you've been busy with this place," said Tang as she looked around the interior of the old bank building.

"I have," said Kit. "Would you like a cup of coffee?"

"I certainly would. The past four days have been long, and I'm tired of flying and driving all over creation and getting nothing done."

"Please go in my office and have a seat. I'll be right in with your coffee. You still take it black?" asked Kit.

"Black and strong, Kit," said Tang.

Kit returned to the office with a fresh cup of coffee, and Tang took it from him without a word.

"Sorry about the chairs," said Kit. "I ordered new ones, but they're not here yet."

"Not a problem," said Tang. "I've sat in worse."

Kit returned to his desk and sat down in the big office chair. "What brings you back to Kemmerer, Tang? Did you come back to see your mom?"

"I did see her and in fact I'm staying with her, but that's not the reason I'm here."

"So, what's the reason for the visit?" asked Kit.

Tang's face took on a serious look, and her skin color seemed to darken.

"I'm afraid something has happened to my grandfather," said Tang.

"I don't seem to remember him. Did he live around Kemmerer?" asked Kit.

"No, he never lived here. He's always been kind of a hermit. I actually haven't seen him for many years," said Tang.

"So why do you think something's happened to him?" asked Kit.

"He always sends me a birthday card, and this year I didn't get one."

"Has that ever happen before?" asked Kit.

"He has never missed a birthday, never," said Tang with obvious emphasis on the word never.

"Have you tried to contact law enforcement where he lives to check up on him?" asked Kit.

"Of course, I have. They were no help at all. Calling them was a waste of time," said Tang.

"Why do you say that?" asked Kit.

"Let me explain the circumstances, Kit. My grandfather has a cabin off the grid somewhere in the mountains in southeast Wyoming. He occasionally comes into town to pick up his mail from his post office box and to buy some supplies. This might happen once a month."

"What town is that, Tang?" asked Kit.

"A small town called Woods Landing. There are less than one hundred people living there. It's in a mountain valley in the middle of an old mining district where they used to mine for copper and gold. All the mines have been closed for years. The only law enforcement is the Sheriff's office in Laramie, and they had no idea who my grandfather was, let alone where he lived," said Tang.

"Have you been to Woods Landing?" asked Kit.

"I just got back from driving a rental car down there. I'd have been better off with a four-wheel drive pickup. The roads there are roads in name only."

"Did you talk to any of the people there about your grandfather?" asked Kit.

"I did. I talked to the people at the post office and the general store. That and a small café are about all there is to the town, Kit."

"Were they any help?"

"Not really. They remembered an old timer coming to town to pick up his mail and to buy supplies. He would cash his government pension check and social security check at the store, and then would then buy supplies. It didn't sound like he was in town more than half an hour at a time. He never spoke to anyone except to ask for something. Most of the time he just brought his supplies to the counter and handed them his checks."

Kit found himself taking notes on a yellow legal pad as he listened to Tang. He looked up and saw Tang was close to tears. Tears from Tang were something he could not imagine. He had never seen her cry.

"What's your grandfather's name?" asked Kit.

"His name is Theodore Kelly, but he went by Ted," said Tang.

"Do you have a picture of him?" asked Kit.

"No I don't," said a now sniffling Tang.

Without saying a word, Kit grabbed a box of tissues from his desk and handed it to Tang. She took the box, pulled out a tissue, and dabbed at her now damp green eyes.

"Can you give me a physical description of your grandfather?" asked Kit.

Apparently, that was the wrong question to ask as Tang began to weep and sob.

Kit felt helpless. This was one of those situations where he had no skillset. All he could think of were those scenes from movies where someone patted the crying person on the back and kept saying, "There, there." It always looked contrived and stupid to Kit, but it left him with nothing helpful to say to Tang.

When Tang finally stopped weeping, and regained her composure, she took a final dab at her eyes with a fresh tissue and looked up at Kit.

"I'm sorry," she said.

"Why can't you tell me what your grandfather looks like?" asked Kit carefully.

Tang paused, as if to take a deep breath and gain control of her emotions. Finally, she looked up at Kit. "I haven't seen my grandfather since I was twelve years old. My family had stopped to visit him in a cabin up in the Bridger Wilderness west of Commissary Ridge. He told us he was moving, and he would be in touch. After that, all I ever got were birthday cards."

"Do you remember where the cards were postmarked?" asked Kit.

"They were all postmarked from Woods Landing, Wyoming."

"Did he write anything on the birthday cards?" asked Kit.

"He just signed his name as Grandpa Ted."

11

"How did he get to town? Did he walk, ride a horse, drive a vehicle?" asked Kit.

"He drove a really old vehicle. The owner of the general store often helped him load supplies and she remembered that Grandpa Ted drove a 1952 Dodge Power Wagon. She said it looked like an old Jeep on steroids."

"Did the vehicle have license plates?" asked Kit.

"The store owner didn't mention any, and I didn't think to ask," replied Tang.

"What color was this old Dodge?"

"I think the paint was pretty faded and unremarkable, because the store owner couldn't remember it," said Tang.

"Did anyone in Woods Landing give you a description of your grandfather?" asked Kit.

"I don't think anyone paid him any attention," said Tang. "The owner of the general store remembered him as old, medium height, white hair with a full beard. He was dressed in old denim work clothes and a beat-up cowboy hat. She did mention Grandpa Ted was wearing what looked like new work boots. She noticed them because everything else Grandpa Ted wore looked old and worn."

Kit put down his pen and looked at Tang. She had regained her composure and she again looked like the tough, smart, and confident woman he had known since he first met her in Kemmerer.

"Is there anything else you can remember about your grandfather that might be helpful in locating him?" asked Kit.

Tang sat quietly in front of Kit, apparently deep in thought. Kit let her think and did not say anything, waiting for her to come to her own conclusions.

After a few minutes, Tang's face suddenly brightened and she looked up at Kit.

"There is this one thing I remember. I guess it was the artifact hunter in me at a young age," said Tang.

"What was it?" asked Kit as he picked up his pen.

"My grandfather's cabin I visited was small and sparse. I remember there was almost no color in the cabin as everything was drab. The exception was the letters he had framed and hung on the walls of the cabin."

"What kind of letters?' asked Kit?

"There were several of them on the walls. I think there were five or six of them. They were letters that a western artist named Charles M. Russell had sent to my great-grandfather. They had been good friends years ago, when they were young and working as cowboys on a big cattle ranch in Montana."

"Why did he have these letters from Mr. Russell framed?" asked Kit.

"Charles Russell was a western artist. He would paint western scenes on the letters with water colors to illustrate them. They were like tiny works of art. My grandfather was very proud of them, especially one letter."

"Why was that?" asked Kit.

"One of the letters to my great-grandfather talked about their days together as night hawks on the cattle ranch. The picture Russell painted on the letter was a night hawk cowboy on horseback wearing a long yellow slicker. Grandpa Tom told me that was his favorite of the letters, because he thought the night hawk in the painting was my great-grandfather. He called it the "Night Hawk" letter."

Kit looked up from his note pad. "Is there anything else you can remember about your grandfather, Tang?" he asked.

"I remember he was pretty short, even to me when I was twelve," said Tang. "I wish I could remember more. I'm sorry I can't."

"You've told me a lot, Tang," said Kit. "What exactly do you want me to do?"

Tang looked directly at Kit. Her green eyes were flashing now. "I want you to find out what has happened to my grandfather, Kit. I need your help. I can't stay here much longer. I must get back to Chicago and my job. I need you to do what I can't do," said Tang.

"I'll do my best, Tang," said Kit.

"I know you will, Kit. That's why I'm here," said Tag. She reached in her purse and pulled out a business card. "This has all my contact information. Please keep me informed of your progress. I don't expect you to do this for nothing, but I'm pretty sure my credit is good with you," Tang said as she got to her feet.

"You know it is, Tang," said Kit as he also got to his feet.

Tang stood in front of her chair as if waiting for Kit to come forward and put his arms around her.

Before Kit could move around the desk, there was a knock on the wooden frame of the office door.

Both Kit and Tang looked back at the open doorway. Standing there was Shirley Townsend.

Shirley was dressed in a blue western shirt and jeans with her blonde hair pulled back in a ponytail. Her bright blue eyes were intense as she took in the sight of Tang standing in the middle of Kit's office.

"I'm sorry, Kit. I didn't realize you had company," said Shirley. Kit instantly got the feeling she wasn't one bit sorry for her interruption. But he was a guy. What did he know?

Kit saw that both women were intensely checking each other out while pretending to be disinterested. "Oh, crap," thought Kit. "This can't be good."

Later Kit would swear to Swifty it was like one of those awkward moments where it felt like all the oxygen in the room had been sucked out and the temperature suddenly dropped by about thirty degrees.

The awkward moment was broken by Tang. "Where are your manners, Kit? Aren't you going to introduce me to your friend?" asked Tang in a strong and almost too loud voice.

Tang's loud voice knocked Kit out of his temporary state of shock.

Kit immediately stepped away from Tang and towards Shirley. "Tang, I'd like you to meet my friend Shirley Townsend. Shirley's a nurse from Boulder, Colorado."

Kit then turned back to Tang and said, "Shirley, this is Mustang Kelly, better known as Tang. She's an old friend who used to live in Kemmerer. She's here as a client and a friend."

Both women stepped forward and shook hands as briefly as possible, and their eye contact was anything but warm.

Kit was stumped for what to say next, but Tang bailed him out.

"I really must be going," she said. "You have my card, Kit. Please keep me informed of any progress you might make." Her words were normal, but they came out like they were encased in ice.

Tang strode past both Kit and Shirley and was quickly out the front door and disappeared from sight.

Shirley turned and looked at Kit. She had her arms folded in front of her. Kit knew that was not a good sign.

"So just how old a friend is this Ms. Kelly?" asked Shirley.

"Have a seat while I get you a cup of coffee, and I'll tell you all about Tang," said Kit. Shirley nodded and sat down on one of the folding chairs. Kit hurried to the coffee maker trying to use this time to come up with something safe to tell Shirley.

When Kit returned to the office with a fresh cup of coffee, he handed it to Shirley. She looked at the coffee and then at Kit.

"You added cream," she said. "I'm glad you remembered."

Kit took a deep breath and took a drink of coffee from his cup.

Then Kit sat back in his chair and proceeded to tell Shirley about how he came to Kemmerer, traded his car to Tang for the old GMC pickup and how he discovered that she was raiding an Indian burial ground for artifacts.

"So, you caught her stealing from an Indian burial ground?" said Shirley.

"Yes, I did. She was trying to pay off her deceased father's debts so she could get back to Chicago. I made her a deal and loaned her the money she needed. She went back to Chicago, got her old job back as an assistant curator at the Field Museum, and since then she paid me back all the money she borrowed. I haven't seen her since I stopped in the Field Museum a few years ago, when I was in Chicago."

"So why was she here in your office this morning?" asked Shirley. Her voice had softened and Kit got the feeling that the tension of the morning was being dialed down.

"She was here on business. She asked to hire me for a search assignment."

"What kind of assignment?" asked Shirley

"She's lost touch with her grandfather, and she's been unable to locate him. She is worried about him and asked me to find him. She flew out here to try to locate him and had no luck. She has to get back to her job in Chicago, so she is hiring me to do what she can't," replied Kit.

"I know this is really none of my business," said Shirley. "Why doesn't she know where her grandfather is?"

Kit then told Shirley about the distant relationship and the birthday cards and why Tang was upset.

"I guess I understand, but it seems really strange to me she has not seen her grandfather since she was twelve," said Shirley.

"Families can be strange," said Kit. "Mine is no exception. My mother and father divorced when I was very young. My mother told me my father was dead, and I believed her. I wound up in Kemmerer by accident and found out my father was not dead, but alive and living here, of all places."

"I guess you're right about that," said Shirley.

"Are you hungry?" asked Kit.

"I'm famished," replied Shirley with a wry smile on her face.

"Let me close up, and we'll go over to the cafe," said Kit.

"Not so fast, Cowboy. Just how good of friends were you and Miss Mustang?" asked an unsmiling Shirley.

"We were just good friends while she was here in Kemmerer," said Kit.

"Did something happen outside of Kemmerer, like say, Chicago?" asked Shirley, still not smiling.

Kit took a deep breath and looked straight into Shirley's bright blue eyes.

"I stayed overnight with her at her apartment in Chicago when I stopped to see her on my way to my relative's farm in Altona," said Kit.

Shirley's hard gaze held, and then began to soften. "I'm still famished. Just how far is this café?"

"You're not mad?" asked Kit.

"Of course, I'm mad. I dislike competition. But I wanted to see if you would tell me the truth or lie to me like most men. You never cease to amaze me, Kit. You are probably the most honest man I ever met," said Shirley.

"Is that a bad thing?" asked Kit.

"It depends on the situation," said Shirley. "There may be times when I want you to lie to me," she said.

"What kind of times would those be?" asked Kit.

"You're pushing your luck here, Cowboy," said Shirley. She turned to go out the office door and then she stopped and turned back to Kit.

"I don't mind being lied to when you tell me how gorgeous and wonderful I am. I give you a free ride to do that anytime," she said, as she flashed her perfect teeth in a big smile.

"Come on, Cowboy, you need to feed me," Shirley said with a laugh.

She turned and walked toward the front door of the building, and Kit hurried to beat her there so he could open it for her.

CHAPTER THREE

Kit led the way across the triangle park to Irma's Café. The triangle park served as the center of Kemmerer's small business district. Kit held open the door and followed Shirley into the small café that exuded the smell of bacon, eggs, and potatoes in various stages of preparation. The café was almost full of customers with not an empty table or booth in sight. As he was looking, Kit saw a large hand extended from a booth in the front of the café up next to the picture window. The hand went down, and a giant Viking with a cowboy hat stood up and waved Kit over to the booth.

Big Dave Carlson's blue eyes lit up when he saw Shirley with Kit. When Kit and Shirley reached his booth, he gave her a big hug and escorted her to the seat opposite his in the booth. Kit slid in beside Shirley.

"The prestige of the town of Kemmerer just went up about fifty percent by having you here, Shirley," said Big Dave. "How did this worthless cowboy manage to pry you out of Boulder and get you to come up to our fair city?"

"He invited me and since I had nothing better to do, I accepted," said a smiling Shirley.

"I ain't sure it's possible, Miss Shirley, but I'll be damned if you ain't somehow got better lookin' than the last time I seen

19

you. Course, that was under kinda extreme circumstances what with Kit getting' hisself shot up and all," said Big Dave.

"Compliments from you are always appreciated, Big Dave," said Shirley.

"You know I only give 'em when they're well deserved," said Big Dave.

"So, how long are you here for?" asked Big Dave.

"I flew into Salt Lake City last night and will be flying out on Monday afternoon," replied Shirley.

"I suppose Kit here has got your social calendar all filled up for your time here," said Big Dave.

"I think so, but he hasn't really given me any details," said Shirley. "He did start this morning off with a bit of a surprise."

"What kind of surprise," said a grinning Big Dave with a pronounced twinkle in his eyes.

"I got introduced to an old flame of his after I found the two of them in his office," said Shirley with emphasis on the words old flame.

"Who the hell would that be?" asked Big Dave. "Kit ain't got no flames I'm aware of, let alone an old flame."

"Are you acquainted with a woman named Mustang Kelly?" asked Shirley.

"You mean old Tang?" said Big Dave.

"That's the one," said Shirley.

"Hell, I ain't seen hide nor hair of her for a couple of years. She left Kemmerer to go to Chicago, and best I know she never came back."

"Well, she was in town this morning and had a meeting with Kit less than half an hour ago," said Shirley.

"Goddamn! Two gorgeous young women in Kemmerer at the same time and I missed it. I must be getting' old," said Big Dave.

"Hey, I'm sitting right here, guys," said Kit who had started to feel like a third wheel in this conversation.

Both Shirley and Big Dave ignored Kit and continued with their conversation.

"Now why would Tang be havin' a meetin' with Kit?" asked Big Dave.

"She claims that her grandfather is missing and she flew out here to find him. She was unsuccessful and had to get back to Chicago, so she hired Kit," replied Shirley.

"I don't recall no grandfather bein' around here," said Big Dave. "I knew her pa. Her ma still lives here in Kemmerer."

"You'd have to ask Kit about that," said Shirley.

Big Dave turned and looked at Kit.

"Her grandpa never lived around Kemmerer. Apparently, he is kind of a hermit and lives in a cabin somewhere in the mountains in southeast Wyoming," said Kit to the unasked question.

"Does Tang know where in southeast Wyoming? This is a pretty big state," said Big Dave with a smile in his eyes.

"She got birthday cards from Woods Landing, Wyoming, so I think his cabin must be somewhere around there," said Kit.

"Woods Landing," said Big Dave. "I ain't been down there in years. They used to have a big dance hall there. The floor had these big springs under it so the floor would give when you were dancin'."

"When were you dancing in Woods Landing?" asked Kit.

"Long before your tenderfoot butt arrived in Kemmerer," replied Big Dave.

"Why is it named Woods Landing?" asked Shirley

"Feller named Woods established it about thirty miles east of Laramie on the Big Laramie River. He had a couple of sawmills there and mainly cut wooden ties for the Union Pacific Railroad," said Big Dave.

"Are the sawmills still there?" asked Kit.

"Naw, they were torn down years ago. As I recollect the only things left are a general store and post office and a small café. There used to be a small resort there and I think there might be a few cabins left, but that's about it," said Big Dave.

"Just where is Woods Landing in connection with the mountains?" asked Kit.

"There are mountains to the north, the west and the south," said Big Dave.

"This is beginning to sound like I might be looking for a needle in a haystack," said Kit.

"If it were me lookin', I'd try south. The Big Laramie River turns south at Woods Landing. I'd follow that drainage and talk to the ranchers located along the river. If some old coot has a place in the mountains off the grid, he's likely got to cross somebody's ranch land to cross the river and get access to the road to Woods Landing," said Big Dave.

"Got room for one more?"

Kit, Big Dave, and Shirley looked up at the short, older man standing at the end of their booth. He was well dressed and looked amazingly like Teddy Roosevelt.

The man stepped forward and gave Shirley a little bow. "Woodrow Harrison, Miss. I don't believe I've had the pleasure of an introduction, but I assume you are Miss Shirley Townsend. If I am correct, then I must extend my sincere thanks for your medical assistance to my friend Kit Andrews up in the Wind River Mountains. My friends call me Woody, and I would be pleased if you did the same."

Kit grinned at Shirley's surprise. She placed her hand in Woody's extended hand and smiled as he took it to his lips and kissed it. Without another word, Woody slid into the booth next to Big Dave.

The waitress magically arrived and took everyone's order. She returned shortly with steaming cups of coffee for Kit, Shirley, and Woody.

"So, what was the topic of the intense conversation I so rudely interrupted?" asked Woody.

"Tang Kelly came to my office this morning to ask me to try to locate her missing grandfather," said Kit.

"I never met the man, but Tang's mother has mentioned him to me," said Woody. "Why does he need to be located?"

Kit went on to explain what Tang had told him about her grandfather and Woody listened quietly and attentively until Kit mentioned the framed letters from Charles Russell to Tang's great-grandfather.

"Oh my," interrupted Woody. "I assume we are talking about Charles Marion Russell, the world-famous cowboy artist from Great Falls, Montana?"

"She said he was a famous cowboy artist," said Kit.

"Russell and Remington are probably the two most famous western artists in American history," said Woody. "If she is talking about original illustrated letters from Russell, she is talking about big money."

"Big money for old letters?" asked Kit.

"I assume you have not yet visited the Buffalo Bill Museum in Cody, Wyoming, Kit," said Woody.

"I can't say that I have," replied Kit.

"It should be on your must do list, my boy. The sooner, the better."

"Why?" asked Kit.

"The museum is one of the true treasures of western history and art. It has five distinct wings. One of them is western art and it includes works from almost all famous western artists. Much of the wing contains works from Russell and Remington. Remington's studio was moved from New

York and rebuilt in the museum. Included in the works of Russell are many of his illustrated letters," said Woody.

"Just how much are these letters worth?" asked Shirley.

"It would depend on the letter and the illustration and the auction they were sold at, but most of Russell's illustrated letters usually sell for one hundred thousand dollars or more," said Woody.

"A hundred thousand dollars a letter!" exclaimed Big Dave.

"That is correct," said Woody.

"So, you're saying this old hermit is living in some cabin off the grid with over half a million dollars in art work hanging on the cabin walls," said Kit.

"If Ted Kelly actually has five or six framed Russell illustrated letters, that is exactly what I am saying," said Woody.

"Holy shit," said Big Dave

"That adds a whole different dimension to his possible disappearance," said Kit.

"Are you thinking that his disappearance may have to do with the theft of those letters?" asked Woody.

"I don't believe in coincidences," said Kit.

"Neither do I, Kit, but there would be a big problem for the thieves of any Russell works of art," said Woody.

"What do you mean?" asked Kit.

"A thief could never sell a Russell work without going through a credible art auction house and they would use a certified appraiser and he would need to verify ownership. Without that, the letters would appear to be copies and not worth a great deal of money."

"So how would a thief get rid of a Russell piece?" asked Kit.

"He'd have to deal with a fence of some sort," said Woody.

"What the hell is a fence?" asked Big Dave.

"A fence is a criminal who has a legitimate business as a front who takes in stolen goods and resells them. In this case, it would be an art dealer who is crooked. He would sell the piece to a private collector who would ask no questions as to prior ownership and be happy to own the piece. People like that keep stolen works of art in vaults or private rooms where only they have access," explained Woody.

"What the hell is the fun in that?" asked Big Dave.

"They are enthralled with the idea they own something no one else has and they revel in the fact that only they can see it," replied Woody.

"Sounds like some sort of fruitcake to me," said Big Dave.

"They are fruitcakes, but unfortunately the world is full of them. They have money and want what they want and they pay little attention to such impediments as the law," replied Woody.

Kit had remained silent during the exchange between Woody and Big Dave.

"You've been awfully quiet, Kit. What are you thinking about?" asked Shirley.

"I'm thinking that I may have gotten into something that may be over my head," replied Kit.

"I don't think so, Kit," said Woody. "Find Mr. Kelly or the letters and you will find a trail that leads you to the other."

"You are probably right, Woody, but I have a bad feeling that I'm probably looking for a dead man. If Mr. Kelly was robbed, then why has his granddaughter not heard from him? She said she had no luck checking with law enforcement in Laramie."

"That's a good place to start your search," said Big Dave. "When are you plannin' to start?"

"I'm not sure. I need to do some research and set up a plan. Then I need to get my gear together. I don't plan to do anything until after Shirley goes back to Boulder."

"Does that mean I'm more important to you than your friend Mustang Kelly?" asked Shirley. The word friend came out with special sarcastic emphasis.

Kit knew this was a trick question. Kind of like answering the question does this dress make me look fat. He paused for a few seconds.

Shirley arched her eyebrows and looked expectantly at Kit.

"Right now, nobody means more to me than you do, Shirley," said Kit.

Silently, all the men at the table breathed a silent sigh of relief.

Kit's luck held, for at that moment the waitress arrived with their breakfasts.

CHAPTER FOUR

Two hours later, Kit had Shirley in his pickup truck headed out of Kemmerer. He took the route out of town paralleling the Ham's Fork River.

"So where are you taking me?" asked Shirley.

"We're headed up the Ham's Fork drainage," said Kit. "The Ham's Fork is the river that runs through Kemmerer. It got its name from a member of Ashley's fur trappers. Guy's name was Ham, and he was the one that found the river."

"I thought today I'd take you on a trip up the drainage to the source of the river. The river is what gave the town life, although coal is the reason there is a town. That and the Union Pacific Short Line Railroad."

Kit continued with his background story for Shirley.

"A surveyor for the Union Pacific named Quealy found outcroppings of coal when he was surveying a route for the Short Line. The Short Line was a spur line that ran to Oregon instead of California. Quealy went to Chicago and met with a mining magnate named Mahlon Kemmerer from Pennsylvania. Together they formed a company, bought up the land where Kemmerer stands, and formed the town of Kemmerer," said Kit.

"Did Mr. Kemmerer live in Kemmerer?" asked Shirley.

"I think he visited the town, but I doubt he ever lived here. Quealy was his on-site man," said Kit.

The paved road ended just past the Kemmerer Reservoir and the ride got a little rougher. As they left the reservoir, the vast plains of sagebrush and buffalo grass gave way to land more and more heavily covered with pine trees.

"The Kemmerer Coal Company virtually owned the town and almost everything in it. Miners got paid in script which they could redeem in Kemmerer's stores. That changed when James Cash Penney came to town. He opened the first J.C. Penney store in Kemmerer. Everyone thought he'd fail, but he managed to succeed. The original store is still here and still open. Penney's home was moved and is in the town park. The United Methodist Church is named after his wife who generously supported the church. Penney built a second store out on the flats, but that mining town failed and so did the store," said Kit.

The road had narrowed, and Kit slowed the speed of his truck to maneuver around pot holes, to keep the ride as smooth as possible. It was now obvious they were driving up a narrow valley with the surrounding hills, getting higher as they drove.

"This area was settled by homesteaders, and they were here before the town existed. One of those homesteads is right up ahead on the left side of the road. If you look at the side of that hill where that grove of trees is located, you might be able to see the ruins of a cabin," said Kit.

Kit brought the truck to a stop and handed Shirley a pair of binoculars. Shirley took the binoculars and adjusted them until she had them properly focused.

"I can see the ruins!" said Shirley excitedly.

"Those are the remains of Big Dave's grandfather's homestead cabin," said Kit.

"Really!" said Shirley as she continued to glass over the area around the ruins.

"Ready to move on?" asked Kit.

"Yes," replied Shirley.

Kit retrieved the binoculars from Shirley and slipped them back into the truck's center console. He put the truck in gear and they headed further up the drainage.

After about thirty minutes of sightseeing, Kit turned off the road at the entrance to a small gravel parking lot. He brought the truck to a stop in the middle of the empty parking lot.

"Look straight across the lot and what do you see?" asked Kit.

Coming out the side of a tall hill was a stream of water. It cascaded down the side of the hill, pausing only briefly on several shelves of rocks which gave the impression of stair steps in the side of the hill. The water splashed over the rocks and down the hill until it entered a large pool of water that began draining immediately down the center of the small valley they had just come through.

"This is Big Spring said Kit. "It's the source of the Ham's Fork River and the primary water source for Kemmerer."

"Wow," said Shirley. "Can I see those binoculars again?"

Kit retrieved the binoculars and handed them to Shirley who promptly scanned the spring and the surrounding wooded hillside.

"Can we hike over to see it up close?" asked Shirley.

"Your wish is my command, fair lady," said Kit with a smile on his face.

Both exited the truck. Kit paused and reached behind his seat for his gun belt and pistol. Kit strapped on the gun belt and moved the holster so it rode properly on his hip.

"Expecting wild Indians, Kit?" asked Shirley with a grin on her face.

"Not unless they're big, furry and have large claws," replied Kit. "You never know what you might run into and I prefer to be prepared. Ready to hike over?"

"Lead on, Cowboy," said Shirley.

They hiked over and up to the spring. Big Spring was even more impressive close up and personal.

"This is gorgeous," said Shirley.

"This is Wyoming," said Kit. "It's gorgeous, but it's also dangerous."

They returned to the truck and soon Kit took them on a side road leading them up to the slope of a large hill.

"What's that sign up ahead of us?" asked Shirley.

"Let's drive up there and find out," replied Kit.

They drove up to the sign. It was an old wooden hand painted sign. The sign read, "Signal here."

"What does signal here mean, Kit?"

"It means this is one of the few places up here where you can get a signal for your cell phone," said Kit with a big grin on his face.

"You're kidding me, right?" said Shirley.

"No, I'm not. The sole purpose of the sign is to help people who need to use a cell phone. Try your phone and see if I'm right."

Shirley got out her cell phone and sure enough, she had three bars for a signal.

Kit put the truck in gear and moved back down the hill about fifty feet. "Try the phone now," he said.

Shirley looked at her phone. It reflected no service.

Kit laughed and headed the truck back down the hill. Half an hour later he turned off on another side road and followed it until it ended in a rough cul-de-sac. He pulled the truck to the end of the cul-de-sac and parked it. Kit and Shirley exited the truck and walked to the front of the truck. They were standing on a small knoll and looked out over miles and miles of plains and mountains. Stretching out before them were hundreds of acres of wild flowers of bright colors. The view was breathtaking.

"See that tall peak in the distance," said Kit. "That's Electric Peak."

"My God this is beautiful, Kit. Thank you for bringing me," said Shirley.

"I wanted to share this with you, Shirley. A good deal of southern Wyoming is high plains desert and while it has its own beauty, it doesn't compare with this," said Kit.

"Hungry?" asked Kit.

"I suddenly feel famished," replied Shirley.

Kit went back to the truck and pulled out an honest to god wicker picnic basket and two folding camp stools. He set up the stools and returned to the truck for a small cooler.

"I thought this would be a good spot for a picnic," said Kit.

He no sooner got the words out of his mouth before Shirley had moved close to him and used her hands to pull his mouth down to hers. The kiss was soft, long, and passionate.

Shirley broke the kiss and whispered in Kit's ear, "I'm still hungry. What's in the basket, Cowboy?"

The basket contained roast beef sandwiches with horseradish sauce, potato salad, potato chips, and two apples, along with plates and plastic silverware. Shirley filled two plates and Kit retrieved two Cokes from the cooler.

Kit and Shirley sat eating their lunch in silence as they looked out over one of Nature's most beautiful scenes in America.

When lunch was finished, Kit gathered up everything and placed it back in the truck. Soon he and Shirley were headed back down the drainage the same way they had come up.

On their way up the drainage, they had seen no other people. Going down the drainage, they met the occasional pick-up truck. Each time they met someone, both parties exchanged waves.

"Everyone seems pretty friendly," said Shirley. "It reminds me of how things are back where I grew up on the western slope of Colorado."

"People out here generally want to be left alone," said Kit. "That doesn't mean they aren't friendly. A person gets in some trouble and there are usually more than a few folks willing to lend a hand. You tend to be more self-reliant when you live in a remote area, and Kemmerer is certainly remote."

"Sometimes remote is not so bad," said Shirley. "I get a little tired of crowds and traffic, living on the front range of Colorado. Boulder used to be smaller, slower, and friendlier. Now it seems to be more and more like Denver."

"I enjoy the advantages of a city, but I like my privacy and value my peace and quiet," said Kit. "I lived in Chicago, and now I live in Kemmerer. I love living in Wyoming."

"Is it true that Jerry Buss, who owned the Los Angeles Lakers grew up in Kemmerer?" asked Shirley

"Mr. Buss lived with his uncle, a local plumber called Old Brownie. Once they had a fight and Old Brownie threw Buss out of the house. It was winter and Buss went to the Post Office which was open twenty-four hours a day, and he slept up on the second-floor hallway. He found an application for a chemical engineering scholarship to the University of Wyoming on a bulletin board. He applied, got the scholarship and after school got a great job in California. Then he got into real estate and made millions and became famous," replied Kit.

"Wow," said Shirley.

"Old Bill Carlisle also lived in Kemmerer," said Kit.

"Who was he?" asked Shirley.

"Carlisle was the last of the train robbers in America," answered Kit.

"So, Kemmerer has had both ends of the famous spectrum," said Shirley.

"You could say that," chuckled Kit.

"Are you going to show me the rest of Kemmerer?" asked Shirley.

"It won't take very long, but I'll show you the few highlights we have," said Kit with a grin on his face.

An hour later, they arrived back at the Kemmerer city limits. They passed through the former town of Frontier, which had been the headquarters for the Kemmerer Coal Company until it was bought out by a subsidiary of Chevron Oil Company.

As they drove slowly through Kemmerer, Kit pointed out several historic sites including the J C Penney store, the old City Hall, and the town museum located in the Triangle Park. He showed her the two cemeteries.

"In the winter, when someone is being buried in the cemetery, flowers are placed on the grave site. You can see moose gathering at the edge of the cemetery waiting for the people to leave so they can lunch on the fresh flowers," said Kit.

When their tour was finished, Kit parked the truck next to the unfinished drive-up/garage.

"Hungry?" asked Kit.

"I'm ashamed to admit it, but I'm famished again," said Shirley. "I'm going to have to work out twice as hard when I get back to Boulder to adjust for all the food I'm eating here."

"You look totally gorgeous to me just the way you are," said Kit.

"Thank you for the compliment, Cowboy," said Shirley as she leaned in to kiss Kit on the lips.

The kiss lingered until Shirley broke away from Kit.

"Where to now, Kit?" asked Shirley

"Let's walk over to Bootleggers for dinner. They serve a mean steak dinner," said Kit.

"Works for me," said Shirley.

They crossed the Triangle Park holding hands.

CHAPTER FIVE

Kit and Shirley spent the next two days visiting sites around Kemmerer, including Kit's father's home and the Carlson home where she met Connie, Big Dave's wife, and Thor, their son. They also visited Skull Point and the Indian burial ground where Kit had discovered Tang stealing artifacts.

Shirley insisted on a tour of the yet unfinished bank building. Kit showed her the two bank vaults on the main floor. One housed records and gear. The second vault contained all kind of guns and ammunition.

Inside the big vault were three gun safes placed next to each other along one wall. Cabinets along the next wall contained dry boxes full of ammunition. Each dry box was labeled with the caliber of the ammunition contained in it. The last cabinet contained materials for loading ammunition. There were containers of shells, bullets, primers, and large plastic jars of powder of various types. Along the third wall was a long reloading and work bench. The bench had shelving behind it that was full of gun cleaning materials, tools, plastic gloves, and hand cleaning supplies, including paper towels. A four-stage reloading press was stationed at one end of the bench.

The vault was well lit with ceiling lights, and the bench contained hand held lamps and a large magnifying glass on a base with a swivel.

"Good lord, Kit, are you expecting World War III?" asked Shirley.

"You can never have enough guns and ammo," said Kit. He was not smiling when he said it. "The world can be a good place, but all too often it has a lot of predators and bad guys running around. This vault insures I'll never be a victim."

"Can you show me some of the guns and explain them to me?" asked Shirley.

"Of course," said Kit. "Over here we have rifles. They consist of bolt-action rifles and semi-automatic rifles."

"What's the difference?" asked Shirley.

"The bolt action rifle requires you to pull the bolt back to eject the cartridge shell of each bullet you have fired through the rifle. A bolt action rifle usually has a clip of between three and five rounds. Let me show you," said Kit. He pulled out a Kimber model 84 bolt action rifle with a telescopic sight. "This one is chambered in .308 caliber. It's a long-range hunting rifle with a Leopold mil dot scope. It's pretty accurate out to about 800 yards," said Kit. Kit worked the bolt and showed Shirley how to load and unload the clip and adjust the scope.

"Wow, this gun is pretty heavy," said Shirley.

"That actually is a good thing," said Kit. "The weight cuts down on the recoil when you shoot the weapon and that makes it easier on your shoulder when you are shooting."

"Good to know," said Shirley. "What's this one?" she asked as she pointed to a black assault rifle.

"This one is an AR-15 semi-automatic rifle chambered in .223 caliber. It's the civilian version of the military M-16. The main difference is that the M-16 has a fully automatic feature. Notice the bullets are smaller than the Kimber in .308. The bullets fit into a magazine. I have both twenty round and thirty round magazines," said Kit. He then showed Shirley how to load and reload the AR-15 and how to pull back on the charger to get a bullet in the chamber of the rifle. He showed her the selector of the left side of the rife that was a safety on the rifle.

"This rifle will fire every time you pull the trigger," said Kit. "Until you run out of bullets," he added with a grin on his face.

Shirley hefted the rifle. "This one is much lighter," she said.

Kit showed her how to turn on and tune the holographic sight on the rifle.

"Wow," she said. "This looks like it would make it pretty hard to miss."

"It's still possible to miss due to distance from the target, cross winds, and humidity," said Kit. "But, under normal circumstances, this sight greatly improves your chance of hitting something you aim at."

Next Kit took her to the pistol section of the vault. "Pistols are broken down into three categories," he said. "A little pistol like this 2 shot derringer is ready to fire each time you pull back on the hammer to cock it and then fires when you pull the trigger. A revolver holds five or six rounds and each time you fire the revolving wheel in the gun turns and allows you to shoot the next round until they are all expended."

Kit then showed Shirley how to load and unload a revolver, using an old Colt Python .357 magnum caliber. He also showed her the difference between single action and double action revolvers.

Then he showed her a Kimber Classic semi-automatic in .45acp caliber as well as a Glock 17 semi-automatic chambered in 9mm. He showed her the difference in the size of the bullets.

"The Kimber is much heavier, but the bullets are much more effective and I personally prefer the .45acp round in the pistols I use," said Kit. "The kinetic energy it delivers on impact has great stopping power."

Kit showed Shirley how to load and unload the weapon and how the Kimber has two safeties, while the Glock has one and it's right in front of the trigger.

Finally, Kit showed Shirley the shotguns. "There are single shot shotguns that you have to cock, but I don't own one," said Kit. "I also don't own a side by side shotgun either. I prefer the over and under." Kit showed her how the barrels were on top of each other and how to load and unload the shotgun.

Kit demonstrated how to hold and aim the shotgun and had Shirley try it.

"This thing is pretty heavy," said Shirley.

"Shotguns are usually in 12 gauge and 20 gauge. The 20 gauge will always be lighter," said Kit. He had Shirley mount a 12 gauge and then a 20 gauge so she could see the difference.

"The 20 gauge is much lighter," said Shirley. "Why would anyone carry the 12 gauge?"

"Most people use a shotgun to hunt birds," said Kit, "but a good 12 gauge is actually the best weapon to safely take down a bear. It can handle a powerful load and a man using slugs is well armed against even a grizzly bear."

"I'm a woman," said Shirley. "What type of gun would be the best for self-defense for a woman like me?"

"For home defense, this would be your best bet," said Kit as he handed Shirley a Remington 870 Defender 12-gauge pump shotgun.

"Why is that?" asked Shirley.

"When something bad happens and you need to use a weapon to defend yourself, a shotgun is the best bet. When something happens, it rarely happens under ideal conditions. It could be dark, it could be partly dark, you might have just woken up and you are a little groggy and maybe you need glasses and you don't have them on. None of those things are conducive to using a hand gun. You would be frightened and your gun hand would be shaking. Those things add up to something less than ideal shooting conditions. The shotgun is the best choice for close quarters."

"What's the difference?" asked Shirley.

"This gun is as reliable as they get. Plus, it has a large magazine. Normally a pump shotgun or even a semi-automatic hold only three to four rounds. This one holds eight rounds. A bonus for you is you don't have to aim it."

"What do you mean, I don't have to aim it?" asked Shirley.

Kit took the shotgun and held it at his hip, with his right hand on the bottom of the barrel and his right hand around the trigger guard and the barrel pointing straight out from him. "All you have to do is point and shoot," said Kit. "Plus, there is a bonus."

"What's the bonus?" asked Shirley.

"When you pull the pump back to eject the empty shell and force a new shell into the chamber, the shotgun makes a mechanical noise that any man on the planet would recognize, even in the dark," said Kit with a smile. "Any crook with half a brain would take off running when they heard that distinctive sound."

"I'd like to try to shoot the Glock and the Remington 870," said Shirley.

"You would?" asked a surprised Kit.

"Do I have to repeat myself?" asked Shirley.

Kit shook his head and grabbed the two guns, some ammo and safety glasses and soundproof ear muffs and led Shirley out of the vault and then down the stairs to the basement. Kit and Swifty were converting the old bank basement into a shooting range twenty-five yards deep. The job was mostly done, but not yet fully complete.

They entered the basement and Kit switched on the lights and a controlled ventilation system. He set up six targets at the end of the range. And then he and Shirley donned safety glasses and hearing protection.

"Do you want me to load the shotgun?" asked Kit.

"Nope," said Shirley. "I can handle it."

She took the shotgun and expertly began loading shells into the magazine. When she was finished, and ready to begin firing, she nodded to Kit.

"The range is hot," said Kit as he stepped back behind Shirley. She stepped up to the firing line, expertly pulled back on the pump and chambered a round in the Remington. Then she shouldered the shotgun and fired downrange at the first target, perforating it with buckshot. She immediately worked the pump, ejecting the spent shell and loading another one. She fired again and perforated the second target.

In rapid succession, Shirley fired, reloaded, and shot until she had perforated all six targets. Then she flicked on the gun's safety and laid it down on the wooden shelf in front of her. Both she and Kit removed their hearing protection ear muffs.

"I guess I forgot to tell you that I grew up on a ranch on the western slope of Colorado and I've been shooting since I was twelve years old," said a smiling Shirley.

"I guess you did," said a shocked Kit. "Are you this good with a rifle and a pistol?"

"I'm best with a shotgun, OK with a rifle and so-so with a pistol," said Shirley.

"So, you were just having a little fun with me?" said Kit.

"I was a little bit, but I did want to see the vaults and all your weapons. You did teach me some things I was not aware of and I'm sure you could teach me a lot more about shooting," said Shirley. "I may be a woman, but I know how to take care of myself."

The two days flashed by and before they knew it, Kit and Shirley were kissing good-bye at the Salt Lake City Airport. Kit pulled away from Shirley and held her at arm's length. "Thank you for coming to visit me, Shirley. This meant a lot to me."

"I wouldn't have missed it for the world," replied Shirley. "Take care of yourself down in Woods Landing."

"I don't think I have much to worry about looking for an old man," said Kit.

"If you find his cabin and those letters are missing, then you might have to change your tune," said Shirley. "Promise me you'll be careful, Kit."

"I promise to be careful, and I'll let you know how the search for Grandpa Ted works out," said Kit with a grin on his face.

"I'll miss you Kit," said Shirley. "Promise me you'll keep in touch."

"Why do you need me to promise that? You know I will," said Kit.

"Because I know unlike most men you always tell the truth and you keep your promises," said Shirley with a smile on her face.

Then Shirley turned and pulled her carry-on bag up to the security station. Kit stood and watched Shirley disappear through the security line, then he made his way back to his truck in the airport parking lot.

As Kit drove back to Kemmerer, he began to think about the job that lay ahead of him. He made a mental checklist of things he needed to look up and find so he could formulate a plan to locate Tang's missing grandfather.

When Kit arrived home, he found himself too restless to sleep, so he opened his computer and began to research the area around Woods Landing.

As he found items of interest, he printed out copies. He also ordered a good topographical map of the area on the internet. When he looked up at the clock on the wall in his office, he was surprised to find he had spent almost four hours on the computer. He shut the computer down, turned off the lights, and made his way upstairs to his apartment. He was fast asleep ten minutes after his head hit his pillow.

Early Tuesday morning found Kit in his office with a cup of coffee in one hand and computer print-outs in the other.

It wasn't long before Swifty slipped into the office and planted himself on one of the metal folding chairs. He too had a cup of coffee in his hand.

"Well, good morning, Sunshine. I see you survived your week-end bout with the ladies," said Swifty.

"Ladies?" said Kit.

"Well, I ain't sure what the hell you call them, but to poor old me Miss Tang and Miss Shirley look to qualify as ladies, especially in good old Kemmerer."

"You never cease to amaze me, Swifty," said Kit.

"I was born amazin'," said a grinning Swifty.

"I'll make a note of that so I can have it inscribed on your tombstone," retorted Kit.

"While you're makin' them notes, be sure to include me in your will cause I'm pretty damn sure I'll outlive your sorry ass," said Swifty.

"The way you live, you'll be lucky to see fifty," said Kit.

"At least I will have lived a full life, you sorry excuse for a cowboy," replied Swifty.

"So?" asked Swifty after the ensuing silence from Kit.

"So what?" asked Kit.

"What happened with the ladies?"

"Tang's gone back to Chicago, and Shirley flew back to Boulder. Satisfied?" said Kit.

"That's all you got to say?" asked Swifty.

"Tang came to see me about a search job," said Kit.

"A search job. Why the hell didn't you tell me that up front?" asked a surprised Swifty.

"You were so busy yukking it up, I didn't have a chance to get a word in edgewise," said Kit.

"Okay, okay, what's the job?" asked Swifty.

"You ever hear of a place called Woods Landing down in southeast Wyoming?" asked Kit.

"Can't say I ever heard of it," replied Swifty.

Kit proceeded to tell Swifty the story about Tang's grandpa Ted Kelly and her fears about his possible disappearance.

When Kit had finished his story, Swifty got up without a word and walked out of Kit's office.

"Where the hell are you going?" asked Kit.

"I'm getting a fresh cup of coffee. Something tells me this is a job that calls for a lot of caffeine," retorted Swifty.

Kit just shook his head and waited for Swifty to return.

Swifty returned with his fresh cup of coffee and again planted himself down in the metal folding chair.

"If I have to sit here and listen to all your wandering bullshit, you need to provide me with a more comfortable chair," complained Swifty.

"Compared to where I think we're going, you're likely to have fond memories of that chair," said Kit.

"Promises, promises," retorted Swifty.

43

Kit picked up a piece of paper from his desk he had just printed out from his computer.

"Here's how I see the plan," said Kit. "We take my truck, a trailer, and two horses with tack. That along with our personal supplies including sleeping bags and a small tent."

"Do we take cooking gear and food and supplies?" asked Swifty.

"Yes. I'll add them to the list," said Kit.

"How about weapons and ammo?" inquired Swifty.

"Pack whatever you think we might need," said Kit, knowing good and well that Swifty always took a small arsenal.

"Once we're packed up, we drive down to Laramie. Our first stop will be the county sheriff's office to see if they have any leads on Mr. Kelly, and if they have any information we don't."

Swifty nodded his head in agreement.

"Then we head over west to Woods Landing and stop in at the general store and post office and talk to those ladies about what they know about Ted Kelly. I forgot to ask Tang if they said when was the last time they had seen Mr. Kelly, so that's something else we can ask them," said Kit.

"Ladies?" asked Swifty.

"Tang told me there were two old ladies who ran the general store and post office. They're the ones who have had contact with Mr. Kelly. He cashed his checks from a pension and social security there and bought his supplies from them," said Kit.

Kit reached to the side of the desk and pulled out a paper copy of a colored photo and handed it to Swifty.

"What's this?" said Swifty

"This is a copy of a photo of a 1953 Dodge Power Wagon. Tang said her grandpa owned one and the ladies at Woods Landing confirmed it to her. My guess is we'll be talking to ranchers in the area and while we don't have a picture of Grandpa Ted, we do have a photo of the type of vehicle he owned and drove. Any rancher I know would notice an old truck like that if they saw it," said Kit.

Swifty looked at the photo, then folded it and placed it in his shirt pocket.

"When do we leave?" asked Swifty.

"Be here at six tomorrow morning and we'll load up and then have breakfast at the café before we leave," said Kit.

"What about the horses?" asked Swifty.

"I'll pick them up at my dad's place along with tack and hay, grain, and water," said Kit.

"I'll get everything else together today," said Swifty

"Sounds like a plan to me," said Kit.

CHAPTER SIX

Swifty showed up a little early. Kit had arrived with the truck and loaded horse trailer about 5:30 A.M. By six A.M. they had loaded all their gear and supplies into the truck. Five minutes later they were sitting down at the café. The waitress brought them steaming mugs of hot coffee without waiting for them to order. They ordered eggs, sausage and hash browns and sipped their coffee while they waited for their breakfast.

"How long do you figure it will take us to get to Laramie?" asked Swifty.

"Why, you got a hot date waiting for you there?" countered Kit.

"No, damn it. I'm just curious," said Swifty.

"Curiosity killed the cat," said Kit.

"It's also a damn good way to find out what the hell is goin' on," replied Swifty.

A short silence ensued as the two cowboys drank their coffee. Kit waited until the waitress arrived with their breakfast order before he mumbled, "About four to four and a half hours towing the horse trailer."

Swifty acted like he hadn't heard Kit, and he raised his mug and beckoned to the waitress that he needed a refill.

Both men were hungry and they quickly devoured their hot breakfast. Neither man spoke. When they were finished with their meal, Kit grabbed the check and walked up to the register and paid the bill, handing the cashier a tip for the waitress. Swifty headed straight to the truck. When Kit reached the truck, Swifty had already made himself comfortable in the passenger seat.

As soon as Kit was seated and had strapped on his seat belt, Swifty spoke. "More like five hours with a panty-waist like you drivin'."

Kit ignored the insult, started the truck and pulled out of his parking spot. Soon they were leaving Kemmerer in their rear-view mirror.

As Kit drove, Swifty shifted in his seat and was soon fast asleep.

"Slacker," mumbled Kit as he looked over at his sleeping best friend.

The trip was uneventful and true to Swifty's estimate, they arrived at the sheriff's office in Laramie just before noon. Kit drove around the block looking for a place to park the truck and horse trailer. He found an open space big enough for his rig and pulled into it.

"Wake up, Sleeping Beauty, we're here. You tend to the horses and I'll head in to see the sheriff," Kit announced to a startled Swifty.

"I'm on it," said Swifty and he bailed out of the passenger side of the truck and went back to check on the horses.

Kit slid out of the truck and walked the two blocks to the sheriff's office. The building housing the sheriff's office was a modern cinderblock building with double glass doors at the entrance. Two flagpoles flanked the entrance with the American flag on one and the Wyoming state flag on the other.

Kit made his way to the front of the office where a middle-aged woman in a deputy's uniform seated at a metal desk with a receptionist sign on it.

"What can I do for you, sir?" she inquired.

"I'm here to see the sheriff or a deputy about a missing person," said Kit.

"Who is the missing person?" inquired the receptionist.

"A senior citizen named Theodore Kelly," said Kit.

"From what location has Mr. Kelly disappeared?" asked the receptionist.

"I believe he has a cabin somewhere around Woods Landing," replied Kit.

The receptionist began typing on her computer keyboard and after a few seconds, she said, "You need to speak with Deputy Parcell. He's the one handing the case of Mr. Kelly."

"Where would I find Deputy Parcell?" asked Kit.

"Second cubicle on my right," she replied.

"Thank you, ma'am," said Kit.

"You're welcome, sir. Have a nice day," she said.

"You too, ma'am," answered Kit.

Kit walked over to the cubicle with a sign on it denoting Deputy Parcell.

"Deputy Parcell?" asked Kit of the uniformed deputy seated at the desk in the cubicle.

"Yeah, what is it?" said the large man seated at the desk as he looked up at Kit.

Deputy Parcell had dirty blonde hair in a crewcut. He had broad shoulders and was built like a man used to hard labor.

Kit extended his hand. "I'm Kit Andrews. I'm with Rocky Mountain Searchers out of Kemmerer. A Miss Kelly asked me to look into the disappearance of her grandfather, Theodore Kelly. I understand you're handling a missing persons case on him."

Deputy Parcell stood and shook Kit's hand. Parcell's hand was big and hard, but unlike some big men, his handshake was firm and smooth.

"Have a seat," said Deputy Parcell as he returned to his chair.

Kit sat on one of the two visitor chairs in front of Parcell's desk.

"Are you a private investigator?" asked Parcell.

"No." said Kit. "My partner and I run a search and tracking company out of Kemmerer."

Kit could see doubt and concern registering in Parcell's eyes.

"Are you ex-military?"

"No, but my partner is," said Kit.

"What branch of service?" asked Parcell.

"He served in the army," replied Kit.

"What outfit in the army?" inquired Parcell.

"He was with the Delta Force," answered Kit.

Kit could see relief and approval come into Parcell's eyes and his hard demeanor softened almost immediately.

"What do you want to know?" asked Parcell.

"I'd like to know if you have learned anything more about Ted Kelly's possible whereabouts," said Kit.

"Let me take a look, Mr. Andrews," said Parcell as he tapped out a few key strokes on his computer keyboard. It took a few seconds for the file to come up. When it did, he swiveled the computer display around so Kit could read it.

"Miss Kelly reported him missing about a week ago. We have no records on Theodore Kelly. He's never been in any trouble in our county. He doesn't show up in voter registration rolls and I couldn't find a vehicle registered to him with the DMV. I called the general store in Woods Landing and they remembered him, but they haven't seen him in over a month and he usually stopped in for supplies at least monthly. I'm afraid that's all I've got, Mr. Andrews," said Parcell.

"Could I possibly have a printout of that report, Deputy Parcell?" asked Kit.

"Officially, no. Unofficially I'm printing it out now," replied Parcell.

Deputy Parcell rose and walked over to a satellite printer and was soon back with the printout.

"Here you go, Mr. Andrews. I trust you'll keep me informed of anything you learn about what's happened with Mr. Kelly."

"Absolutely, Deputy. By the way, my name's Kit. Mr. Andrews is my old man," said Kit with a smile.

"Roger that, Kit. Good hunting," said Parcell.

When Kit got back to the truck, he found Swifty leaning against the front fender of his truck.

At Kit's approach, Swifty slipped into the passenger seat. When Kit was seated, and belted in, Swifty asked, "Learn anything useful?"

Kit handed Swifty the printout and Swift read it quickly. "Wow, I can't believe the law was actually helpful. That certainly runs against the grain of recent experience."

"Deputy Parcell was a stand-up guy. I think he might be helpful if we run into any issues in this county," said Kit.

"Miracles never cease," said Swifty. "Where do we go now?"

"Next stop is Woods Landing which is about thirty miles east," said Kit.

"How about some lunch first?" asked Swifty.

"I see McDonalds about two blocks ahead on the left. It looks like they have a large parking lot with room for trucks and trailers," said Kit.

"Big Macs all around," said a grinning Swifty.

Fifteen minutes later they were eating cheeseburgers, fries, and Cokes while they were driving east toward Woods Landing.

The trip took about half an hour. As they crossed the bridge over the Big Laramie River they saw a large wooden historical site sign on their left emblazoned with Woods Landing on it.

Kit turned the truck and trailer off the highway and down a slight incline to a large gravel parking lot. To his left was an old wooden general store with a small post office attached to it. In front of the general store were two ancient gasoline pumps.

West of the general store was a larger wooden building with a sign proclaiming it to be a café. In the window of the café was a small neon sign indicating the café was open. Between the general store and the café was an entrance made of two large wooden poles on each side and one at the top connecting the two side poles. Past the entrance were several wooden cabins that were nestled in a grove of pine trees.

To the left of the general store, Kit could see the Big Laramie River flowing south. Kit pulled the truck to a stop about thirty yards from the general store.

"Shall we?" asked Kit.

"You go ahead. If there are two old ladies running that place, we don't want to scare the shit out of them," said Swifty. "I'll wait out here."

Kit exited the driver's side of the truck and walked up to the door of the general store. As he opened the door and stepped inside, a small bell tinkled above his head announcing his presence.

In front of Kit was a glass enclosed counter with a cash register on top. Behind the counter was a short, small elderly lady with pure white hair. Behind her and off to her left was a slightly larger version of the first lady. Both women looked at Kit with curiosity, but neither spoke.

Kit could see the walls of the store contained shelving of various types and the shelves were filled with goods and sundries. A large floor to ceiling cooler took up part of the wall to his right.

Kit decided to take the initiative. "Good day, Ladies, my name is Kit Andrews."

Neither of the two ladies had moved and neither of them spoke a word in return to Kit's greeting.

"This is not going to be as easy as I had hoped," thought Kit.

"And who might you ladies be?" asked Kit.

That got the shorter of the two elderly ladies' attention and she replied, "I'm Thelma and this here is Louise."

"You're Thelma and Louise?" asked an incredulous Kit.

"That's right, Thelma and Louise," replied Thelma as Louise nodded her head in agreement.

"You're kidding me, right?" said Kit.

"Why would I kid you about our names," said a confused Thelma.

Then it dawned on Kit, these two elderly ladies had never seen the movie and didn't understand his surprise.

"I'm sorry, ladies, I meant no disrespect, I was just confused there for a second," said Kit.

"What can we do for you, mister," said Thelma.

"I'm looking for an older man whose granddaughter reported as missing," said Kit.

"Missing?" asked Thelma.

"Yes," said Kit. "She hasn't heard from him and when she did it was from mail sent from this post office," said Kit.

"What is this man's name?" asked Thelma.

"His name is Theodore Kelly, probably better known as Ted Kelly. He's short and drives an old 1952 Dodge Power Wagon. It's my understanding he cashed his social security and pension checks here and then bought his supplies here as well. We think he came in about once a month," said Kit.

"Oh yes. I remember him. He's a nice old gentleman, not like all the young riffraff we too often see around here," said Thelma.

"When was the last time he was here in the store?" asked Kit.

"Let me think. I believe he was in about six weeks ago," said Thelma. "Is six weeks ago, about right?" Louise nodded her head in agreement.

"I don't have a picture of him," said Kit. "Can you describe him to me?"

"He's about five and a half feet tall, white hair, brown eyes, and a full white beard," replied Thelma.

"He usually dressed in old, worn jeans with an old Carhart jacket over a denim shirt. He did have almost new boots and a ratty old cowboy hat."

Thelma turned to look at Louise. "Am I leaving anything out?" she asked.

Louise pointed to her eyes.

"Oh, yes, I forgot. He wore wire rimmed glasses," said Thelma.

"What kind of supplies did he usually buy?" asked Kit.

"He bought food and staples, lamp oil, matches, and he occasionally would fill up his truck at the gas pump," said Thelma. "Am I forgetting anything?"

Louise shook her head in the negative.

"That's all I can remember," said Thelma. "Do you think he's all right?"

"I hope he's fine, but we won't know until we find him," said Kit. "Thank you for all your help ladies," said Kit and he waved good-bye as he slipped out the door of the general store.

Swifty woke up from a nap when he heard the driver's side door open. "What took you so long?" Swifty asked.

"Did you just sleep while I was talking with the two old ladies?" asked Kit.

"Course not," replied Swifty. "I went into the café, which used to be the dance hall, and found out we can rent one of the cabins at the old lodge. They have a free corral so we can keep the horses there and they provide hay, oats, and water for a daily fee," replied Swifty with a smirk or his face. "I can't help it if I'm a lot quicker than you."

"That's a complaint I hear from a lot of your lady friends," retorted Kit.

"Baloney," said Swifty. "Hundreds of women, never a complaint."

"Which cabin is ours?" asked Kit.

"You rented cabin number two, and you owe me the fifty bucks I paid as a deposit," said Swifty.

Kit pulled out his wallet and handed Swifty a fifty-dollar bill. Swifty stuffed the bill in his shirt pocket.

Kit started the truck and drove through the entrance of the old resort and parked in front of the cabin with a big number two painted on the door.

It took the two about half an hour to unload the horses into the corral, unhitch and park the horse trailer and bring much of their gear into the cabin. They left most of their weapons and ammo in the truck along with some other field gear.

The cabin was small, but neat and clean. There were two beds, two chairs, a dresser, and two night stands with lamps on them. There was an open closet and a small, but serviceable bathroom. The cabin had a window on the front wall and the back wall. Heat was provided by a propane fueled space heater.

"This will do nicely," said Kit as he unpacked his duffel bag and placed clothing in the drawers of the dresser. Swifty just plopped his duffel bag down next to the dresser and flopped down on the bed nearest to the bathroom.

"Where do you think we should start searching?" asked Kit to the almost comatose Swifty.

"I looked at the map and there are four roads leading into Woods Landing. There are mountains to the north, the west, and the south. I think we should pick one and stop at each home or ranch and ask if they've ever seen the old Dodge Power Wagon. I think you're right about people remembering the old Dodge, but not the old geezer," responded a surprisingly alert Swifty.

"Should we search together or should we split up?" asked Kit.

"We only have one truck, but I think two men on horseback will get a lot better reception from the locals than two cowboys in a big truck," replied Swifty.

"I agree," said Kit. "Which road do you want to start out on?"

"We'll flip a coin and go clockwise," said Swifty.

"I've got a quarter," said Kit.

"We'll flip in the morning, you moron. I need some beauty sleep, and then I'll need some dinner. You feed me a good steak and some top shelf booze for dinner and you can bring me back here and have your way with me," said Swifty.

"I'll agree to dinner and pass on the rest," replied a grinning Kit.

"I don't get no respect," groaned Swifty.

Kit took off his boots and sat on the edge of his bed. He turned to ask Swifty a question, but Swifty was fast asleep and snoring loudly.

Kit set his small travel alarm clock for 5:30 P.M. and rolled over on his back. Ten minutes later he was out like a light.

CHAPTER SEVEN

Kit awoke to the sound of a big semi-truck's air horn coming from the highway. He looked over at his alarm clock and it was ten after five. "Close enough," he thought.

"Boots and saddles, Cowboy," said Kit as he ripped the blanket off a still sleeping Swifty.

"What in the wide world of sports is goin' on!" exclaimed Swifty. "Are we under attack? Is the cabin on fire?"

"It's mornin' you moron," said Kit. "Get your ass out of the sack, we're burnin' daylight."

"Man, you just messed up a really good dream. How about I go back to sleep and try to find the same channel I was on," complained Swifty.

"I'll get dressed and see if I can rustle up some breakfast at that café. I'll see you there," responded Kit.

"You could mess up a wet dream," said Swifty. "And I think you just did," he said as he slowly slid out of bed and landed on his feet on the cold, cabin floor.

By the time Kit had showered and gotten dressed, Swifty was still sitting on his bed in his underwear mumbling to himself about some slave driver.

"See you at the café," said Kit as he opened the cabin door and stepped out into the cool air of an early dawn.

Kit walked over to the café and looked at the sign on the door. The sign indicated that the café was open for lunch and dinner, but there was no mention of breakfast. He tried the door. It was unlocked so he opened it and stepped inside and found himself in a small bar area with several small round tables with chairs. An older woman with white hair done up in a bun was behind the bar and three older men were seated on bar stools, drinking coffee.

Kit sniffed the air. He could smell coffee brewing and bacon frying. He surmised the café was like many he had experienced in Wyoming. They were often unofficially open for things like breakfast for the locals.

"Can I help you, Mister?" asked the bartender.

"I'm stayin' at one of the cabins," said Kit. "Is it possible to get some breakfast here?"

"Pull up a bar stool, Mister," said the white-haired bartender.

Kit followed her instructions and as soon as he was seated, she plunked down a steaming hot mug of coffee.

"You take anything with your coffee?" asked the bartender.

"Cream and sugar, if you got it," said Kit. "Otherwise black is fine."

The bartender handed Kit an old-fashioned glass sugar dispenser and a small pitcher of cream. "I'm Tess," she said. "What name do you go by?"

"Kit Andrews, ma'am," said Kit as he extended his right hand. Tess took his hand and gently shook it.

"May I see a menu," said Kit.

"There ain't no menu on account of we ain't open for breakfast, but I got eggs, bacon, sausage and hash browns," said Tess.

"I'll take three eggs over easy, sausage, and hash browns," said Kit.

"Comin' up," said Tess as she disappeared through a door at the end of the bar. After a couple of minutes, she returned through the same door.

Kit sipped on his coffee and looked around the room. He and the three other men were the only customers.

"You fellas ranch around here?" asked Kit.

The three men looked at each other in surprise. They had been taking in everything Kit and the bartender had said, but hadn't uttered a sound.

"We all owns spreads, hereabouts," said the biggest of the three. All three of them were older men dressed in well-worn denims and cowboy hats.

The man extended his hand. "I'm Eustace Cassidy, but my friends just call me Hoppy."

"You mean like Hopalong Cassidy?" said Kit.

"You look too young to remember old Hopalong," said Eustace.

"I saw way too many old westerns on television when I was a kid," said Kit.

"This here galoot is Calvin Biggs," said Hoppy as a second man stood and extended his hand. He had a weather-worn face with a handlebar mustache.

"Howdy," said Biggs as he shook Kit's hand. "Call me Cal."

"The last gent is Shorty Dawson." Shorty slipped off his bar stool and revealed why he was called Shorty. He stood about five feet five inches tall. Shorty extended his hand and Kit shook it.

The three men returned to their respective bar stools and reacquainted themselves with their mugs of coffee.

"What brings you here to Woods Landing?" asked Hoppy.

"Well," said Kit, "me and my partner work for an outfit called Rocky Mountain Searchers out of Kemmerer. We're here looking for an old gent that seems to have gone missing."

"What's this old gent's name?" asked Hoppy.

"His name is Ted Kelly. He's got to be pushing eighty and his granddaughter hired us to find out where he is and if he's ok," said Kit.

"Name don't ring no bells to me," said Hoppy. "How about you guys?" he asked as he looked to Cal and Shorty.

Both men shook their heads.

"You got any other description, other than him bein' an old fart?" asked Hoppy.

"He drives an old 1952 Dodge Power Wagon," said Kit.

"What color?" asked Shorty.

"I'm not sure. I think the truck is so old there might not be much paint left, so it could be down to the bare metal," replied Kit. "I have a picture of a 1952 Dodge Power Wagon, but it isn't the one Ted owns." Kit reached in his shirt pocket and pulled out the folded picture and after unfolding it, he passed it over to the three old ranchers.

"I remember those old Dodge Power Wagons," said Cal. "They looked a lot like an oversized Willy's Jeep if I remember right."

"An oversized old Willy's Jeep," said Shorty. "I remember seein' one of them a couple of times in the past year. I'd never seen one before and weren't sure what the hell it was."

"Do you remember where you saw it?" asked Kit.

Before Shorty could answer, Tess appeared and placed a plate of hot eggs, sausage, and hash browns in front of Kit.

"Sorry to interrupt fellas, but when foods hot, it's time to eat, not yak," she said.

"Thank you, Tess," said Kit.

"You're welcome, Kit," said Tess.

"Eat your breakfast, Kit. I kin talk while you eat," said Shorty with a grin.

"I saw this here Dodge at least three times in the past year on County Road 10, just south of here. All three times it was heading north goin' towards Woods Landing," he said.

"Do you remember how far south of Woods Landing you saw this truck?" asked Kit.

"I sure don't. I'm sorry, but I remember the truck, and I can't be sure just exactly where I saw it," said Shorty.

Kit was about to ask another question when the door to the café opened and in stepped a rather bleary eyed Swifty.

He quickly looked around and said, "I smell breakfast."

Shorty turned to Kit and said, "Well, at least his nose is workin'."

Everyone except Swifty broke out in laughter. When the laughter subsided, Kit introduced Swifty to Hoppy, Cal, Shorty and most importantly, Tess.

"What can I get for you, honey?" asked Tess.

"I'll have what he's havin'," said Swifty as he pointed to Kit's still full plate.

"Coming up," said Tess and again she disappeared through the door.

Swifty took a seat at the counter where he found a fresh, hot mug of coffee waiting for him. Tess was nothing if not thorough.

Kit explained to Swifty what Shorty had told him about sighting the old Dodge Power Wagon on County Road 10.

"Did you see the old Power Wagon on the same day of the week every time?" asked Swifty.

"Well, sonny," said Shorty, "At my age I don't keep track of the days of the week anymore. Got no need to. Bath on Saturday night, church on Sunday, and the social security check comes on the fourth Wednesday of the month is pretty much my schedule."

Swifty grinned at Shorty's answer.

"Was there a particular time of day when you saw the Power Wagon?" said Swifty as he tried again.

"Let me think," said Shorty. "Now that I think of it, I'm pretty sure I saw the Dodge on my way home after havin' breakfast here at Woods Landing. Yep, I'm sure of it. I was headin' south and the Dodge was goin' north."

"Where do you live from here?" asked Swifty.

"I ain't sure that's none of your business, sonny," said Shorty.

"I'm just trying to figure out where you might have seen the Dodge between here and where you live," said Swifty.

"Well, tarnation, why didn't you say so in the first place," said an exasperated Shorty.

"My mistake," said Swifty. "I'm sorry if I got too personal."

"Shorty lives about four and a half miles south of here," said Hoppy. "That's about as far as you can go south and still stay in Wyoming."

"What do you mean by that?" asked Swifty.

"The state line is about five miles south of here. The road continues on for about thirty miles until it comes to a T," explained Hoppy. "Most of the road is in Colorado."

"He's right," said Cal. "The road is paved until you get to Colorado, and them cheap bastards have gravel the rest of the way."

"How close is the nearest town south of here?" asked Kit.

"Glendevy is about twenty miles south, but you have to take the right fork at the T intersection," said Hoppy.

"Glendevy ain't nothin' but a hole in the road," said Cal.

"So, Woods Landing is the closest place with a general store and a post office for quite a ways south?" asked Kit.

"Yup," said Cal.

"So just what are you two boys plannin' to do?" asked Hoppy.

"We're staying here in one of the cabins, and we plan to ride our horses down County Road 10 and stop at each ranch and ask if they've seen the Dodge Power Wagon. We figure old Ted must have a cabin off the grid and that probably means he's up in the mountains and would probably need to cross someone's ranch land to get across the river and down to County Road 10," said Kit.

"That's likely right thinkin'," said Cal. "There's several old cabins up in the high country that I know of, but most of them are in pretty bad shape."

"What the hell is "off the grid"?" asked Shorty.

"It means there's no electricity or phone service," replied Kit.

"Hell, I spent most of my life off the grid if that's true," said Shorty.

"Most of them old cabins are located near some water source," said Cal. "Usually a spring of some sort."

"You're likely to see a good number of houses and summer cabins along the river that are down pretty close to the road," said Hoppy. "I'd skip them and deal with the ranches only. If old Ted is up high, he likely has to come down through someone's ranch."

"Are you boys here for breakfast every morning?" asked Kit.

"If the café is open, we're here," said Hoppy with a grin.

"Good to know," said Kit. "We might have more questions for you later."

"We'll be here and happy to try to answer any questions you come up with," said Cal.

"Thanks," said Kit.

Kit and Swifty finished their breakfast and when Kit asked Tess for the check, she pulled it out of her apron pocket.

Kit reached for his wallet and pulled out some bills and gave the check and the bills back to Tess.

"Whoa," said Tess. "This is way too much money."

"It should cover our bill and the three old ranchers. The rest is for you," said Kit.

"Well, thank you, Mister. I look forward to you comin' back in here for breakfast," said Tess with a grin.

Kit reached for his cowboy hat, which rested crown down on the counter top, and he and Swifty were soon out the door and headed back to their cabin.

CHAPTER EIGHT

"If you can get the horses out and saddled, I'll get all our gear together and we can get started on this hunt for old Ted," said Kit.

"What the hell do you mean, if I can," said Swifty. "I'll have that done before you're done takin' a piss, you greenhorn tenderfoot."

Kit just grinned and headed for the truck while Swifty walked over to the corral.

Fifteen minutes later, Kit was shoving a model 94 Winchester rifle into the leather scabbard attached to his saddle. Swifty was already mounted and he too had a Winchester repeating rifle secure in his scabbard. The spurs on Kit's cowboy boots jingled as he swung his right leg over his horse's back and settled into his saddle.

Swifty looked back at Kit and said, "Head 'em up and move 'em out."

Kit smiled at his friend's antics. Swifty often acted a little crazy, but he was one of the wariest and most alert men Kit had ever met. Swifty had taught Kit to always scan your surroundings and look for things that didn't belong. That one skill had served Kit well. He had also learned from Big Dave to occasionally stop and use his eyes, his ears, and his nose. That skill had served him well countless times since he had moved to Wyoming.

Robert W. Callis

The two cowboys rode their horses south on County Road 10. They passed several houses and rough roads reaching up the hills to the east. They had ridden for about a mile before they came to their first ranch. The road was on the east side of the Big Laramie River and the ranches occupied the narrow valley the river had created between the foothills that paralleled the river on both sides. The range of foothills to the west were much higher and they were covered with pine and aspen trees.

The drive from the road to the ranch was gravel and bordered by a barbed wire fence. The mailbox on the road had the name "Rocking R Ranch" printed on the side. Kit stopped his horse and took a small spiral notebook with a small pen attached out of his shirt pocket. He wrote down the ranch name and returned the notebook to his pocket.

Kit and Swifty walked their horses down the ranch lane and were soon approaching a rather non-descript ranch house that looked overdue for a paint job. There were several outbuildings and one of them was a good-sized barn or stable. Kit could see at least two corrals.

As they rode closer to the ranch house, the obligatory dogs rushed to challenge them. There were three dogs and all of them were of the Heinz 57 variety. The dogs were barking furiously, but making no aggressive moves against the horses. The noise brought a middle-aged woman out the front door of the ranch house. She had light brown hair tied back in a ponytail. She wore faded jeans and a long sleeved brown shirt.

Kit and Swifty brought their horses to a halt. The women yelled at the dogs and they respectfully retreated to a shady spot under the front porch of the ranch house.

"Howdy, ma'am," said Kit as he touched the brim of his cowboy hat.

"Howdy yourself," responded the woman. "What brings you to the Rocking R Ranch?"

"I'm Kit Andrews and this here is Swifty Olson. We're with the Rocky Mountain Searchers out of Kemmerer. We're here looking for a missing person we believe may have lived in the area."

Swifty also touched his hat in greeting.

"I'm Jenna Richards," said the woman. "Me and my husband own the Rocking R. Just who is this missing person you're lookin' for?"

"We're looking for an older gentleman by the name of Ted Kelly," said Kit. "We think he may have been living in an off the grid cabin up in the foothills."

"Do you have a picture of this Mr. Kelly?" asked Jenna.

"We don't," said Kit, "but we do have a picture of the type of vehicle he was known to drive. We figured if he was living up in the foothills, he would have to come through some one's ranch to get to the road to drive to Woods Landing for supplies."

"Can I see the picture?" asked Jenna.

Kit pulled the picture from his shirt pocket, unfolded it, and handed it to Jenna.

"This looks like some kinda' Jeep," said Jenna. "It says here this was made in 1952! My God, I wasn't even born in 1952."

"Have you seen a vehicle like this one around here?" asked Kit.

"Can't say I have," said Jenna. "Do you have a copy of it I can show my husband when he gets home? He might have seen it and he's out a hell of a lot more than I am."

"You can keep that picture and here's my card. You can reach me at the cell phone number. If I don't answer, please leave a message. Sometimes I'm out of range of a signal," said Kit.

"Ain't we all most of the time," said a smiling Jenna.

"Thank you for your time, ma'am," said Kit.

"You're welcome, mister. Good luck findin' that old man," said Jenna.

Both Kit and Swifty tipped their cowboy hats, turned their horses around and headed back down the ranch lane.

When they reached the end of the lane, they halted their horses. Kit took the notebook out and briefly wrote an account of their meeting with Mrs. Richards.

"Well, that's one down," said Swifty.

"And God knows how many more to do," replied Kit.

They turned their horses south and moved on down the road. The sun was up over the foothills to the east and they could feel its warmth on their faces. Red wing blackbirds fluttered between cattails growing on the marshy edges of the Big Laramie River. There was almost no breeze. As Cal had alerted them, there were no ranches on the east side of the road. All the ranches were situated along the Big Laramie River which flows south on the west side of the county road.

After they had ridden a little over a mile, they came to another mailbox and another ranch entrance road on their right.

Swifty pulled his horse up next to the mailbox. "No name on the mailbox," he said.

There was no formal sign of any kind announcing what might be at the end of the ranch drive.

"Curiosity may have killed the cat," said Kit, "but it's also a peachy way to find things out."

"Peachy?" asked Swifty. "Did you actually use the word peachy? What the hell is wrong with you? Pretty soon you'll be wantin' to stop for a spot of tea. Good God, Andrews."

Kit just grinned at his friend's antics and led the way west on the ranch drive.

As they rode west, Kit could see a grove of cottonwood trees and what looked like a small ranch house and some outbuildings ahead. Cottonwood trees in the West were a sure sign of water.

As Kit and Swifty got nearer to the grove of cottonwood trees, it became clear the house and the small outbuildings were in a state of neglect. Not a spec of paint could be seen, and the roofline of the ranch house looked like a swaybacked mare.

As they drew close to the front of the old ranch house, they could see an old man with a bushy white beard sitting on a rocking chair on the decrepit front porch. A small cooler sat on the porch within easy reach of the rocking chair's occupant.

"It ain't even nine o'clock in the morning and that old coot is already drinking beer," whispered Swifty.

"Maybe that's his breakfast," Kit whispered back.

Kit and Swifty reined in their horses in front of the old gent on the porch.

"Howdy," said Kit.

"Howdy, yerself," said the old man in a high squeaky voice.

"I'm Kit Andrews and this here is my partner, Swifty Olson. We're with Rocky Mountain Searchers out of Kemmerer, and we're looking for a fella who's gone missing."

The old man scowled at the two riders and said nothing.

"I don't think I caught your name?" said Kit.

Finally, the old man spoke. "I'm Randolph Scott. My friends call me Randy, but most of them have gone under."

"Good to meet you, Randy," said Kit. "This your place?"

"Been my place since my daddy left it to me in 1962," replied Randy.

"Did you say your name was Randolph Scott?" asked Swifty.

"Yes sir, I surely did," answered Randy.

"You wouldn't be pullin' our legs with that name, would you, old timer?" said Swifty.

"What the hell do you mean, pullin' your leg? It was my name when I was born, it's my name today, and it'll be my name tomorrow. I don't cotton to no man makin' fun of my good name," said Randy in an even higher voice than before.

Old Randy remained seated in his ancient wooden chair, but he raised both of his arms up in anger and Kit could now see the can of Pabst Blue Ribbon beer he held in his right hand. The sudden motion caused some of the beer to fly out of the can and land on Randy's face.

"Dammit all to hell," bellowed Randy. "Now look at what you made me do, you young smart ass."

It was hard for Kit to keep from laughing out loud, but he managed to keep his mouth shut and his face impassive. Anyone who looked at his eyes could see the laughter reflected in them.

"I'm sorry, Randy, I meant no harm," said Swifty, as earnestly as he could manage without breaking into laughter.

Randy lowered his arms and took a long swig out of his now less than full can of beer. When Randy finished the beer, he opened the cooler at his side and fished out another can. He popped the top of the can and took a long swig of beer. Then he wiped his mouth with his sleeve, as he attempted to dry off his beer drenched face.

Kit noticed the old man made no attempt to offer a beer to his guests, and he wasn't surprised. He decided to try to change the subject and deflect Randy's anger.

"So this is your ranch," Kit said.

"Yup, it shore is," replied Randy.

"What are you running on it?" Kit asked.

"I run two dozen Herefords on four hundred acres. I got goats, chickens, and a few pigs to boot."

"That must keep you busy," said Kit.

"That's for damn sure," said Randy. "All them animals keep me hoppin."

"You got any horses?" asked Swifty.

"Nope. I got rid of them damn oat swizzlin' bastards. I got me one of them ATVs, and it does everything they did, and all I got to do is put a little gas in it. Hell of a lot easier for me to get on and off, and my butt ain't sore at the end of the day," said Randy.

"Well, we still ride horses," said Kit. "Sometimes we need to go places only a horse or a mule can go."

"I got no interest in goin' anyplace my ATV can't go," said Randy. "Now why are you boys here on my place?"

"As I said earlier, we're with Rocky Mountain Searchers out of Kemmerer. We're looking for an old man who seems to have gone missing. We understand he was living in a cabin up in the foothills somewhere around these parts," said Kit.

"What's this old galoot's name?" asked Randy.

"His name is Ted Kelly," replied Kit.

"You got a picture of this Kelly feller?" asked Randy.

"No, we don't. We know he's short and has white hair and a full white beard," said Kit.

"Lot of folks around here fit that description," said Randy as he fingered his own long white beard.

"We do know he drives a unique vehicle. He has a 1952 Dodge Power Wagon. Most of the paint is gone, so it's down to the bare metal," said Kit.

"A Dodge Power Wagon," said Randy. "I don't think I've seen one of them things in twenty years."

"I have a picture of one," said Kit as he pulled a copy out of his shirt pocket. "It would look a lot like this," he said as he handed the picture to Randy.

Randy unfolded the copy and looked at the picture of the Dodge. "I ain't seen nothing that looks like this, Mister," he said.

"Keep the picture and if you should see the truck, please give me a call," said Kit as he handed Randy his business card.

Randy took the card and looked up at Kit. "I ain't got no phone, but if I do see the truck I reckon I can mosey over to the neighbors and use their phone."

"I'd appreciate it and so would Mr. Kelly's family," said Kit.

"Good luck finding that old galoot," said Randy.

Kit and Swifty turned their horses to head back out the ranch drive. Behind them they could hear the distinct sound of another beer can being opened by old Randy. Both men looked at each other and grinned.

When they reached the county road, they halted their horses. "What the hell is it with the people around here with the same names as movie characters and actors, and then they act like they never heard of the famous people or movies with the same names?" said Swifty.

"I have no idea," said Kit. "I'm guessing old Randy is so buzzed by noon, the old Dodge could drive by the front of his ranch house and he'd never see it."

Swifty laughed.

Kit took out his note book and wrote down his summary of their encounter with Randy Scott. Kit put the notebook back in his shirt pocket, and both men urged their horses on as they moved further south on County Road 10.

"Did you notice that old Randy didn't have a dog?" asked Kit.

"Dog probably died of a bad liver from drinkin' all that cheap beer," said Swifty.

CHAPTER NINE

They traveled less than a mile when they came to the next mailbox. The name on the mailbox was Snyder and under it was the name, Laramie River Ranch. An entrance in the fence led to a long ranch drive that showed signs of being recently graded. The drive was made of good quality gravel. The drive was bordered on both sides by a split rail fence. An entrance had been built of three large logs. Two logs were vertical and made up the sides and the third log lay horizontally at the top of the two logs. The logs had been skinned and treated with some substance that made them appear golden in color. Hanging down from the horizontal log was a wooden sign suspended by two chains. The sign proclaimed, "Laramie River Ranch."

"This place looks a lot more prosperous than old Randy's spread," said Swifty.

"Four hundred acres ain't much of a ranch in Wyoming," said Kit.

"More like a small farm," said Swifty.

"I bet this place is a lot more than four hundred acres," said Kit.

"Let's see if anybody is home," said Swifty and he led the way down the graded lane.

As the two men rode down the lane, they soon saw the ranch house and outbuildings of the Laramie River Ranch. The ranch house was a two-story stone and cedar wood siding affair. The roof was green metal. The house looked to have been built recently. The outbuildings were freshly painted and in excellent condition. There was a riding corral and two metal fence holding corrals. There were two late model Ford pickup trucks parked near the ranch house. One truck was an F-150 and the other was an F-350. Both trucks had dust and dried mud on them.

As Kit and Swifty approached the house on their horses, two Labrador retrievers bounded off the covered front porch of the ranch house where they had been lying in the shade. The two dogs charged toward the horsemen, but their tails were wagging as they approached. Neither dog barked, which surprised Kit.

"Friendly dogs for ranch dogs," said Swifty.

"Especially for a place this big and this nice," replied Kit.

As they approached the large, covered front porch of the ranch house, they could see expensive patio furniture on the front porch including an antique porch swing suspended from the ceiling of the porch.

There was a sturdy wooden hitching rail mounted in front of the porch, so they rode up to it and dismounted. As they were tying their horses' reins to the rail, the front door of the house opened and out stepped a very attractive older woman. She was dressed in what Kit would consider designer jeans, highly polished cowboy boots, and a red silk blouse. "This is definitely not typical ranch style clothing," thought Kit.

The woman was tall and thin and had dark hair. She strode to the front of the porch and then stood there with her hands on her hips. Her posture exuded confidence. "This was a woman who was used to giving orders, not taking them," thought Kit.

"What can I do for you gentlemen?" asked the woman.

"Howdy, ma'am," said Kit. "I'm Kit Andrews, and this here is my partner Swifty Olson. We're with Rocky Mountain Searchers out of Kemmerer, and we're out here lookin' for an old gentleman who has gone missin'."

"I see," said the woman. "I'm Priscilla Snyder. My husband Ned and I own this ranch. What's this old gentleman's name?"

"His name is Ted Kelly," said Kit. "He's elderly, rather short, and has white hair and a full white beard."

"Do you have a photograph of this Mr. Kelly?" asked Priscilla.

"I'm afraid we don't, Mrs. Snyder. We do have a picture of the type of vehicle he was seen driving, and we are hoping that someone might have seen the vehicle as it is quite distinctive," replied Kit.

Kit pulled out the picture of the Dodge Power Wagon and handed it to Mrs. Snyder.

"Oh my, that is a rather distinctive vehicle. It says below the picture that it's a 1952 Dodge Power Wagon. It looks like some kind of experimental Jeep with those squared off fenders," said Mrs. Snyder.

"Yes, ma'am, it surely does."

"I haven't seen anything like this in my entire life," said Mrs. Snyder. "My husband is away from the ranch today, but let me check with our foreman. He's much more likely to have seen such a vehicle than anyone else on the ranch."

With that she pulled a small black and yellow object from a holster on her belt. Kit recognized it as a radio transmitter and receiver. She looked at the radio and punched two buttons and then put the radio to her right ear.

After a few seconds a buzz was heard and Mrs. Snyder spoke into the radio. "Trace, this is Mrs. Snyder. I have two gentlemen at the ranch house that have some questions I think you might be able to answer. Please come to the house immediately." After listening to a response, she shut off the radio and replaced it in the holster.

"My foreman will be here shortly. I'm sure he can be of more assistance to you. If you both will have a seat on the front porch, I'll have some iced tea brought out to you," said Mrs. Snyder.

Before Kit could offer a polite refusal, Mrs. Snyder had quickly turned and disappeared into the ranch house.

Kit looked at Swifty and shrugged his shoulders. Both men took chairs at a glass topped table and prepared to wait.

Swifty started to say something, but Kit put his finger to his lips to signal to Swifty to remain silent. Swifty complied.

A few minutes later, a middle-aged Hispanic woman emerged from the house with a tray containing a pitcher of iced tea and two tall glasses. She was dressed in a white blouse and blue jeans with a light blue apron. She set the tray down and placed the pitcher and glasses on the table. She picked up the tray and disappeared back into the ranch house without uttering a word.

"I think these folks must have a pile of money," whispered Swifty.

"Shut up," whispered Kit back.

Kit and Swifty sat on the porch, drinking ice tea and studying their surroundings while trying not to be too obvious about it.

"This is a really high end spread," said Kit.

"No shit, Sherlock," retorted Swifty.

After about ten minutes, both men could hear the unmistakable whine of a small engine. The noise got louder until a man dressed in denims and wearing a grey cowboy hat drove an ATV into the farmyard from behind the largest barn. He pulled the ATV up next to the farm house and killed the engine. He swung off the ATV and walked up to the porch where Swifty and Kit sat.

"Howdy, boys, I'm Trace Bitters," he said as he extended his right hand. Both Swifty and Kit rose to meet Trace, shaking hands, as Kit and Swifty introduced themselves.

"Mrs. Snyder called me and said you had some questions for me. How can I help you?"

"We appreciate you coming in, Mr. Bitters," said Kit.

"Hell, son, Mr. Bitters is my old man. I'm Trace to everyone I know or give a shit about," said Bitters.

"Okay, then Trace it is," said Kit. "We're looking for an old man who's gone missing. His name is Ted Kelly and while we don't have a picture of him, he's old, short, and has white hair and a full white beard. He lives like a hermit, and we think he has a cabin off the grid up in the foothills. He was last seen about six weeks ago, at the general store in Woods Landing. He has a rather unusual vehicle you might have seen. He drives a 1952 Dodge Power Wagon which has lost most of its paint and is pretty much down to the bare metal. We think he must have had to come down through someone's ranch to get to the road to Woods Landing. Here's a picture of a 1952 Dodge Power Wagon. We were wondering if you had possibly seen him or the Dodge."

Trace took the picture Kit offered and looked at it. "Damn, I haven't seen one of these since I was knee high to a grasshopper. I don't recall seeing either the old man or the Dodge. If I can keep the picture, I'll check with my hands to see if any of them have seen either the old man or the truck."

"Keep the picture," said Kit. "Here's my business card. We're staying at one of the cabins at Woods Landing. If you can't reach me on my cell phone, please leave a message with Tess, the bartender at the café."

"I'll do that," said Trace. "Nice meetin' you boys. I got to get back to work, but I'll make sure I talk to all of our hands by no later than tonight."

"We'd appreciate that," said Kit. The three men shook hands and within seconds, Trace and his ATV were out of sight with only the whine of the ATV's engine to mark his presence.

Kit went to the front door of the ranch house and knocked. The Hispanic woman opened the door. "Please extend our thanks to Mrs. Snyder for her assistance and the tea. It was delicious," said Kit.

The woman nodded, said nothing, and closed the door.

Kit and Swifty mounted their horses and headed back out the ranch lane to the road.

"Real talkative gal," said Swifty. "I could hardly get a word in edgewise."

Kit just laughed.

CHAPTER TEN

When the two men reached the road, they halted their horses and Kit made notes in his little notebook. Then they turned south and were interrupted only once when an old GMC pickup passed them heading south for Colorado.

"You think the guy could have slowed down so he didn't raise so much dust when he passed us," groused Swifty.

"When's the last time you extended that courtesy to anyone you passed?" asked Kit.

"Hell, a little dust never hurt anyone," said Swifty.

"Then quit complaining." said Kit.

"I ain't complainin' I'm just commentin'," mumbled Swifty.

"I have a hard time telling the difference," said Kit.

"That's just 'cause you ain't too bright," snorted Swifty. "When God gave out brains, you thought he said trains and you asked for a slow freight."

"Whereas you are a paragon of virtue and knowledge," replied Swifty in a voice dripping with sarcasm.

It was getting near noon, and they came to the next mailbox. The box was old and a bit rusty, but still intact. The name on the mailbox was Nordstrom.

"Looks like we got us a Swede rancher on this spread," said Swifty.

"How do you know he's not Norwegian or Danish?" asked Kit.

"Because my name is Olson and I'm a Swede. A guy named Nordstrom is a Swede. I had one in my unit in Delta," said Swifty with a knowing sneer.

"Let's try to avoid asking him about his nationality. We need answers to our questions about old Tom Kelly, not pissing off someone about their nationality," said Kit.

"My lips are sealed, Master," said Swifty as he made a motion with his hand like he was zipping his mouth shut.

"That'll happen when pigs fly," said Kit.

While the two men had been talking, their horses had taken them closer to the ranch. The ranch house was small and modest, but in good condition. The outbuildings were in good repair and neatly kept.

As they rode up to the ranch house, they could not see any sign of life. Just as they neared the hitching post in front of the ranch house's front porch, a very large black dog appeared as if out of nowhere. The dog did not bark, but he placed his large frame squarely between the two mounted men and the front of the ranch house.

"I don't like the looks of that dog," whispered Swifty.

Kit studied the dog and saw that his fur was more like a sheep than a dog. The dog remained motionless and silent.

Kit carefully swung down out of his saddle and handed his reins to Swifty who was perfectly content to remain mounted and out of reach of the large black dog.

As Kit slowly began to approach the ranch house porch, the dog remained motionless, but the dog never took his eyes off Kit.

Kit stopped about three feet from the dog. The dog moved forward until his right shoulder was up against Kit's legs. Kit had nowhere to go. As he stood there he could feel pressure from the dog on his legs. The dog was trying to move Kit away from the ranch house.

The dog was so powerful that Kit was forced back a few inches. Kit was confused and unsure what to do.

Before he had to make a choice he might regret, a strong voice rang out loudly.

"Boonie, back."

Kit looked toward the sound of the voice on his right and there was a tall blonde man dressed in worn denims, wearing tired cowboy boots and a battered cowboy hat. The man was neither young, nor old. He stood about six and a half feet tall and looked like he should have been more appropriately dressed like a Viking.

The dog immediately retreated to the porch, where he sat down and watched Kit intently.

"Don't mind Boonie," said the tall man. "He's a herding and guard dog by breeding, and he uses his body and his strength to keep any threats away from the ranch house or the herd. He's a Bouvier and he won't hurt you unless he perceives you as a threat."

"I come in peace," said a chastened Kit with his arms extended above his head.

The tall man laughed.

"I'm Kit Andrews and this is Swifty Olson, my partner. We're with the Rocky Mountain Searchers out of Kemmerer. We're looking for an old man who's gone missing from this area," said Kit

The tall man stepped forward and shook Kit's hand. "I'm Nels Nordstrom and I own this ranch. You say you're looking for a missing old man. What's his name?"

"His name is Ted Kelly. He's old, short, has white hair and a white full beard," said Kit.

"You got a picture of this Kelly feller?" asked Nels.

"No, we don't," said Kit, "but we do have a picture of the rather unusual vehicle he was known to drive."

"May I see the picture?" asked Nels.

Kit handed Nels the picture of the Dodge.

"I hadn't seen one of these old Dodge Power Wagons for years," said Nels.

"What do you mean, you hadn't seen one?" asked Kit.

"I've seen one like this here picture several times in the past year, but the one I saw got no paint. It was down to the bare metal," said Nels.

"Where did you see the old Dodge?" asked Kit.

"About a year or so ago, some old coot drove up to the ranch in it," said Nels. "He had rented some old cabin in the foothills up behind the ranch to the west, and he needed a way to drive up to it 'cause there ain't no road. I told him he was welcome to use our ranch roads and lanes to get down to the county road as long as he promised to close and latch all the gates he went through."

"I think that must be old Ted," said Kit. "When was the last time you saw him?"

"I ain't rightly sure, but I think I saw him about two months ago, heading back up to the foothills. I can't swear to the exact time, but that might be pretty close," said Nels.

"Anybody else ask for permission to drive through your ranch to get up to the foothills?" asked Kit.

"In the fall, I get some hunters, but I only allow folks I know or people who've been vouched for by folks I know," said Nels.

"Just hunters?" asked Kit.

"I've had a few hikers and mountain bikers over the past few years, but not many. We still get 'em though," said Nels.

"What do you mean you still get 'em?" asked Kit.

"These people today, especially the young ones, they pay no attention to fences, gates, or signs. They never ask permission, they just trespass, leave gates open, cut fences, and leave garbage behind. Pisses me off."

"You have any trouble with them?" asked Kit.

"I've confronted a few of them and between my size and obviously pissed off attitude and the presence of Boonie, they're usually on their way off the property before I can finish talking to them," said Nels with a wry smile.

"Never had any of them retaliate and cause some damage?" asked Kit.

"Not really. I think some still manage to sneak onto the property, usually with those damn ATVs. I've seen tire tracks on my roads, but never seen them ridin'. Some of my hands have heard their motors, but they're always gone by the time my men have ridden over to the source of the noise," said Nels.

"How far up the foothills does your ranch land go?" asked Kit.

"My property line is just short of the peak of the foothills. The other side is government land managed by the BLM and open to public use. That's harder ridin' for them, but that's how they usually get access to the trails up in the foothills," replied Nels.

"Do you happen to know where Mr. Kelly's cabin is located?" asked Kit.

"I'm not sure," said Nels. "I've ridden the summit of the foothills, and down the other side for about a mile when I've had lost cattle, but I don't recall seeing a cabin. 'Course there's a lot of timber up there, and it'd be hard to find it unless you were lookin' for it."

"Can we have your permission to use your ranch roads to reach the foothills?" asked Kit. "We promise to shut and latch all the gates we pass through."

"I'm happy to help you find that old man. Feel free to use my ranch roads if you need to. Tie off those horses, and I'll get us some coffee and draw you a map of my roads that lead to the summit of the foothills," said Nels.

With that Nels headed into the ranch house. Swifty dismounted, and he and Kit tied their horses' reins off to a hitching post. Then they walked up to the porch and sat on the wooden steps. Boonie remained between them and the front door to the ranch house and he eyed them warily.

"Iced tea and now coffee," said Kit. "I wonder what we'll be drinkin' next."

"If you're a Swede, it's always coffee time," said Swifty. "I should know."

Nels soon returned and invited both Kit and Swifty into the ranch house. He led them into a wood paneled living room and then into a large eat-in kitchen with tile floors, cherry wood cabinets, and granite counter-tops. Nels gestured towards a round kitchen table with four chairs. Already on the table were three large coffee mugs, a small pitcher of cream, a container of sugar and a plate of what looked like toast.

"Have a seat boys, the coffee will be ready in a minute," said Nels.

Kit and Swifty seated themselves, and waited for a couple of minutes until the coffee maker made a small beep. Nels scooped the glass coffee pot off the machine and brought it to the table. He proceeded to fill all three mugs full of hot, dark coffee. Then he returned the coffee pot to the machine and seated himself at the table.

Nels added cream and sugar to his coffee, stirring it with a spoon. After taking a sip of coffee from his mug, he sat the mug down on the table. Then he picked up one of the pieces of toast from the plate and dunked it into his coffee before eating it.

"Is that toast you're dunking into your coffee?" asked Kit.

"Not exactly," said Nels with a grin on his face. "It's a dry Swedish bread that we call rusk. You can get it in different flavors. I order it from a Swedish bakery in Denver because I can't get it around here, and my wife can't find a recipe that turns out as good as the place in Denver."

Kit reached out and took a piece of the toast and dunked it in his coffee. Taking a bite, he found it to be quite good. Swifty quickly followed to make sure he was not missing out on something.

"You mentioned your wife?" asked Kit.

"Oh, my yes," said Nels. "She's gone up to Laramie for groceries and supplies today. My wife's name is Betty. We've been married for twenty-seven years and we've lived on this ranch for the past twenty-five years. I'm sorry she wasn't here to meet you. She is always delighted to have visitors, which isn't very often."

"Please extend our thanks for your kind hospitality," said Kit.

"I certainly will, Mr. Andrews. She'll be sorry she missed both of you."

"You mentioned a map," said Swifty.

"I almost forgot," said Nels. He got up from the table and went to a built-in desk in the far side of the kitchen. He opened a drawer and pulled out a tablet of paper and a pen.

Nels returned to the kitchen table and began to draw on the paper, pausing now and then to review what he had written and to take a sip from his mug of coffee. Finally, he laid his pen on the table and picked up the paper for a final examination. Satisfied with what he saw, he tore the page off the tablet and laid the paper map on the table, turning it to face Kit and Swifty. Then Nels used his finger to point out the various ranch roads and lanes to them.

Kit carefully followed Nels' explanation of the map and noted that Nels had written a large N at the top of the map with an arrow indicating the direction of true North.

Kit took the map and folded it and placed it in his shirt pocket. He and Swifty shook hands with Nels and thanked him for his help. Soon they were out of the ranch house and mounting their horses. Boonie stood sentry by the front steps and watched both of them carefully.

"I think we should head back to Woods Landing and feed and water the horses and have some lunch at the café before we head up into the foothills," said Kit.

"Lunch was the word I heard," said Swifty with a grin.

Both men wheeled their horses and began riding back down the ranch lane to the county road. Boonie stood still and watched them until they rode out of sight.

Before long they reached Woods Landing. Kit fed and watered the horses and put them into the corral, while Swifty went to the truck and pulled out pieces of gear for their trek to the foothills. By the time Kit was done with the horses, Swifty had placed several items in their saddle bags and then both men headed over to the café.

As they approached the entrance to the café, Kit could see the neon "OPEN" sign was lit. They walked into the bar and nodded at Tess. She pointed to the open door at the end of the bar and when they walked through it, they found themselves in a dining room.

A young girl with a white apron pointed to an empty table, and Kit and Swifty pulled out chairs and seated themselves. The dining room had about ten tables and over half of them were full of diners.

The young waitress returned with glasses of ice water and menus, and it didn't take long for them to make their selections. Both men ordered cheeseburger plates with onion rings and a small salad. Kit ordered a Dr. Pepper to drink and Swifty ordered coffee.

"What's the plan for this afternoon?" asked Swifty.

"After lunch, I'll look over our maps and set up some search zones," said Kit. "We should be able to complete at least one zone this afternoon."

"Works for me," said Swifty.

The two men devoured their lunch and fifteen minutes later they were headed back to their cabin. Kit went into the cabin and Swifty continued to the corral.

By the time Kit had gone over his maps and divided the foothills above the Nordstrom ranch into search zones, Swifty had the horses saddled and their gear repacked.

When Kit walked out of the cabin with his map in hand, Swifty was already mounted and holding the reins to Kit's horse.

"Let's get movin' Andrews. We're burnin' daylight," said Swifty.

Kit just grinned and mounted his horse.

Soon, both men were mounted, and they had their horses at a trot as they headed south on County Road 10 toward the Nordstrom ranch.

In less than an hour, they were riding west on the Nordstrom ranch lane. Kit stopped them at the gate on the north side of the ranch lane and reached down from his horse and unlatched the gate. Still astride his horse, Kit opened the gate and after he and Swifty were through, he closed and latched the gate behind them.

They followed the two track in the grass and dirt of the pasture they had entered. After half an hour, they crossed the Big Laramie River on an old wooden bridge and soon they were stopped by yet another gate. Kit repeated his latching and unlatching of the gate, and they proceeded on. This time they were in a lane fenced on both sides. The lane ran on for over a mile, and then they came to another gate. Once through this gate, they were on a faint two track in the grass. Kit could see no fences beyond them and was sure they were off the Nordstrom ranch and onto BLM land as they neared the crest of the foothill.

As they rode up toward the crest of the foothill, both men were on full alert and were constantly scanning their surroundings and listening carefully.

They soon reached the crest, and they brought their horses to a halt. The two track they had been following had petered out. Kit pulled out his map and studied it while he compared it to their surroundings.

"Are we lost yet?" asked Swifty.

"You've been lost most of your life," said Kit. "Why should today be any different."

"So, I guess that means we're lost," responded an unrepentant Swifty.

Kit ignored Swifty. "I think we keep about thirty yards apart and move laterally from where we are to the south over to that clump of Aspen trees," said Kit.

Swifty nodded his agreement and quickly both riders were riding south thirty yards apart on a route that had them moving parallel to the foothill crest on the western slope.

Both riders took their time and carefully scanned their surroundings ahead of and below them. When they reached the clump of Aspen trees, they dropped lower on the western slope and rode back to the north, keeping their thirty-yard interval as they rode.

A large rock nestled close to the crest of the foothill marked where they had initially started their search. When they reached a spot below the rock, they again dropped lower on the slope and rode to the south to a spot below where the clump of Aspen trees stood.

The two men repeated this process for almost four hours. By that time, they had ridden the western slope of their search zone from the crest to a spot about a mile and a half lower on the slope.

Kit brought his horse to a halt and Swifty followed suit. "I think we'll call it a day," said Kit. "We go much longer, and we'll be losing the light." With that he took out his GPS and marked their final spot as a waypoint after the portable GPS had acquired enough satellites to be operative. Then Kit pulled out his cell-phone and took a couple of pictures of the area they had searched.

"Are you done here, professor?" said Swifty with some annoyance.

Kit put his GPS and cell phone away and just grinned at Swifty.

Both men turned their horses toward the crest of the foothill and an hour later they were riding into the area in front of their cabin. Kit and Swifty unsaddled their horses and Swifty led then into the free corral where he fed and watered them. Kit put their gear back in the truck.

"Hungry?" asked Kit.

"Does a bear shit in the woods? Of course, I'm hungry after an afternoon of riding over hell's half acre and findin' nothin'," replied Swifty.

"Dinner is on me," said Kit.

"It sure as hell better be," snorted Swifty.

Both men entered the café and were surprised to see a different bartender behind the bar. The bar was empty.

"What can I get you boys?" asked the bartender. She was almost a carbon copy of Tess, only much younger.

"What happened to Tess?" asked Swifty.

"She finished her shift. I'm her daughter. My name is Bess. Who are you boys?"

Kit and Swifty introduced themselves to Bess and she quickly fulfilled their request for two cold beers.

The two men sat at a small table and each took a welcome swallow of cold beer.

"Damn, that hit the spot," said Swifty.

"It sure did," agreed Kit.

"So, do we chalk up today as a waste of time?" asked Swifty.

"A search has to begin somewhere, and today was just a start. We've got a lot more area to search up on the foothills," said Kit.

"How long do you figure it will take us to search all of it?"

"It could take us over a week, but we could find the cabin without searching the entire area, so our search could be over tomorrow, if we're lucky," replied Kit.

"The sooner, the better. We make awful tempting targets ridin' up there in the open," said Swifty.

"I don't think anyone is gunnin' for us, Swifty," said Kit.

"Easy for you to say. Ridin' out in the open and movin' slowly makes me downright uncomfortable," said Swifty.

They finished their beers and headed into the dining room. The waitress told them to sit anywhere they wanted as the dining room was almost deserted except for one table occupied by two older couples.

"We must have beat the rush," said Swifty.

"I have no idea if there is a rush on a week-night at this place," replied Kit.

The waitress brought them glasses of ice water and took their orders. Swifty ordered a steak and Kit settled on fried chicken. They each ordered another cold beer. They were halfway through their beers when their meals arrived. Both men dug into their food.

"That's one good thing about you and food," said Kit.

"What's that?"

"The one time I can count on you bein' quiet is when you're eating."

"Kiss my ass, tenderfoot," mumbled Swifty between bites of his steak.

CHAPTER ELEVEN

After riding for about an hour the next morning, they found themselves turning into the ranch lane for the Nordstrom Ranch. As they approached the ranch house, Kit had Nels' home-made map out. He stopped them at a fence gate on the right side of the lane just before they reached the yard of the ranch house.

Kit unlatched and opened the gate while still on horseback. Soon he and Swifty had passed through the last gate on the Nordstrom Ranch after closing and latching the gate. They rode to the top of the foothill, Once on the crest, they stopped to carefully view the area around them.

Kit listened carefully and sniffed the air. Nothing that he saw, smelled, or heard gave him any indication of the cabin's location.

Swifty dismounted from his horse and handed his reins to Kit.

"What're you doing, Swifty?" asked a confused Kit.

"Your system sucks," said Swifty.

"What do you mean, it sucks?"

"It's a stupid plan. It might work on a small snow field, but it makes no sense on an area this big."

"What's your alternative?" asked Kit.

"I got an idea," said Swifty.

"Swifty has an idea," exclaimed Kit. "God help us, Swifty finally has an idea!"

Swifty ignored Kit's sarcasm. "The old man was drivin' a heavy old truck. Even if he only made a few trips, he and the truck had to leave an imprint. It can't be that hard to find."

Swifty began to walk slowly in ever widening circles around the spot where they had stopped on the summit of the foothill.

Kit realized Swifty was looking for sign and trying to cut the trail that Mr. Kelly might have made driving the heavy old Dodge truck over the summit. He had seen Swifty try to cut trail many times before. Kit sat patiently on his horse and waited for Swifty to finish and come back for his horse.

Swifty's tracking circle had widened until he was about forty yards out from where Kit waited. Suddenly Swifty stopped and went down to one knee. He used his hand to move the grasses aside. He moved more grass with his other hand and then began to crawl forward in a southwesterly direction. After about five minutes of crawling and moving grasses aside, Swifty rose to his feet and signaled Kit to come to him.

Kit urged his horse forward leading Swifty's horse with him. When he reached Swifty, Kit halted the horses.

"Find anything?" asked Kit.

"Traces of tire tracks that look like they belong to an old Dodge truck," said Swifty with a satisfied smile on his face. "I'm sure this is the faint two track old Kelly made when he drove between his cabin and the Nordstrom Ranch. I'm gonna follow it on foot, and you stay behind me with the horses."

Kit nodded his understanding and waited until Swifty had advanced about twenty yards before he and the horses followed.

Swifty came to a halt and turned to face Kit. "I knew your plan of searching was crap, tenderfoot," he said defiantly. Then he turned back to his tracking.

Almost an hour later, Swifty was leading them through several clumps of trees on a faint path just wide enough for an old Dodge Power Wagon. Fifteen minutes later, Swifty called a halt and walked back to Kit and the horses. Swifty took his canteen off his saddle horn and took a long drink. "Thirsty work," he said as he replaced the canteen. Without another word, Swifty resumed his tracking efforts. He led the way as they wound around and through groves of trees and went further down the west side of the foothill.

Kit referred to his portable GPS and could see they were headed in a southwesterly direction.

As Swifty led them around a large boulder, he came to a sudden stop. "Bingo," said Swifty.

Kit rode up to find out what Swifty had seen. When he was next to Swifty, he reined in his horse and found himself looking at a large cave. The entrance was shielded on both sides by large pine trees.

Kit dismounted and tied off their horses to a nearby pine tree. Both men walked forward to the entrance to the cave. As they got closer they could see the cave was about nine feet high and about ten feet wide. The cave went back into the foothill for about forty feet. Sitting inside the cave was a 1952 Dodge Power Wagon with more bare metal showing than paint.

"Quite the garage," said Swifty.

"It certainly is," said Kit. "The cave slopes slightly uphill so water from above just runs around it and on down the slope."

"It's like having a bomb shelter for your truck," said Swifty.

"Let's check out the truck," said Kit.

Both men entered the cave, one on each side of the truck. The dusty truck was unlocked and they opened the side doors. The truck was empty except for a plastic water bottle on the passenger side of the seat.

Swifty went back to his horse and pulled a screwdriver out of his saddle bag. He opened the hood of the truck and propped it open. Then he used the screwdriver to make a connection between the battery and the starter. The move caused a few sparks and the starter turned over.

"Battery is still charged," said Swifty. "Old Mr. Kelly drove this beast not too long ago."

"Let's see if we can find the cabin from here," said Kit.

Swifty lowered the hood on the truck and replaced the screwdriver in his saddlebags.

"Did you see this?" asked Kit.

"What?" replied Swifty.

"There are four five gallon cans of gas under a tarp a little further into the cave," said Kit.

"Are they all full?" asked Swifty.

After checking the cans, Kit replied, "Three are full, one's empty."

"Smart old coot," said Swifty.

Kit exited the cave and he untied the reins to the horses. Then he joined Swifty who was searching the area around the front of the cave for signs.

"Cabin can't be too far from the cave," said Swifty.

"Why do you think that?" asked Kit.

"He had to haul his supplies, and at his age, the closer to the cave and the shorter the trips, the better."

"You lead, and I'll follow," said Kit.

"As it should be," snorted Swifty.

Swifty began to study the ground carefully, when he paused and said, "Aha."

"What is it?" asked Kit.

"I see what looks like the faint tracks of two small, parallel tires. Might be from a small cart," replied Swifty.

"That makes sense, using a cart to get things from the cave to the cabin," said Kit.

With Swifty again in the lead and Kit and the horses following behind him, they slowly made their way through a heavier growth of pine trees on a path now much narrower than the one Swifty had tracked to the cave.

Swifty came to a pile of rocks and stopped. He held up his right hand. Kit and the horses halted.

"Listen," said Swifty.

Kit listened intently and soon he heard the faint sound of splashing water. Swifty led the way around the rock pile and soon discovered the source of the sound. There was a small spring coming out of the side of the rock pile, and at the base of the rocks was a naturally hollowed out basin of rocks full of water. The water overflowed the basin and made a very small stream of water headed downhill from the rock pile.

"I'd guess this was the old man's water source," said Swifty. "The cabin can't be far from here."

Kit nodded his agreement. They let the horses water in the basin and then both men and their horses moved out with Swifty in the lead.

They moved through a heavy screen of pine trees and suddenly the cabin was in front of them. It was small and built out of logs. Kit estimated the cabin was about twenty feet long and fifteen feet wide. The roof was made of old metal, and it was rusty in color. A crude chimney of stone was at the north end of the cabin. They tied off the horses and Kit watched the front of the cabin, while Swifty silently circled around the old building. When he returned to where Kit stood guard, Swifty gave Kit the sign for all clear.

"Any other doors?" whispered Kit.

"Nope. One window on the front, and one on the east and south side. No lights on," whispered Swifty.

There was no noise, nor smells coming from the small, dark cabin. The front door was closed. Next to the front door was a small two-wheeled cart with bicycle-sized tires. Swifty motioned for Kit to cover him. Kit pulled out his Kimber 45. When he was set, he nodded to Swifty.

Swifty had also pulled out his Freedom Arms 454 Casul caliber revolver and carefully made his way to the door of the cabin. Once he was next to the door, he laid his head next to the door and listened. When he was satisfied that he could hear nothing from within the cabin, he reached for the door handle and pushed open the cabin door, while remaining next to the door and not in front of it.

The door swung open and there was nothing, but silence. Swifty entered the cabin and after a few seconds, he reappeared at the door and motioned for Kit to join him.

Kit entered the cabin with his gun in his hand. Swifty was inside the dark cabin, moving around. Suddenly there was a burst of light. Swifty had found a kerosene lantern and lit it with a match. With the sudden addition of light, both men could clearly see the interior of the cabin. The cabin was one large room with a small, but efficient kitchen equipped with a wood burning cook stove. There was a small propane powered refrigerator. The kitchen sink had a drain that went into an empty five-gallon pail under it. A five-gallon pail of water sat on the counter next to the sink.

A large blanket hung over a rope separated the sleeping area from the rest of the cabin. The stone fireplace had a battered rug in front of it. There was a small pile of split firewood stacked next to the fireplace and a rough-hewn table with two mismatched wooden chairs. A long pole was attached to the log wall and several articles of clothing hung from it. A large metal wash pan and a scrub board hung from a hook on the wall.

Swifty lit another hurricane lantern and now the interior of the cabin was well illuminated. Both men stood and carefully studied their surroundings.

"Check out the walls, Kit," said Swifty.

Kit looked carefully at the walls and saw what Swifty had observed. There were six spots on the walls that were darker than the rest of the walls. They were rectangular, and slightly larger than an eight and a half inch by eleven-inch piece of stationary. Kit stepped forward to one space on the wall and found a nail in the log where the frame would have hung.

"Looks like old Ted did have the letters sent to his father by Charley Russell," said Kit.

"It don't look like old Ted left the cabin on his own," said Swifty.

"How do you figure that?" asked Kit.

"The front door was unlocked. The three windows all got shutters, and they ain't closed and latched. Then there's the fact his truck is still parked in the cave," said Swifty. "You see what you can uncover in here, and I'll take a look outside and see if I can find any sign of old Ted."

Kit agreed, and Swifty was quickly out the door. There wasn't much to search, but Kit carefully went through everything in the small cabin. In the makeshift bedroom, he found a small shelf attached to the log wall. On the shelf, he made a discovery. A red envelope sealed and stamped and addressed to Mustang Kelly in Chicago. Kit picked it up and put it in his vest pocket.

The rest of the cabin revealed nothing helpful. Kit found a half loaf of moldy bread in a drawer in the kitchen and some moldy cheese in the small refrigerator. He checked the propane bottle supplying the refrigerator and it was almost empty. A spare propane bottle was nestled next to the refrigerator.

Satisfied he had thoroughly searched the cabin, Kit closed and latched the window shutters Swifty had mentioned. Then he blew out the two hurricane lanterns. When he was finished, Kit stepped outside the cabin door.

Once outside, Kit latched the front door and walked back to where they had left the horses. There was no sign of Swifty. Kit grabbed his canteen on his saddle horn and unscrewed the lid. He took a long drink and after replacing the lid, he replaced the canteen.

Kit took out his GPS and activated it. When the unit emitted a signal indicting it had acquired the necessary number of satellites, Kit took a reading of the cabin's location by longitude and latitude and stored it in the unit's memory as a waypoint. When he was satisfied that the location had been stored in the GPS, he shut it off and returned it to his shirt pocket.

Kit sensed movement to his left and his hand dropped to his pistol as his head turned to face a possible threat.

"Take it easy there, partner. It's just me," said Swifty as he emerged from behind a large pine tree. "Find anything interesting in the cabin?"

Kit pulled out the obviously un-mailed birthday card addressed to Mustang Kelly. "This's why Tang never got the card. It never got mailed."

"It looks more and more likely that old Ted's sudden disappearance was not by his choice," said Swifty.

"What makes you so sure?" asked Kit.

"The cabin was not buttoned up like a smart old codger like Ted would have done. He didn't mail the card. He didn't take his truck. At his age, just how far do you think he would have gotten on foot, and why would he when he had the truck?" asked Swifty.

"I got no idea," replied Kit.

"Well, I damn sure do," said Swifty. "I found some interesting prints in the dirt under all them pine needles back of the house."

"What kind of prints?" asked Kit.

"Looks to me like two or three of them ATVs with them all-terrain tires came in behind the cabin. There's also some boot prints. Looks to be at least three sets. Prints show them going to and from the cabin. Somebody tried to sweep them out with a branch," said Swifty as he held up a four-foot long pine branch that was still green. Bits of dirt and debris were still stuck in the branch's pine needles. "Found this where someone tossed it in the weeds."

"Did you find where the tracks lead from the cabin?" asked Kit.

"I got a general direction, but that was over a month ago, and the trail is cold and hard to find," replied Swifty.

"We still got daylight," said Kit. "Let's see if we can follow the trail."

"Let's walk and you lead the horses like we did before," said Swifty. "The trail might get better when we get further from the cabin."

"Sounds like a plan," replied Kit.

Swifty walked to the rear of the cabin with Kit following and leading their horses. After a couple of circles walked by Swifty, he began to move down the slope from the cabin and Kit followed.

They walked for over two hours. Several times Swifty lost the trail and had to circle to cut it again. One time both men were startled when a large mule deer doe jumped out from behind a screen of pine trees and bounded away in the opposite direction.

Both men stood there with their pistols drawn. "False alarm," said Swifty, and both men holstered their pistols.

Each time the trail turned, it took them down slope, but at angle that moved them in a northwesterly direction.

Finally, the trail led them to a well-defined ATV trail that showed signs of heavy traffic. They had come upon one of the ATV trails on BLM land that Nels Nordstrom had mentioned to them.

Both men took a break to drink from their canteens, and Kit handed Swifty an energy bar he pulled from his saddlebags. Both men sat on the ground and ate their bars and drank from their canteens.

"Can you tell which direction they went on the ATV trail?" asked Kit.

"There's been too much traffic," replied Swifty. "Them ATVs all use pretty much the same tires to tell me anything. I think we follow the trail to the northwest and see where it goes."

"Works for me," said Kit. He pulled out his GPS and when it was active, he marked the junction of the two trails as a waypoint.

The two men swung into the saddles of their horses and headed down the ATV trail. Swifty led and Kit followed, both men scanning the sides of the ATV trail for any signs of tire prints leaving the trail.

They rode for over an hour and then came to a fork in the ATV trail. One fork went west and the other fork went north. They stopped their horses and contemplated their next move.

"Which way do we go from here?" asked Kit.

"There's no way of telling which fork those bastards took," replied Swifty.

"Let's take a break," said Kit. "I want to look at my maps."

"Works for me," replied Swifty.

The two men dismounted and tied off their horses. Swifty lay down on the ground and tipped his cowboy hat over his eyes.

Kit just grinned at his partner. Swifty had learned this in the army. Never pass up a chance to get some shut-eye was his motto. Kit retrieved his maps from his saddlebags and unfolded them on the ground in front of him.

Kit determined their current location on the map and looked for some indication of the ATV trails. There were some trails on the map, but the trail they were on was not on it. Kit moved his finger on a northwesterly direction on the map and came to the small town of Albany.

Kit decided he needed to look up Albany on the internet when they got back to the cabin and a wireless source. He wasn't sure Albany had anything to do with their search, but at the moment, he had nothing else to go on.

Kit interrupted Swifty's beauty sleep and was met with curses and disapproval of the interruption of his nap. Kit just grinned at his partner's protests.

It was almost dark before the two horsemen made their way back to their cabin at Woods Landing. After unsaddling their horses and leaving them in the corral with grain, hay, and water, they made for the café.

CHAPTER TWELVE

Bess welcomed then as they entered the café. They headed into the dining room, pausing only to say hello to Bess. They found the dining room almost full. They found an empty table and were immediately furnished with menus and ice water.

The young waitress started to leave, but Swifty asked her to hold up. "We don't need to look at the menus," said Swifty. "Just bring us two of the biggest steaks you got with all the trimmin's."

"We'll each have a glass of your best bourbon while we're waitin'," said Kit.

"Make sure you give the check to the rich guy," said Swifty.

The waitress smiled at them and hurried off. She could tell the two tall men were impatient for their meal. She quickly returned with their drinks, smiled at them, collected their unused menus and left.

Both men sat back in their chairs and relaxed. They were both tired from a hard day in the saddle and too hungry to talk.

"Here's to old Ted," said Swifty as he raised his glass.

"I'll drink to that," said Kit as he clinked his glass against Swifty's.

"Hell, you'll drink to anything, tenderfoot," snorted Swifty as he took a long swig out of his glass.

Kit just grinned and pulled his iPad out of a small leather case.

"Is that one of them smart thingies?" asked Swifty.

"It's an iPad and yes, it's pretty smart," answered Kit.

"Ask it where we can find some fast women and some cheap whiskey."

"You ask it," said Kit.

"I don't know how to work that damn thing."

"All you have to do is ask it," said a smiling Kit.

"You mean talk to it?"

"That's exactly what I mean," said Kit.

"That thing and me don't speak the same language," snorted Swifty.

"Just give it a try."

"Oh, hell," said Swifty. "Where can I find loose women and cheap whiskey?"

After a short pause, the iPad responded with a feminine voice, "In your dreams, pal."

Kit burst out laughing, startling several nearby diners.

"Goddamn smart ass machine. This is what I get for listenin' to the likes of you, tenderfoot."

Kit ignored his protesting friend and began tapping on the keys of the iPad. While he was tapping, Swifty called the waitress over and asked for another round of drinks, which arrived almost immediately.

"Whatcha lookin' for in that thing?" asked Swifty.

"I'm looking up Albany, Wyoming. Seems they have a fairly sizeable lodge there."

"Lodge? In Albany? Hell, there can't be hardly any people in that place," said Swifty.

"According to the last census, there are about eighty people in Albany," said Kit.

"Eighty people in that little place?" said a surprised Swifty.

"It also says the lodge isn't so small. It can handle about one hundred and eleven guests in their hotel, cabins, houses, and suites."

"Really," said Swifty.

"Guess what one of their main activities in the summer is," said Kit.

"I ain't got no idea," replied Swifty.

"Ridin' ATVs on trails," said Kit with a smile on his face.

"I suppose this means we're gonna pay Albany a visit tomorrow," said Swifty.

"Yeah, it does," replied Kit. "But this time we just take the truck. I think we should be able to get all the information we need at that lodge."

"In that case, let's order another round of drinks."

Kit just sat back in his chair and grinned at his friend.

Their steak dinners arrived and the steaks were so large they covered the entire plate. The sides were served on separate dishes. The waitress also brought another round of drinks.

"Hey, Miss, we didn't order another round," said Kit.

"These are courtesy of Bess, the bartender," replied the smiling waitress.

Kit and Swifty asked her to extend their thanks to Bess and they dug into their steaks. After dinner, they personally thanked Bess on their way through the bar. Once the two men returned to their cabin they were both sound asleep in minutes.

Both were awake early and soon were pushing the door open to the café, although the open sign was clearly not lit.

Sitting at the bar were Hoppy, Shorty, and Cal while Tess was busy behind the bar washing glassware.

"Hello, boys. What'll it be this morning?" asked Tess.

"I'll have three eggs over easy, sausage patties, and hash browns," said Kit.

"I'll have the same," echoed Swifty.

"Coffee?" asked Tess.

"Hot and black," said Swifty.

"Add some cream and sugar," said Kit.

"Coming up," said Tess.

"You boys have any luck findin' that old man?" asked Hoppy as the two men took seats at the bar.

"We made a little progress," answered Kit.

"How's that?" asked Shorty.

"Thanks to Swifty's trackin' skills, we found the old boy's cabin."

"Where was it?" asked Cal.

"It was over on the western slope of the foothill just west of the Nordstrom Ranch," replied Kit.

"That area is pretty wooded, as I recall," said Hoppy.

"Lots of pine, fir, and spruce, with a little aspen thrown in," said Swifty.

"Any sign of the old guy?" asked Shorty.

"Nope," said Kit.

"Maybe he just took off for a while," offered Cal.

"He left his truck, and he didn't lock up and secure his cabin," said Swifty.

"That don't sound good," said Hoppy.

"You boys get much ATV traffic on your spreads?" asked Kit.

"Too damn much and none of it welcome," said Cal.

"Punk kids with no respect for private property and the law," echoed Hoppy.

"Why do you ask?" said Shorty.

"I found sign around the cabin that looked like it had been visited by folks on three or four ATVs," said Swifty.

"I wouldn't put nothing past those punks I seen trespassing on my place," said Hoppy.

"Have you had any trouble with people on ATVs in the past couple of months?" asked Kit.

"Can't say I have," said Hoppy.

"Have you heard of any of your neighbor's havin' trouble?" asked Kit.

"I heard old Randy Scott was having some trouble. Course he has trouble with everybody," said Cal.

"That old buzzard would have trouble with Christ if he stopped in for a visit," said Hoppy.

"Not if he was bringin' a cooler of Pabst Blue Ribbon," injected Swifty. All five men burst into laughter.

"Well, we best be goin'," said Kit.

"Good luck lookin' for the old guy," said Hoppy.

"Yeah, good luck," echoed Cal and Shorty.

Tess just kept washing glassware.

Both men stepped out of the café. As Kit turned to go to the cabin, Swifty grabbed him by the arm.

"Take a look at that," said Swifty as he pointed to the front of the old general store. Tied to the hitching post was a mule harnessed to a small two-wheeled cart.

"That looks like something out of the great Mormon trek to Salt Lake City," said Swifty.

Kit had to admit it was the first mule drawn two-wheeled cart he had ever seen. It was a strange sight, even in Woods Landing.

While the two men were standing in front of the café gawking at the cart, a short, stout, white haired woman in men's clothing and boots walked out of the general store.

Her arms were full of supplies, and she was loading them into the cart.

"We could be gentlemen and help the old lady," said Kit, but Swifty was already moving toward the cart.

"Can we give you a hand, Ma'am," said Swifty.

The old woman looked up in surprise. She quickly took in the two tall cowboys and her eyes became suspicious.

"Help me with what?" she said in a high voice.

"If you've got more supplies to load, we'd be happy to give you a hand," said Swifty.

The old woman looked carefully at Swifty and then at Kit. Finally, she spoke. "I 'spose it'd be all right if you two young whelps promise to be careful with my stuff."

"We'll be real careful," responded Swifty.

Both men followed the old lady inside the general store and were soon carrying her purchased supplies out to her cart. When they were finished, she untied the mule, got up on the seat on the cart and left without a word to the two men.

"I'm overwhelmed with her thanks," said Kit.

"Yeah, she just gushed over with gratitude" said a grinning Swifty.

"I bet we don't see her again," said Kit.

"Why do you say that?" asked Swifty.

"She had enough supplies for a couple of months by the looks of them," said Kit.

"It did seem like an awful lot of stuff," agreed Swifty. "It looked like almost too much for one person."

"Maybe she's got a boyfriend," said Kit with a snicker.

"I pity that poor old bastard," said Swifty.

Both men resumed their walk back to their cabin. They had only taken a few steps when Kit came to a halt. Swifty also stopped and threw a puzzled look at his friend.

"What's wrong?" asked Swifty.

"I got an idea," said Kit.

"This idea thing is gettin' out of hand," said Swifty.

Kit laughed and led Swifty over to the general store. Kit led the way through the door and made his way to the counter where Thelma stood, with Louise working on a shelf behind her.

"Pardon me, Thelma," said Kit.

"Yes," replied Thelma, obviously surprised the young man remembered her name.

"That older lady who was just here. The one we helped load up her supplies. Do you happen to know her name?" asked Kit.

"The lady with the mule-drawn cart?" replied Thelma.

"That's the one," said Kit.

"I believe her name is Eleanor," said Thelma. "You know, like the President's wife."

"Which President?" asked Swifty.

"Why FDR of course," said Thelma.

"How silly of me to forget," said Swifty, biting his tongue.

"It was Eleanor, wasn't it, Louise?" said Thelma.

Louise nodded in agreement.

"Do you happen to know Eleanor's last name?" inquired Kit.

"No, I don't believe I do," said Thelma. "Do you know, Louise?"

Louise shook her head no.

"Will there be anything else, gentlemen? We have a store to run," said Thelma.

"No, no there is nothing else," said Kit as he led Swifty out of the general store.

"That Louise just can't seem to shut up," said Swifty.

"Maybe that's a good thing," said Kit as the two men walked back to their cabin.

111

CHAPTER THIRTEEN

After they finished feeding the horses and making sure there was enough water in the trough, Kit and Swifty climbed into their pickup truck and headed out of the Woods Landing parking lot.

According to Kit's map, Albany was about five miles away on County Road 12. Kit drove just below the speed limit of forty-five miles per hour, as they rolled along the blacktop two-lane road.

Before long, they saw signs welcoming them to the lodge. Kit pulled into the lodge parking lot and then up to the front of the hotel. The hotel was a long, two-story building of wood and stone. A covered wrap-around porch dominated the hotel.

Kit and Swifty exited their parked pick-up truck and walked up the steps to the porch and the large double doors that served as the entrance to the hotel.

They stepped into a large foyer with vaulted ceilings of polished tongue and groove wood. The theme was mountain lodge with a large stone fireplace and various mounted heads of bears, elk, deer, and even a buffalo decorating the walls. The floors were a smooth stone.

Kit made his way to the counter and asked the attendant for the lodge manager. He gave the attendant his business card. Kit waited while she made a phone call and after she hung up the phone, she asked him to wait in the lobby. Kit and Swifty found two large overstuffed leather chairs by the fireplace and each took a seat.

About five minutes later, a dark haired, attractive middle-aged woman dressed in designer jeans, a silk blouse, and a buckskin fringed jacket strode into the lobby. She had on designer boots that looked like cowboy boots, but were not.

"Mr. Andrews?" she asked as she approached Kit and Swifty.

Both men rose to their feet. "My name is Kit Andrews," said Kit as he offered his hand to the lady. "This is my partner, Swifty Olson. We're with Rocky Mountain Searchers out of Kemmerer."

The lady took his hand and shook it and did not offer her hand to Swifty. "Please, sit down, gentlemen," she said. "My name is Sheila, I'm the manager of the lodge. What can I do for you?"

As soon as all three of them were seated, Kit spoke up. "We're looking into the disappearance of an elderly man who was living off the grid in a cabin in the foothills just south of Woods Landing."

"I'm sorry to hear someone is missing, but what does that have to do with my lodge?" asked Sheila.

"We suspect foul play," said Kit. "We believe he may have been abducted by persons unknown using ATVs. We tracked the ATVs until we came to one of the main trails, and we think the trail may have led to your lodge."

"I see," said Sheila thoughtfully. "Excuse me while I get a copy of one of our trail maps."

With that Sheila rose and disappeared behind the main counter. She was back quickly with a colorful map. She opened it on the coffee table in front of them and pointed to the various trails depicted on the map.

"Each trail has a different color code and the Rimrock Trail is the yellow one," said Sheila. "As you can see, it runs slightly southwest from the lodge and stays on the west side of the foothills all the way down to Colorado."

"I think that's the trail we are looking for," said Kit. "May we keep this map?"

"Of course, please keep it with my compliments," said Sheila. "And here is my business card. Please feel free to call me if you have any further questions."

"Thank you," said Kit as he accepted her card. "I'll be sure to do that."

"Please use it to call me if you ever have any interest in staying at the lodge, or anything else," said Sheila.

"Thank you, ma'am," said Kit. "I'll be sure to do that. Thank you for your kindness and your help."

"Good luck with your search for the poor, unfortunate old man. I hope you find him," said Sheila, as she offered her hand.

Kit took her hand and felt her grip his back and hold on for a little longer than she had originally. He and Swifty said good-bye and headed out the door of the lodge.

As soon as they were on the porch of the lodge, Swifty started in on Kit.

"My, oh my, I do believe that Miss Sheila is hopin' Mr. Kit will call her lookin' for something else," said Swifty with a voice that was dripping with sarcasm.

"I have no idea what the hell you're talking about," replied Kit.

"The hell you don't. Why that woman was practically panting after you, tenderfoot."

"That woman is at least ten years older than me, Swifty."

"Ten years older means she has more experience than you and there's no substitute for experience," said Swifty, who was grinning from ear to ear, enjoying Kit's discomfort.

"I got no interest in Miss Sheila," said Kit.

"But she's got plenty of interest in you, tenderfoot. I bet this ain't the last you hear from her," said Swifty.

"I'll never hear from her. I told her my name and your name, and I didn't even give her a business card," said Kit.

"Oh, she's got your business card," said Swifty.

"How can that be?" said a puzzled Kit.

"'Cause I slipped her one on our way out," said Swifty who burst out laughing and continued to laugh all the way to their parked pick-up truck.

When they reached the truck, Kit stopped before opening the truck door. "Before we go, let's take a look at the lodge's ATV rental place and see where the trails come into the lodge."

Kit led the way and Swifty followed, but he continued his barrage of suggestive remarks about Kit and Sheila until Kit stopped in his tracks and confronted Swifty.

"We're here on business. Shut the hell up."

Swifty acted like his feelings were hurt and gave Kit his hurt puppy look. "Yessur, yessur, Mr. Big Shot," but he did shut up. He knew from experience getting Kit pissed off would not end well.

They followed the signs to the ATV rental shop. There they found a young boy manning the counter. Kit asked for the shop manager and the boy excused himself and went through a door into a back room that looked like a shop for working on the ATVs.

A bearded man appeared through the door and approached Kit and Swifty.

"I'm Clem, the shop manager. How can I help you?" he asked.

Kit introduced himself and Swifty and explained they were looking into the disappearance of an old man and why they were at the lodge inquiring about the ATV trails.

"I ain't sure how I can help," said Clem, "but ask away."

"Do you get a lot of rentals for ATVs or do most folks bring their own?" asked Kit.

"We keep a fleet of about twenty ATVs and UTVs for rent," said Clem.

"What's a UTV?" asked Kit.

"It's easier to show you than to try to explain," said Clem. He took Kit and Swifty out the back of the shop and stopped at a four-wheel vehicle with a bench seat and a steering wheel. "As you can see, a UTV is like a small pick-up truck. We even have them with two bench seats that seat four people. That model has gotten more and more popular. I'll probably buy more for next season."

"You still rent the ATV type?" asked Kit.

"Yes, but not very much. The UTV is a lot more popular, especially with the novice riders and the families who come here. Most of the experienced riders usually bring their own vehicles in on trailers," said Clem.

"Thank you, Clem," said Kit. "You've been very helpful."

"How about you and your partner take one for a test drive," said Clem. "I can put you on the trail you were asking about, and you can see what you think."

"Oh, I don't think so," said Kit.

"Hey, it's on the house. No charge," said Clem.

"We'll take it," said Swifty before Kit could respond to Clem's offer.

Ten minutes later, Kit and Swifty were roaring down the trail marked in yellow on the map Shelia had given them. Swifty was at the wheel and Kit was hanging on for dear life.

After about ten minutes of Swifty transforming himself into Parnelli Jones and scaring the crap out of some other UTV riders they met on the trail, Kit shouted to make himself heard over the wind and the engine noise. "Slow down, dammit."

Swifty turned to Kit and smiled and finally took his foot off the UTV's accelerator. When they had slowed down enough to be heard, Swifty said, "I gotta get me one of these things."

"Not with me, you're not," responded Kit.

"Spoil sport, chicken shit tenderfoot," retorted Swifty.

The UTV speedometer indicated they were rolling along at thirty-five miles per hour. Even at that speed on the clear, ten-foot-wide trail, most of what they passed was a blur to Kit.

In the next half hour, they met several other UTVs and passed several. Finally, Swifty took his foot off the accelerator pedal and the UTV slowed down. After about ten minutes, Swifty brought the UTV to a stop.

"We're here," said Swifty.

"Where's here?" asked a suspicious Kit.

"This is where we cut the main trail when we were following the trail from the cabin," said Swifty.

"How can you be sure?" asked Kit.

"I know 'cause I marked that tree limb over there," said Swifty pointing to a branch about five feet off the ground on the left side of the trail. There on the branch Kit could see some white toilet paper wrapped around it.

"Toilet paper? You used toilet paper to mark a tree?" said an amazed Kit.

"I don't leave home without it," said a grinning Swifty.

Both men got off the UTV and walked over to the tree. Sure enough, Kit could see their boot prints next to the tree and it was obvious where the thieves' ATVs had rolled into the main trail.

"How long do you think it would have taken them to get from here back to the lodge?" asked Kit.

Swifty thought for a few seconds and then responded. "I'd guess they would be driving pretty normal. They'd want to be careful of them framed letters and they wouldn't want to draw any attention to themselves. I'd say maybe an hour, maybe a little less."

"Shit," said Kit.

"What?" asked Swifty.

"I must be losing it. We should have checked for security cameras at the lodge. I'll bet those three ATVs were filmed when they left the lodge and when they came back."

"Maybe so, but we don't know the dates that this all happened. All we know is it happened sometime within the last two months," said Swifty.

"It's still worth looking into," said Kit. "There can't be that many groups of three ATVs going in and out of the lodge trail."

"There is one other thing," said Swifty.

"What's that?" asked Kit.

"Clem at the lodge shop said that most of the traffic now is UTV, not ATV. That could make the search easier," said Swifty.

"Are you sure they were on ATVs, not UTVs?" asked Kit.

"I'm sure, and I can prove it," said Swifty. He walked over to the old trail from the cabin and he used his feet to measure the distance between the tire marks in the grass. Then he moved back to their UTV and did the same thing between the rear tires. "The distance between the UTV tires is wider than on the ATV," said Swifty.

"Let's head back to the lodge and see if we can get permission to look at the tapes," said Kit.

"You bet," said a grinning Swifty. "I'm sure your new girlfriend will be happy to see you again."

"Swifty," said Kit.

"Yes?"

"Bite me," said Kit.

Swifty roared with laughter as he fired up the UTV and did a two-wheeled high speed U-turn on the trail. The only thing behind them was some toilet paper in a tree branch, fluttering in the wind.

CHAPTER FOURTEEN

Swifty had them back at the lodge in less than forty minutes. Clem came out of the shop to greet them.

"Well, what did you boys think of her?" asked Clem.

"I loved it," said Swifty. "I just told old Kit here, I got to get one of these things."

"If you boys come around at the end of the season, we sell off the older ones and you can get a pretty good bargain," said a grinning Clem.

"I'll keep that in mind," said Swifty. "Thanks for the chance to try one out. It was a lot of fun."

"How about you?" said Clem to Kit.

"I think Swifty was more impressed than I was, but it was a lot of fun."

"Glad to hear it," responded Clem.

"That said, I have another favor to ask of you, Clem," said Kit.

"Ask away," replied Clem.

"Do you folks have security cameras that would show any units entering or exiting the trail at the lodge?" asked Kit.

"We installed a new security system last spring and that includes cameras that record everyone who enters the trail at the lodge and, of course, anyone who exits the trail, as well," replied Clem.

Robert W. Callis

"Our insurance company required it. I can't tell you where all the cameras are located on the property for security reasons, but I see no problem in showing you the ones that record the access to the trail."

"Is your system tape or digital?" asked Swifty.

Clem looked surprised at Swifty's question. "It's digital. It was more expensive, but with the old tape system, we recycled the tapes so we only had recordings for thirty days back. This way we store everything they record," replied Clem.

Kit looked at Swifty and then turned to Clem. He explained that they were looking for three ATVs traveling together sometime within the last two months.

"I got to check with Sheila, the lodge manager, but I'm sure she would have no objections," said Clem.

Clem went back into the shop to call Sheila.

"We may just get lucky," said Kit.

"We could use a little luck on this one," replied Swifty.

Clem reappeared and told them Sheila had no objections to them viewing the security footage of the access to the trail only.

"How do we proceed?" asked Kit.

"I'll take you back into the shop and get you set up," said Clem.

"We really appreciate this," said Kit.

"No problem," replied Clem.

Fifteen minutes later, Swifty and Kit were seated on some folding metal chairs in front of a thirty-inch monitor in a small room separate from the rest of the shop. Clem explained how to work the security unit and how to pause, back up, and go forward, as well as how to slow the pictures down.

"You boys want something to drink?" asked Clem when he was done explaining.

"Thanks for the offer, but we're fine," replied Kit.

"If you need me for anything or have any problems, I'll be working in the shop just outside the door," said Clem.

Kit and Swifty thanked Clem and then proceeded to start viewing scenes beginning with two months prior and working their way forward.

The pictures were very distinct and at first both men watched as the camera's recordings came to life in front of them. After an hour, they decided to switch off viewing with each man taking a twenty-minute shift to keep alert and not have their eyes glaze over.

They had been viewing footage for almost three hours when Swifty yelled, "Got you!"

Kit had been sitting next to him with his eyes closed when he jerked to attention with Swifty's yell.

"What is it?" said a startled Kit.

"I got three tricked out ATVs leaving the lodge and returning three hours later. This was a month ago," said Swifty.

"How do you know it's them?" asked Kit.

"I'll show you," said Swifty.

Swifty started the footage with when the three ATVs entered the trail. He froze the footage and pointed to the rear of the ATVs. "See those plastic cargo boxes strapped behind each of the ATVs?" asked Swifty.

"I see them," replied Kit.

"Each of them is slightly bigger than those picture frames would be and they are deep enough to each hold two or three frames. All the other ATVs we've watched had backpacks or soft bags strapped on the back. Nobody else has had what looks like cargo boxes. I'm sure they're our boys," said Swifty.

Then Swifty advanced the footage until he reached the spot he wanted, and he stopped the film advance. The monitor screen was filled with the sight of the three ATVs returning to the lodge. The ATVs were moving much slower than when they left the lodge. The cargo boxes were tightly strapped behind each of the ATVs.

"We need to get a look of the footage of the parking lot. They brought those ATVs to the lodge and we need to see if we can identify their vehicle and trailer," said Swifty.

Kit called Clem into the security room and explained what they had found and requested the footage of the parking lot for the same day shown on the trail access footage. He also requested still pictures of the three ATVs from the footage. Clem agreed to print pictures for them.

"I'll have to call Sheila again and get permission to look at the parking lot footage," said Clem, "but since you found them on the trail access camera, I'm pretty sure she'll let us view it."

Clem left the security room and both Kit and Swifty got up from their chairs. Both men were stiff from over three hours of sitting.

Clem was back within a few minutes. "Sheila said she was fine with it. Let me spool it up for you," he said.

Soon he had the camera footage of the lodge parking lot on the monitor. Once he had the correct day, he began to advance the footage. Since they had the times the ATVs had accessed and exited the lodge trail, it did not take Clem long to find the truck and trailer that had transported the ATVs to the lodge.

The truck was parked going away from the lodge with the back of the trailer closest to the lodge camera. Kit had Clem enlarge the picture to get it as clear as possible and then had Clem get still pictures of the truck and trailer. When the footage showed the thieves loading the ATVs back on the trailer, Clem took still pictures of the action.

Finally, they backtracked to catch the footage where the truck first entered the lodge parking lot and got still pictures of the front and side of the truck and trailer.

Clem produced the still pictures, and Kit offered to pay for them.

"Sheila told me to help you and so as far as I'm concerned, the pictures are on the house. I hope you catch up with those guys," said Clem.

Soon, Swifty and Kit were striding toward the lodge with a folder full of still pictures.

"My belly's rubbin' against my backbone," said Swifty.

"Mine feels the same way," replied Kit.

Without another word spoken between them, the two friends headed for the lodge restaurant.

Fifteen minutes later, they were seated at a table in the restaurant. Both men had ordered the deluxe half-pound cheeseburger with fries and a salad. Before their food arrived, each of them had downed a cold beer.

While they waited for their food, Kit and Swifty sorted through the still pictures from the folder.

"There's no sign of old Ted on any of the three ATVs when they returned to the lodge," said Kit.

"Likely they ditched him somewhere along the trail," said Swifty.

"They had to know where the cabin was, and they had to know about the framed letters," said Kit.

"How so?" asked Swifty.

"They knew where they were going, and they had those cargo boxes to transport the framed letters safely," replied Kit.

"How could they know where the cabin was? Nobody we talked to knew anything about the location," said Swifty.

"Somebody found out somehow. My guess is somebody stumbled on the cabin and for whatever reason, old Ted let them in. Once inside the cabin, they saw the framed letters and knew what they were. When they left, they went back to wherever they came from and planned to come back and rob the old man. Or they told somebody else, and they came up with the idea to rob him," said Kit.

"That's a whole lot of what's, if's and maybe's," said Swifty.

"It's the best I can come up with right now," said Kit.

"Maybe your brain will work better when it gets fed," said Swifty.

No sooner had Swifty spoken, then the waitress arrived with their orders.

"Please bring us another round of beers," said Swifty to the waitress. She nodded her agreement and left. Five minutes later she interrupted their meal with two more cold beers.

The men consumed their meals like hungry wolves. Swifty caught the waitress's attention and ordered a piece of cherry pie and coffee for both of them.

"How did you know I wanted cherry pie?" asked Kit.

"I didn't give a shit what you wanted, and I wanted cherry pie," said Swifty.

"Lucky for you I do like cherry pie," said Kit

"Who doesn't," responded Swifty.

Kit just shook his head as he ate his pie.

Their pie finished, the two men sat back and sipped on their hot coffee. While they rested, Kit again rummaged through the photos in the folder.

"If I had a magnifying glass, I'm sure I can make out the license plate on the front of the truck when it was pulling into the parking lot and the plate on the trailer when it was parked in the lot," said Kit.

"Well, I ain't got no magnifying glass, but I bet I know someone who does," said Swifty.

"Who?"

"I'll bet Deputy Parcell back in Laramie has one and what's more, he has access to find out who the truck and trailer are licensed to, once we find out the plate numbers," said Swifty.

"You're right," said Kit. "What's more, this is looking more like a crime than a simple missing person's case."

"And we ain't no law enforcement," said Swifty. "We gotta be careful not to get our noses in something we ain't supposed to. I'm not in no mood to have to deal with lawyers, courts, and such."

"Before we go to Laramie, I think we need to finish one task," said Kit.

"What task is that?"

"We got hired to find old Ted Kelly, and we need to find him."

"Just how do you propose we do that?"

"I think we go back to the shop and rent a UTV from Clem and go back and search the lodge trail and then backtrack to the cabin and see if we missed something," said Kit.

"That ain't gonna be easy," said a reluctant Swifty.

"Nobody said the job was going to be easy," said Kit.

"All right, you win. Let's go for another wild goose chase and see what we can find," responded Swifty.

Kit and Swifty made their way back to the shop and were soon talking to a surprised Clem. Kit explained that they wanted to rent a UTV. Clem wrote up the paperwork, took Kit's credit card and fifteen minutes later, the two men were heading south on the lodge trail. This time Kit was driving, over Swifty's protests.

"I need you looking for signs and you can't drive and do that at the same time. Swifty reluctantly agreed and Kit kept the UTV at a slower, but steady pace as they made their way south on the lodge trail.

After an hour, they came to the branch still wrapped with toilet paper, and Kit drove the UTV off the lodge trail and came to a stop.

"Where do you think they might have taken old Ted and dumped him?" asked Kit

Swifty thought for a minute and then spoke. "I think they might have taken him on foot somewhere and then dealt with him. Keeping him on one of those ATVs already loaded with cargo boxes would have been almost impossible."

"Let's head back to the cabin, and we'll take a look," said Kit.

Kit guided the UTV slowly as Swifty kept checking the area they passed through for sign. By the time they reached the cabin, Swifty had seen nothing helpful.

Kit pulled to a stop about thirty yards from the cabin and shut off the engine. Both men slipped from their seats and Swifty led the way to the side of the cabin. He carefully made his way to where he had found the signs of the ATVs. When he reached the spot, he stopped and turned toward the cabin. He began to slowly make his way in half circles back and forth until he reached the walls of the cabin.

"Find anything?" said Kit who remained standing at the spot where the ATVs had been parked.

Swifty shook his head and moved to the other side of the cabin. Again, he started slowly making half circles starting at the cabin wall and working his way out from the cabin. He worked his search until he was about forty yards from the cabin. There he stopped and stared at the ground in frustration.

After a few seconds, Swifty moved to the front of the cabin by the entrance door. There he again started his slow and methodical search of the ground. His half circle searches were done with agonizing slowness. Swifty worked his way out from the front of the cabin until he reached a distance of about forty feet. Then he came to a stop and went to one knee and began to carefully move the grass and weeds with his hands.

"Got something," said Swifty.

"Can I come up to where you are?" asked Kit.

"Yes, but do it in a straight line from where you're standing," said Swifty.

When Kit reached the spot where Swifty was kneeling, he came to a stop and leaned over Swifty so he could see what Swifty had found.

Swifty parted some grass and leaves with his hand and said, "Look at this."

Kit leaned closer and saw a cigarette butt next to Swifty's finger.

"A cigarette butt? What does that mean?" asked Kit.

"There were no ashtrays in the cabin and the only smell was of wood smoke, not tobacco smoke. Plus, I've found no evidence of any other cigarette butt in my search. This butt is new, not affected by any rain, snow, or even dust," said Swifty.

"So, we might have a cigarette butt from one of the thieves, who was a smoker?"

"That and as I looked just beyond the cigarette butt, I found boot heel marks in the ground. Let's see what they might tell us," said Swifty.

Swifty moved forward on his hands and knees and carefully moved grass, weeds, and dead leaves aside as he searched for more clues. He kept this up for about ten minutes. Then he stopped and got to his feet.

"What is it?" asked Kit.

"As nearly as I can tell, two dudes took Ted for a walk in the woods. They left one guy behind to watch the cabin and their ATVs. We need to follow their trail and see where they took old Ted," said Swifty.

"Let's do it," said Kit.

"First, I need you to go back to the UTV and get my pack. I've got rope, flashlights, and a first aid kit in it. We might need it," said Swifty.

Kit hurried back to the UTV and retrieved Swifty's backpack. As soon as he returned, Swifty began walking slowly forward into the woods to the south of the cabin.

The faint trail led them through thick woods for about fifteen minutes and then the trees thinned and they were moving on more open ground. After they had walked for almost forty minutes, they came to a small bluff. Below the bluff was a ravine that was thick with brush. The drop to the ravine was about eighty feet.

Swifty studied the ground carefully and then moved to the edge of the bluff. He peered down into the ravine and motioned to Kit to come forward.

Kit moved up next to Swifty, who reached into the backpack Kit was carrying and removed a small set of binoculars. Swifty adjusted the binoculars and then used them to slowly scan the brush filled ravine that lay below them.

"We need to get down to that ravine," said Swifty.

"You think Ted is down there?" asked Kit.

"I ain't sure," said Swifty. "From what I can tell, the signs indicate the two men struggled with Ted here by the edge of the bluff. Old Ted must have put up more of a fight than they expected. It looks like they beat him up and then tossed him off the bluff, and he ended up in the ravine. If you look carefully here, you can see some faint traces of dried blood on these two leaves."

"They killed him?"

"I don't think so. I think they hurt him and then pushed him off the bluff. A man his age ain't gonna do well with an eighty foot drop into a ravine. They probably felt Mother Nature would take care of Ted, and if anybody ever found his remains, it would look like he fell off the bluff," said Swifty.

"Shit," said Kit.

"I agree, but we got to get down to that ravine. I can see from here that a bunch of those bushes are bent out of shape like something might have crashed on top of them. If I'm right, we might find old Ted down there in them bushes," said Swifty.

Swifty replaced the binoculars in the backpack and began to look for a trail or a way to take them down from the bluff to the ravine below.

After a short search, Swifty found a game trail and the two men followed it down the side of the bluff. When they reached the bottom, they followed the base of the bluff until they came to the ravine.

The ravine was almost impassable, as it was rocky and choked with heavy brush.

"This isn't going to be easy," said Kit as he examined the entrance to the ravine.

"Maybe not," said Swifty. He was examining the entrance to the ravine and then began backing away from the entrance. He turned and studied the ground in front of him. He reached down and picked up a large leaf.

"What is it?" asked Kit.

"I found a leaf with dried blood on it. I also see scrape marks in the ground that look like they were made by someone crawling and dragging their toes into the dirt," said Swifty. "I think old Ted survived the fall and crawled out of the ravine."

"Where would he have gone?" asked Kit.

"I ain't got no idea, but I intend to find out," replied Swifty.

Swifty slowly followed the trail he had found and Kit followed at a short distance. Fifteen minutes later, they came to a small spring of water. Swifty found more dried blood on some leaves and some rocks next to the spring.

"Old Ted must have known about this spring," said Swifty. "He came here for water."

"Where would he have gone from here?" asked Kit.

"I don't know," said Swifty. "I'll check for tracks around the spring."

Swifty followed a faint trail from the spring for about a hundred feet when he came to a wall of bushes acting almost like a hedge. He made his way through the bushes and suddenly found himself on a well-worn trail about six feet wide.

"Kit, come here," yelled Swifty.

Kit plunged through the bushes and came out almost right next to where Swifty was standing. Both men looked at the trail in disbelief.

"Where the hell is this trail on the map?" asked Swifty.

"Let me check the map," said Kit.

Kit pulled the trail map from his shirt pocket and unfolded it. He looked up at the direction of the sun and oriented his map accordingly. After a few seconds, Kit said, "I don't see this trail on the map."

Kit took out his portable GPS unit and waited until it spooled up. Then he took a reading and made the location of the spot they were standing a waypoint.

"Got it marked?" asked Swifty.

"Yep," replied Kit. "Which way from here?"

Swifty looked at the sky and then his watch. "I think we're runnin' out of daylight. Better to start back here tomorrow when we have plenty of light. I think we'd do better on horseback as well."

"I hate to stop now," said Kit.

"Wherever old Ted is, one more day ain't gonna make much difference," said Swifty. "If we find him we're gonna need time and help to get him outta here."

"I guess you're right," said Kit.

After double checking the waypoint as stored in the GPS, the two men began to retrace their steps back to the cabin. Kit stopped at the spring and marked it as a waypoint on the GPS unit. When he was finished, they headed back up the game trail to the top of the bluff. It was almost dark by the time they returned to the lodge.

Kit parked the UTV outside of the shop and went inside to give the keys back to Clem.

"Did you have any luck out there?" asked Clem.

"We found some clues, but we need to go back tomorrow," said Kit.

"Should I reserve a UTV for tomorrow for you?" asked Clem.

"We're gonna take the horses tomorrow," replied Kit. "It's pretty rugged country and not many trails wide enough for a UTV."

"Good luck," said Clem.

"Thanks," said Kit. "We'll need it."

CHAPTER FIFTEEN

Dawn the next morning found Kit and Swifty in the saddle and heading south down County Road 10 to the Nordstrom Ranch. Each man had downed a to-go cup of coffee Kit had begged from Tess at the café.

They rode side by side in the chill of the early dawn. The only noise was from the sound of the horses' hooves on the roadway.

"I sure could use somethin' to eat and make my belly quit complainin'" said Swifty.

"Try a couple of these," said Kit as he pulled a small paper bag out of the inside of his coat.

"What the hell you got in the bag?" asked Swifty.

"I had Tess toss in a few day-old biscuits," said Kit.

Swifty took a couple of biscuits out of the bag and handed it back to Kit. Kit took out a biscuit and stuck the sack back inside his coat.

Swifty bit into his biscuit and savored it. "This is damn good for day-old," he said.

"I agree," said Kit as he also bit into a biscuit. "We need to thank Tess when we get back to the café."

They rode in silence for a while. Then Kit heard Swifty mumbling something.

"What'd you say?" asked Kit.

"I was talkin' to myself," retorted Swifty.

"Well, what were you telling yourself?" asked Kit.

"I can't believe I didn't search all sides of the cabin the first time we got there. I can't believe I made such a basic mistake," said Swifty.

"It doesn't matter that you made a mistake, Swifty. What matters is that you made up for it, and now we have a good idea that Ted might be alive."

"I'm still pissed at myself," said Swifty.

""Better to be pissed off, than pissed on." is what Big Dave would say," said Kit.

Swifty couldn't keep himself from laughing out loud.

"As soon as we find out what happened to Ted, we need to take everything we've learned and give it to Deputy Parcell in Laramie," said Kit. "That keeps our hands clean so we're not involved in the criminal aspect of this deal."

Swifty nodded his agreement.

As they turned into the Nordstrom Ranch lane, the top of the sun appeared over the foothills to the east. The sun and its warmth were welcome after the chilly ride from Woods Landing.

The two horsemen were about to open the first gate when Nels rode up on his ATV.

"Morning, boys," said Nels.

"Morning, Nels," responded Kit and Swifty.

"I'm surprised to see you out here this early in the morning," said Nels.

"We're heading back to take up where we left off yesterday," said Kit.

"Have you had any luck?" asked Nels.

"Some," said Kit. "We found the cabin and are pretty sure old Tom was jumped by some dudes on ATVs that came from the lodge over in Albany. They robbed him, beat him up, and tossed him off an eighty-foot bluff into a ravine."

"They killed him!" said an astonished Nels.

"We don't think they got the job done," said Swifty. "We found no body in the ravine, but we did find tracks leading to a spring. It looked like somebody had crawled there. Then we found a pretty wide trail about a hundred feet from the spring."

"Then the old man is still alive?" asked Nels.

"We don't know," said Kit. "This happened about a month ago. We're headed back to the place where we found the spring and see if we can pick up any kind of a trail."

"Well, good luck to you. Do you need any help from me and my hands?" asked Nels.

"Less people is better when I'm looking for signs," said Swifty. "If we find Ted, then we might need your help."

"Just give me the word, and we'll come arunnin'," said Nels.

"We'll be sure to do that," said Kit as he leaned forward to open the gate.

"Before I forget, I rode out here to tell you boys one of my hands heard the sounds of ATV motors just about half an hour ago from up on the top of the foothill behind my ranch. It may be nothin', but I thought you might want to know," said Nels.

"Could be anyone," said Swifty, "But thanks for lettin' us know."

Kit and Swifty rode in silence as they made their way through the gates and lanes of the Nordstrom Ranch, making their way uphill towards the summit of the foothill. When they closed the last gate, Swifty broke the silence.

"I just felt somthin' cold goin' through the hairs on the back of my neck."

"I just felt the same thing," said Kit.

Without another word, both men pulled their rifles from their scabbards and checked them. After replacing their rifles, they pulled out their pistols and checked them as well. Satisfied, they holstered their pistols and resumed their ride up the foothill.

By the time they reached the summit of the foothill, the sun was completely up over the foothills to their east. The morning chill was quickly chased away.

"Who do you think was ridin' an ATV up here this morning?" asked Kit.

"I got no idea, but I don't like coincidences," said Swifty.

"I don't believe in coincidences," said Kit. "After all our visible activity yesterday, it wouldn't take much for word to travel about our investigation and the trips we took on the lodge trail. Places like lodges are just like small towns. Word travels fast."

"Too damn fast, if you ask me," said Swifty.

Before long, they had arrived at Ted's cabin. Swifty didn't bother to dismount and urged his horse on the same route he had followed on foot the day before. After about fifteen minutes they arrived at the edge of the bluff.

Swifty dismounted and handed his reins to Kit. "Wait here while I scout the way down. Keep your eyes peeled. I got a feelin' we may not be as alone as we might think," said Swifty in an ominous tone.

Kit took the reins and nodded his agreement. Still in the saddle, Kit drew out his rifle and rested it across the front of his saddle.

Swifty moved to the left of the bluff and soon disappeared into the brush and trees. He was back in less than ten minutes.

"I found the trail down to the bottom of the bluff," said Swifty. He took the reins from Kit and mounted his horse.

Then he led the way as they moved through some heavy brush. They found themselves on a rocky trail that led down to the ravine below the bluff.

Once they reached the ravine, it was a short ride to the spring. There they stopped to rest and water the horses.

"I think I'll scout on foot and make sure I didn't miss any signs from yesterday," said Swifty. "I want you to follow me, but keep back at least thirty yards. While I'm lookin' for sign, I want you armed and scanning the area around us."

"Looking for what doesn't belong," said Kit.

"Exactly," said Swifty. With that he began to move in half circles around the spring as he moved to the south. Kit again pulled his rifle from the scabbard and rested it on his saddle. Kit kept his head on a constant swivel, scanning the area around him and moving his gaze from the top of his view down side to side and then working down.

Swifty had reached the thick bushes that created the hedge. Before he went through the hedge, he went down to his knees and studied the hedge. Like Kit, he ran his gaze from side to side, starting at the top of the hedge.

"Aha," said Swifty.

"What is it?" asked Kit.

"I think old Ted went through this hedge, and he tore off a piece of his shirt doin' it," said Swifty, holding up a scrap of red, black, and white checkered flannel cloth.

Swifty then studied the ground at the base of the bushes. Leaning forward, he slowly crawled into the bushes. After he was almost halfway through the bushes, Swifty came to a halt. Kit could see him brushing aside some leaves on the ground.

Swifty then backed out of the bushes and got to his feet. "Let's get to the other side of these bushes. It looks like Ted had help getting through them."

Swifty led the way on foot, and Kit followed with the horses. When they made their way to the other side of the bushes, they found themselves on the wide trail they had found the day before.

"What did you find in the bushes beside the piece of shirt?" asked Kit.

"I found signs of boot prints about half way through. From the depth of the heel marks, looks like someone found Ted and dragged him out of the bushes. The boot prints are small, like a young person or a woman," said Swifty.

"What do you think happened?" asked Kit.

"I think old Ted made it to the spring and was revived enough by the water to stay alert. I think he heard someone on the trail and crawled through the bushes, trying to get to the trail. Either somebody on the trail heard him in the bushes or he called out. They found him and pulled him out of the bushes," said Swifty.

"Now what?" asked Kit.

"Now we got to try to look for sign on this trail," said Swifty. "It's a good trail, but based on the weeds growin' in it, the trail ain't heavily used."

Kit remained mounted while Swifty began to move slowly back and forth over the trail as he moved away from the bushes that lined it on the north side.

Swifty had made his fourth pass over the trail when a shot rang out and a bullet plowed into a small tree on the other side of the trail. The tree was directly behind where Swifty had been in a half crouch searching for signs.

Swifty dove for the ground. Kit bailed out of his saddle, taking his rifle with him. When Kit hit the ground, he rolled over several times to reach a bush on the south side of the trail. A second shot rang out and a bullet whizzed about a foot over Kit's head.

"Where's the shooter?" yelled Swifty.

"I think he's up on the bluff," said Kit. "Move closer to the thick bushes, Swifty."

Swifty quickly wormed his way to the cover of the bushes, crawling on his belly.

Kit slipped behind more bushes and paused. Then he crawled to the east for several yards. Once he had reached a sizeable tree, he rose to his knees so he could peek around the tree trunk.

A third shot rang out and leaves exploded out of the bush Kit had previously been hiding behind.

This time Kit saw the muzzle flash from up on the bluff and he quickly brought his rifle to bear on the spot.

"Do you see him?" asked Swifty from his prone position behind the thick bushes.

"I think so," said Kit.

"Shoot the sonofabitch," snarled Swifty. "I can't spend all day down here in the dirt getting' acquainted with these damn bushes."

Kit waited. He knew patience was a necessity. He knew the shooter would get curious and try to take a peek at what he had done.

A minute passed, then another. Kit kept his rifle sights on the same spot he had seen the muzzle flash. Then he saw movement at the spot and he got a quick look at a man dressed in woodland cammo with a rifle. Sure enough, the man rose up slightly to take a peek down at the ravine area. Kit took in a deep breath and then slowly let half of it out and softly squeezed the trigger. The rifle fired and after the recoil, Kit tried to reacquire his target. He saw nothing.

"Did you get him?" yelled Swifty.

"I'm not sure," said Kit.

"Well, who the hell is sure?" yelled an angry Swifty.

Kit ignored his angry partner and waited. Five minutes passed and nothing moved up on the bluff. Kit began to crawl to his right. When he reached a grove of trees, he got to his feet and began to move at a half crouch with his rifle at the ready.

Nothing happened. There was no sound and no movement Kit could see. He quickly moved to the trail Swifty had used to lead them down from the bluff to the ravine.

Kit moved as quietly as he could up the trail, while still moving quickly. He was almost to the top of the bluff, when he heard it. The distinct sound of an ATV engine starting and then accelerating. Kit reached the top of the bluff and scanned his surroundings. He saw nothing at first.

As he carefully searched the area at the top of the bluff, something glinted in the sunlight. Kit walked over to it and found three spent rifle casings. He picked them up and put them in his shirt pocket. He knew most rifles ejected to the right side of the weapon, whether it was semi-auto or bolt-action. He searched to the left of where he found the casings and saw a reasonable amount of fresh blood on the leaves, grass, and dirt.

He marked the spot with his GPS, and then pulled out his iPhone and took a picture of the blood-stains. Then he made his way back down the bluff to where Swifty sat in the dirt of the trail with his back to a large pine tree.

"What happened?" asked Swifty.

"I hit him, but then I heard him get away on an ATV," said Kit. "I picked these up," he said as he handed Swifty the three spent cartridge casings.

Swifty looked at the casings. "30-06," said Swifty. "That's pretty old school for a rifle."

"Lots of rifles chambered in 30-06 still around," said Kit.

"Well, we got a wounded shooter who uses a rifle chambered in 30-06 who took a dislike to us searching for old Ted," said Swifty.

"Speaking of old Ted. We still need to find him if we're ever going to get any answers as to what's really been going on," said Kit.

"Back to work," said Swifty as he rose to his feet. "You better do a damn better job of providin' security for me when I'm trackin', than you been doin'."

"I promise," said Kit with a grin on his face. He took the reins to Swifty's horse in his hand, and mounted his horse. "Lead on, Oh Mighty Swifty."

"Kiss my ass, tenderfoot," said Swifty as he resumed his search of the trail.

Swifty carefully made his way down the trail to the east and after he had gone about one hundred yards, he came to a halt. "I got nothing goin' this way. I'll give the west side a shot," said Swifty.

Swifty returned to his starting point and then began to make his way west on the trail as he moved in half circles back and forth.

Kit followed on horseback, keeping his rifle out and his eyes alert scanning the area around and above them.

After Swifty had searched about fifty yards west on the trail, he came to a halt. He went down to his knees and began to carefully study the ground of the trail in front of him.

"Find anything?" asked Kit.

"Maybe," said Swifty. "Give me a minute."

After a couple of minutes of sweeping his hands over the trail, Swifty rose to his knees and waved for Kit to come forward.

"What is it?" asked Kit.

"I ain't positive, but it appears I found some traces of what looks like wagon wheel imprints in the dirt in several places," said Swifty.

"What kind of wagon wheels," asked Kit.

"I hesitate to say," said Swifty, "but I think I'm lookin' at the tracks from a horse drawn cart."

"You sure you don't mean a mule-drawn two-wheeled cart," said Kit.

"It sure could be," said Swifty.

"Are we talking about the old lady we saw with the cart at the general store in Woods Landing?" asked Kit.

"This trail is too narrow for a horse drawn wagon, but it is the right size for a two-wheeled cart," said Swifty.

"So, you think it's the old lady, what was her name?"

"I think it was Eleanor," said Swifty.

"That was it, Eleanor. So, you think she might be the one who found old Ted?"

"It's possible. Someone found him and managed to cart him away cause there ain't no sign of him here," said Swifty.

"So how do we find where this Eleanor lives?" said Kit.

"We could go on a wild goose chase down this trail and hope for the best, but I'd say our chances might be better if we talked to them two old ladies at the general store in Woods Landing," replied Swifty.

"So, we need to go back and talk to Thelma and Louise," said Kit.

"We need to talk to Thelma. Past experience says we ain't gonna get much conversation out of Louise," replied Swifty.

"So, we head back to Woods Landing?"

"Let's see where this trail takes us if we continue to the west," said Swifty. "I don't think we'll find her place on this trail, but you never know. We're here, let's finish searching this trail."

"Sounds like a plan to me," said Kit. "Lead on, Oh Mighty Swifty."

"At least you recognize your betters, tenderfoot."

Swifty took the reins from Kit and mounted his horse. Then the two men began riding slowly west on the grassy trail.

Wary of another ambush, Swifty led the way, with Kit trailing him on horseback at least thirty yards behind him. Swifty was not interested in providing easy targets for the unknown shooter.

As Swifty rode slowly around a sharp bend in the trail, he had his head down, searching for any signs. Suddenly his horse reared up and began bucking, as the horse backed away from the side of the trail. Swifty was not balanced in the saddle when the horse reared and threw him off balance. The first buck tossed him from the saddle. He wound up unceremoniously dumped in the weeds on the other side of the trail.

Kit rode up quickly, unsure of what had happened to Swifty and his horse. When he reached the spot where Swifty lay sprawled on the ground, he brought his horse to a halt and vaulted out of the saddle.

He quickly reached Swifty's side and asked, "Are you all right?"

Swifty looked up at Kit with a disgusted look on his face.

"Of course, I'm all right, you stupid tenderfoot. The damn horse got too close to a rattler and decided to go all rodeo on me," snarled Swifty.

Kit helped a pissed off Swifty to his feet and while he was dusting himself off, Kit gathered up both of their horses. He handed the reins to Swifty.

Swifty looked at his horse right in the face and proceeded to call him a worthless piece of dried up horseflesh, among other pleasantries.

When Swifty was finally finished, he looked around at the scene of the crime, but the snake was long gone. The snake was no fool.

Swifty slapped his cowboy hat back on his head and both men mounted their horses. Swifty took the lead and began riding slowly to the west on the trail without saying another word.

CHAPTER SIXTEEN

Kit waited for about ten minutes before he dared to say anything. After he felt enough time had passed, Kit spoke up.

"You reckon the shooter will have to see a doc or go to a hospital?" he asked.

"Depends on how bad he got shot and where you hit him," replied Swifty.

"Judging from the blood I found up on the bluff, I think he's going to need some kind of medical help," said Kit.

"The guy has to be careful. Doctors and hospitals have to report gunshot wounds to law enforcement," said Swifty.

"How about veterinarians? Do they have to report gunshot wounds?" asked Kit.

"Not unless the victims are human, and vets don't see too many of them as patients I'm aware of," retorted Swifty sarcastically.

They came to a small spring up on the side of a hill feeding a tiny stream running down through the trail. The two horsemen halted and dismounted, letting their horses drink their fill from the small stream. Kit took a drink from his canteen and then tossed it over to Swifty. Swifty took a drink and tossed the canteen back to Kit.

"Why the hell would someone follow us and then shoot at us?" asked Swifty.

"Maybe someone involved with robbing Ted heard about our investigation and was following us to make sure we weren't getting anywhere," said Kit. "Then when he saw we were getting close to old Ted's trail, he shot to try to scare us off the case."

"That might sound good on some half-baked television show, but that first shot was too damn close for comfort. Warning, my ass," said Swifty.

"You have a better theory?" countered Kit.

"The only theory I got is three idiots beat up and robbed an old man and left him for dead. Then one of the idiots tried shooting at us and got shot himself," said Swifty. "Them three idiots were worried, and now they're scared. One of them is more than scared. Nobody shoots at me and gets away with it. We're gonna find those three rascals and hog tie them and then dump them on the sheriff's front porch."

"Kind of a ridiculous plan, but at least it's a plan," said Kit with a grin on his face.

Swifty saw him and grinned back. "Those dumb bastards picked the wrong two cowboys to piss off," he said.

"Let's see if we can find old Ted first," said Kit. "Then I'll join you in kicking their asses."

They mounted their horses and resumed their ride on the trail. They hadn't ridden for more than ten minutes when Swifty put up his hand as a signal to halt. Both men brought their horses to a stop.

"Listen," said Swifty.

Kit leaned forward in his saddle and strained to hear what Swifty was hearing. The sound was getting louder and it was unmistakably the sound of an ATV engine.

"Get off the trail," shouted Swifty.

Both men rode their horses off the trail and into the tall grass that bordered the trail on the north side. Five minute later a UTV drove into sight. The driver was a man in his late thirties, and his passenger was a woman about the same age. Both of them were dressed in designer style cowboy outfits, complete with brand new Stetson hats with feathers adorning the sweatbands.

The man saw the two horsemen by the side of the trail and slammed on the brakes and the UTV slid to a halt next to them.

"Howdy," said the driver. The woman just laughed. It was obvious to Kit and Swifty that both UTV riders were roaring drunk. There were empty beer bottles on the floor of the UTV and the woman was holding a whiskey bottle that appeared to be about half full.

"Oh shit," said Swifty under his breath.

"Howdy yourself," replied Kit. "Just where are you folks headed?"

"Oh, we been out seein' the sights and having a good time, ain't we Judy Ann?" said the man.

Judy Ann just laughed harder and took a swig from the whiskey bottle.

"I meant where are you headed on this trail?" asked Kit.

"Why we's headed back to the lodge, if it's any of your damn business," said the suddenly belligerent man.

"Well, I hate to tell you this, mister, but this trail don't lead back to the lodge. You folks have gotten off the main trail," said Kit.

"Says you, Mr. Cowboy. I say we're headed back to the lodge. Ain't that right, Judy Ann?" said the drunken man.

"You tell 'em, Eugene. You tell 'em," said Judy Ann as she took another swig from the bottle.

"All right," said Swifty. "I've had enough of this shit. Look asshole," said Swifty as he pulled out his Freedom Arms Casul 454 and pointed it over the heads of the drunken couple.

"You shitheads are lost and you're headin' away from the lodge. Now turn this heap around and get the hell out of our way."

"Yes sir, yes sir," said the suddenly sober Eugene. "Right away, sir." With that Eugene executed a three-point turn, and within less than a minute Eugene and Judy Ann were headed back the way they had come.

Kit waited until the UTV was out of sight and the dust marking their departure had finally settled back to the ground.

"Do we feel better now?" Kit asked Swifty.

"Actually, I feel much better. Nothing gets the blood up like telling some shitheads to get the hell out of my way," said Swifty.

"Are we ready to get goin'?" asked Kit.

"Born ready," replied Swifty.

"You take the lead," said Kit.

"Then let's move out," said Swifty as he rode his horse back onto the trail and took the lead positon as they headed west once more.

Kit and Swifty rode slowly west, taking their time and studying the area on each side of the trail, looking for any signs.

"At least we know this trail runs into the lodge trail," said Kit.

"Maybe it does and maybe it doesn't," said Swifty.

"Where else could those two drunks have come from?" asked Kit.

"Those two chuckleheads could have come from Mars," said Swifty. "God knows how they got on this trail and what stupid shortcuts they took to get here."

"Well, at least they were entertaining," said Kit with a chuckle.

"You have strange tastes in entertainment," said Swifty.

"You should talk," said Kit. "Your idea of entertainment is fairly limited."

"My idea of entertainment is and has always been fast horses, loose women and cheap whiskey," said Swifty.

"I rest my case," said Kit.

"Right now, I'd rather rest my ass. This has been a long ride," said Swifty.

Swifty pulled his horse to a halt and Kit did likewise.

"Do you hear that?" asked Swifty.

Kit listened, and he heard the faint sound of ATV engines in the distance.

"I think we're getting close to the lodge trail," said Swifty.

"The sooner the better," said Kit. "My butt is as tired as yours is."

"Your butt didn't get slammed into the dirt by a stupid horse afraid of snakes," retorted Swifty.

Kit started to reply to Swifty's remark, but he noticed Swifty was standing up in his stirrups and seeming to sniff the air.

Kit began sniffing the air, and he soon smelled what had alerted Swifty.

There was a definite smell of wood smoke in the air. There was little wind, so Swifty and Kit began trying to determine the source of the smoke.

"The smoke is comin' from above us to the north," said Swifty.

"I don't see any sign of smoke," said Kit as he turned his horse to face north.

"Maybe you can't see it, but it's there," said Swifty.

"Shall we check it out?" asked Kit.

"We didn't ride all this way today, get shot at, and dumped on the trail to go home empty-handed," said Swifty.

The two horsemen dismounted and led their horses off the trail to a small clearing where they tied them off to a dead pine tree.

Swifty pulled his rifle from the scabbard, and Kit quickly extracted his rifle.

"You stay here with the horses," said Swifty. "I'll scout around and see if I can find a trail or something that will lead us to the source of that smoke. If you hear a shot, come arunnin'."

Kit nodded his understanding, and Swifty quickly disappeared into the brush.

Kit found a fallen tree nearby and took a seat as he waited for Swifty's return. He kept his rifle across his lap and he kept scanning his surroundings. Kit also listened for any sounds and kept sniffing the air. The smell of wood smoke remained.

Almost fifteen minutes had passed. Fifteen minutes is not a long time unless you're waiting and fearful of what you might be waiting for.

As suddenly as he had disappeared into the brush, Swifty magically emerged from it. Kit had heard nothing and seen nothing of Swifty until he suddenly appeared.

Swifty motioned Kit over to him. Kit grabbed his rifle and moved next to Swifty.

"I found a cabin up about a quarter of a mile," said Swifty. "It's well hidden and so is the side trail that leads up to it. The side trail comes out about thirty yards behind us. You have to look carefully to see it. There's smoke coming from the chimney and there's a mule in the corral and a two-wheeled cart parked next to the cabin," said Swifty with a broad grin on his face.

"Sounds like you found Eleanor," said Kit.

"Hopefully more than just Eleanor," replied Swifty.

"How do you want to do this?" asked Kit.

"I want you to go up the side trail to the cabin. Stay in the open and make a little noise, so she can hear you comin'," said Swifty. "I'll circle around behind. She may be unfriendly, 'cause she sure wasn't friendly at the general store. I want you as a diversion, so I can get behind her."

"Just don't let the old bat shoot me," said Kit with a look of concern on his face.

"Don't worry," said Swifty. "You're in good hands, tenderfoot."

"Not very reassuring," said Kit.

By the time Kit got the words out of his mouth, Swifty had disappeared into the brush.

"Goddamn, Swifty," said Kit under his breath.

Kit checked the action on his rifle and flipped the safety on and started walking back to the entrance of the side lane to the cabin.

Once he knew where the side lane was, it was not hard to find. Old brush had been pulled in front of it to shield it from view from the trail. Kit pulled the brush aside and headed up the side lane.

Kit did as Swifty had instructed and kept to the middle of the side lane, deliberately stepping on twigs and pieces of bark lying in his way.

Before long he could see the smoke from the cabin's chimney, and then he could make out the cabin just ahead of him. Kit continued walking toward the cabin until a shot rang out, and he immediately dropped to the ground.

"What the hell are you doin' trespassin' on my property," came to him in a high-pitched voice. He looked up from his prone positon on the ground. Standing in front of the small cabin was Eleanor, dressed in old men's clothes with a floppy hat on her head. She was carrying an old double barreled shotgun. Smoke was drifting from one tube she had just fired.

Kit stayed on the ground, not sure how he was going to answer Eleanor's challenge.

Before he came to a decision, Swifty had slipped up behind Eleanor and disarmed her. Now Eleanor was yelling and cussing at Swifty.

Kit got to his feet and quickly joined up with Swifty, who was holding a screaming Eleanor at gun point. Swifty had emptied her shotgun and tossed it in the grass.

"Calm down, Eleanor," said Kit. "We're the two men who helped you load supplies at the general store. We aren't going to hurt you. We're looking for an old man who's gone missing. His name is Ted Kelly. His granddaughter sent us to find him."

What Kit said suddenly registered with Eleanor and she stopped screaming and struggling and Swifty let her go. When he did, she just seemed to collapse, and fell to the ground. Kit and Swifty helped her up and half carried her to the tiny porch at the front of the cabin. They assisted her to the steps where she sat down.

Eleanor was sobbing and breathing so hard it seemed she was having some kind of attack. Kit looked at Swifty and he just shrugged his shoulders. He had no more idea than Kit about what to do with an old woman who might pass out on them.

Kit decided to wait until the old woman ran out of sobs or finally came to her senses, whichever came first.

After about five minutes of constant sobbing, Eleanor suddenly stopped and fearfully looked up at Kit and Swifty.

"Please don't hurt him or me," she said.

"Who is he?" asked Kit.

"Mr. Ted, the man I found on the trail that you people tried to kill," replied Eleanor in a halting voice.

"I told you, Eleanor, we're here to help, not hurt anyone. Mr. Ted's granddaughter sent us. She hasn't heard from him and she's worried," said Kit in the most soothing voice he could muster.

Eleanor blinked twice, and then looked at Kit with very clear grey eyes. "You're sure you won't hurt him anymore?" she said.

"I told you we never hurt him in the first place. We were sent here to help him," said an exasperated Kit.

"Oh God, I hope I'm doin' the right thing," moaned Eleanor.

"Please, Eleanor, just tell us where Mr. Ted is," pleaded Kit.

Eleanor didn't reply. She just sat there on the small porch of the cabin. Finally, she raised her arm and pointed to the door of the cabin. "Mr. Ted's in there," she said softly.

"Thank you, Eleanor. We really appreciate your help, and I'm sure Ted's granddaughter does too," said Kit.

Kit sat with Eleanor and used his hand to motion Swifty to check out the cabin.

Swifty moved behind Eleanor and Kit and slowly opened the door to the small cabin and slipped inside.

The cabin was small, but clean and tidy. Two small windows let in a fair amount of light, but it was semi-dark in the cabin. After Swifty's eyes adjusted, he saw Ted Kelly lying on the only bed in the one-room cabin. Swifty went to the bed to check on him. Ted Kelly was sound asleep. Swifty could see that both his right arm and his right leg were set in a cast of plaster.

Ted's color looked good and his breathing was regular. Swifty decided to not wake him and slipped back out the cabin door and returned to the small front porch.

"He's inside. He's fast asleep and I didn't wake him," said Swifty. "He's got a cast on his right arm and his right lower leg. His color is good and his breathing seems normal. Can you tell us what happened, Eleanor?"

Eleanor took a deep breath and turned so she could see both Kit and Swifty. "I was comin' back from getting' some grain for my mule, Annie," she said.

"Your mule's name is Annie?" said Swifty.

"I named her when she was young," said Eleanor.

"Eleanor, you are aware that Annie is a gelding?" said Swifty."

Eleanor paid no attention to Swifty or his disclosure that Annie was a he, not a her. "I was passing by a spot on the trail where I knew there was a spring, 'cause sometimes I stop there and let Annie get a drink. I heard this sound. It sounded like a moan, and then I thought I heard a voice say "Help", but it was very faint and weak soundin'. I stopped and yelled out, "who's there?," and heard the same voice say "Help" again but it was a little louder. I peered into the bushes and saw the bloody head of a man."

"I got on my knees and crawled into the bushes and grabbed him by the shoulder and tried to pull him out. He cried out in pain, and I couldn't move him. He was stuck in them damn bushes. So, I back out of the bushes and got a rope from my cart. I crawled back in them bushes and tied the rope around his chest. His shirt had a lot of blood on it. He was cryin', real soft like."

"I crawled back out of the bushes and tied the other end of the rope on the back of my cart. Then Annie and I pulled poor old Mr. Ted out of them damn bushes," said Eleanor.

At this point, Eleanor started to tear up and she was breathing heavily. She stopped talking.

"Get some water, Swifty," said Kit.

Swifty went back into the cabin and found a water barrel and a dipper. He filled the dipper with water and returned to the porch. Swifty handed the dipper to Eleanor who took it and sipped greedily until the dipper was empty.

"What happened then, Eleanor?" asked Kit softly.

Refreshed by the water, Eleanor continued with her story. "Once I got him out, I cleared a space in the cart and I helped poor old Mr. Ted to his feet so I could slide him into the cart. He was in a lot of pain. Me and Annie took him back to my cabin, and I helped him inside. I got him into my bed, and then I got water and cleaned him up. He was all cut up from the fall into that ravine and from crawlin' through them damn bushes. I got him undressed and figured out he had a broken arm, a broke leg, and some beat-up ribs. I set the arm and leg and made a cast for them. I wrapped his ribs up pretty tight and been keepin' him quiet and fed," she said.

"How did you know his arm and leg were broken and how in the world did you set the bones and put a cast on them?" asked an amazed Kit.

"I was a nurse in the army, back when I was young and stupid," said Eleanor as though she thought it should be obvious to anyone.

"Why didn't you take him to a hospital?" asked Swifty.

"How in the hell would I do that?" snarled Eleanor like she was a mother lion, protecting her cub. "He had a broke leg, and I got a mule drawn two-wheeled cart. The nearest hospital is in Laramie and there ain't no one there can do more than I can for poor old Mr. Ted."

"I'm sorry, Eleanor. I didn't mean to upset you," said a startled Swifty.

"Ellie, is that you?" came a man's voice from inside the cabin.

"Oh, damn it, you done woke old Mr. Ted up," said an exasperated Eleanor.

"Ellie, Ellie, where are you?"

"I'm out here on the porch with some friends of yours," yelled Eleanor.

"Friends of mine? Who the hell would that be?"

"They say your granddaughter sent them," said Eleanor.

"Mustang sent them?"

"That's what they say," said Eleanor.

"Well, hells bells, bring them rascals in so I can git a look at 'em," said Ted Kelly in a clear and strong voice.

"You heard the man," said Eleanor. "Let's go inside so you boys can introduce yourselves to Mr. Ted."

Kit and Swifty followed Eleanor into the small cabin. Eleanor lit a kerosene lantern on the small table by the tiny kitchen. The added light helped reveal an old man sitting upright in the bed. He had some sort of makeshift night shirt on. He had white bushy hair, but he was clean shaven.

"I thought Ted had a full white beard," said Kit.

"Oh, he did when I found him, but that damn thing got in my way and I didn't like it anyhow, so I shaved it off," said Eleanor.

Kit and Swifty grinned at each other and then stepped up to the bed and introduced themselves to Ted Kelly.

Kit explained to Ted and Eleanor how Tang Kelly had come to him after she failed to receive her birthday card and after coming to Wyoming to search unsuccessfully for her grandfather.

"Tang hired us to do what she couldn't do. She tried to find you, but she ran out of time," said Kit.

"Sounds like my granddaughter. Most of my relatives are worthless as warm spit, but that gal has spunk," said a smiling Ted.

Eleanor dragged a couple of old wooden chairs in various states of disrepair toward the bed. Kit and Swifty took them and pulled them up next to Ted's bed and seated themselves. Eleanor took one of the remaining chairs by the table and stayed there. Far enough away to let the men talk, but close enough to hear what was being said.

"Do you feel like talking, Mr. Kelly?" asked Kit.

"Mr. Kelly was my old man, and he's dead. I'm Ted, and it's good to see you boys. What is it you boys want me to say?" asked Ted.

"We found your cabin and were able to figure out that three dudes on ATV's had showed up there. It appeared to us they abducted you, and then tossed you off the bluff into the ravine below. We think they left you for dead. Can you tell us exactly what happened, Mr. Kelly, err, I mean Ted," said Kit correcting himself.

"You're right about the three galoots who showed up at my cabin. I was surprised, 'cause I ain't hardly never had no visitor to the cabin. The old coot who built the cabin is long dead, and he had no relatives I know of. Them three busted into my cabin and knocked me in the head. Then they tied me up on the floor. They went outside and brought in these plastic boxes. Then they took my dad's framed letters off the wall and put them in them boxes. Them letters were to my dad from his old friend, Charley Russell out of Great Falls, Montana. You heard of him?" asked Ted.

"Yes, Ted, we've heard of Charley Russell," said Kit.

"Well, they took them boxes out and tied them on them damn motor bugs they rode in on."

"You mean ATVs?" asked Swifty.

"Whatever the hell you call them noisy, smelly, contraptions," said Ted. "Then they come back in the cabin and untied my legs and got me to my feet. They told me we were goin' for a walk. I was pretty sure that weren't gonna work out too well for me, but I had no choice."

"They led me out of the cabin and we started headin' south. I kept lookin' for landmarks. I know that part of the country pretty good and I wanted to make sure I knew where I was bein' taken. Finally, we got to the top of Fox Bluff."

"Fox Bluff?" asked Kit.

"Yeah, it's a bluff about two miles south of my cabin. I call it that cause the first time I found it, a red fox was sitting there, eatin' a mouse she'd caught. After that I called it Fox Bluff," said Ted.

"I see," said Kit.

"They untied me and I thought maybe they was gonna let me go, but they grabbed me by the arms and threw me off the bluff. I thought I was a goner for sure, but them bushes in the ravine broke my fall when I landed. I must have hit some rocks cause my leg and arm hurt like hell. Later I found out they was busted. Those sonofabitches didn't even come down to see if I was dead or alive. Didn't really give a shit, I suppose," said Ted.

"You were lucky they didn't come down to check on you. If they'd found you alive, they probably would have finished the job," said Swifty.

"You're probably right about that, sonny, but I'd love to get the chance to get my hands on those young bastards," said Ted with anger in his voice.

"So, you crawled out of the ravine and made it to the spring?" asked Kit.

"Yep. I knew the spring was there. It hurt like hell to crawl. That's when I figured out my leg and arm were in bad shape," said Ted. "I felt a little better after drinkin' my fill of water from the spring. Then I heard Eleanor and her cart comin' down the road. I tried to crawl over to the trail, but that damn hedge was in the way. I tried to crawl through it, but I got stuck. That's when Eleanor found me and got me out of there and over to here."

"You're lucky Eleanor came along and found you. She was resourceful in getting you out of there and thankfully she was trained as a medical professional and able to treat your injuries," said Kit as he made sure he was giving Eleanor as much recognition as he could.

"Yeah, I was damn lucky," reflected Ted.

"I have a few questions for you about those three galoots you mentioned," said Kit.

"Fire away," said Ted.

"Had you ever seen any of them before?" asked Kit.

"Never laid eyes on them before," answered Ted.

"Can you describe them?" asked Kit.

Ted thought for a moment before he responded to Kit's question. "All of them were wearin' jeans, leather boots, black t-shirts, heavy canvas coats and ball caps. They was all wearing fancy sunglasses. The tall one of them had a beard. He had dark hair. The other two were blondies and they had half-ass mustaches."

"Half-ass mustaches?" asked Kit.

"Half assed. The kind young punks try to grow and looks more like a crop failure than a mustache," said a grinning Ted.

Kit nodded that he understood. "Anything else about them you can remember?" he asked.

"They was all under six foot. The dark-haired galoot was a little taller. He had some muscle on him, the others were just fat. They all had tattoos," said Ted.

"Can you describe the tattoos?" asked Kit.

"The usual weird crap," said Ted. "The dark-haired galoot had a skull and cross bones on his upper right arm. The blondies had all kinds of shit and some of them were on their necks runnin' up to their ears."

"Do you have any idea how they knew where your cabin was?" asked Kit.

161

"I ain't got no idea," said Ted.

"How did they know you had those Charles Russell letters framed on your walls?" asked Kit.

"How'd you know they was on the walls of the cabin?" asked Ted.

"Tang told us about the letters, and we noticed the darker spots on the wall where they had been," said Kit.

"Good job of figurin' that out," said Ted. "I got no idea how they knew about the letters. I ain't never told nobody outside of my family about them. I ain't seen none of my family for at least ten years."

"Somehow they knew where the cabin was and they knew the letters were in the cabin. They came ready to steal the letters and get you out of the way," said Kit.

"It don't make no sense to me," said Ted. "Who the hell would go to all this trouble just to get some old letters that don't mean nothin' to anyone but me and maybe my family," said Ted.

"Those letters are actually quite valuable," said Kit.

"To who?" asked Ted incredulously.

"To any collector of western art," said Kit. "Russell wrote many letters to his old friends and he adorned them with personal artwork, usually watercolors. Those letters are considered as much art as his paintings and sculptures."

"I had no idea. Just how much would them art collectors pay for one of old Charley's letters?" asked Ted.

"The folks I talked to said that a Russell letter at an art auction would bring north of one hundred thousand dollars," said Kit.

"U.S dollars?" asked Ted.

"Absolutely," said Kit.

"Holy shit," said Ted. "I had no idea. I liked them because they were letters to my dad. One in particular was a favorite."

"Which one was that?" asked Kit.

"One he wrote my dad about their days workin' as night hawks on a big cattle herd in Montana. The letter has a painting of a cowboy on horseback. He's dressed in a yellow slicker, and he's ridin' herd on a passel of ponies. My dad told me he was sure the painting was of him. I kept it because I thought it was my dad. I called the letter "The Night Hawk." It was always special to me. Every time I looked at it the letter reminded me of my dad. He was a hell of a cowboy, you know."

Ted was looking off into space, seeing something that no one else was a party to.

"I'm sorry about what happened to you and the theft of your letters. We'd like to help you get them back," said Kit.

Ted snapped out of his spell. "I want them letters back, and I want them lowlifes strung up for what they did to me," said a suddenly angry Ted.

"Swifty and I understand how you feel, but what happens to those galoots is up to the law, not us. But, we can help find them and get your letters back," said Kit.

"Ain't no justice in this world anymore," said Ted. "My old man and old Charlie would have hunted them down and strung them up to the nearest cottonwood tree."

"Maybe so, Ted, but that was then and this is now. If we can find those assholes and bring them to justice and retrieve your letters, that should be enough," said Kit.

"It's gonna have to do," said an obviously disappointed Ted. "I really do want them letters back."

"We'll find them and the letters, Ted. I promise you," said Kit.

"Did you have any visitors of any kind at the cabin in the past six months?" asked Kit.

Ted thought for a minute. "I can't say I'd call them visitors, but I did get a surprise visit about three months ago."

"What kind of surprise visit?" asked Kit.

"I was pullin' my cart back from the cave where I parked my truck. It was rainin' hard. We was havin' a damn thunderstorm with lots of thunder and lightning. The trail was gettin' muddy. I was in a hurry, 'cause it had gotten dark in a hurry and I wanted to get them supplies in the cabin. I had them covered with a tarp, but it was so damn windy the tarp kept tryin' to fly off."

"I was halfway back to the cabin when I heard a cry for help. At first I thought I was imaginin' it. Then I heard it again. I stopped the cart and walked toward the cries for help I was hearin'. The cries were coming every few seconds. As I got nearer, the cries got louder. I came around a stand of aspen trees, and there was these two young gals. They had them mountain bikes and one of them had a flat tire. They was wet and scared and were havin' no luck in trying to fix that tire."

"How old would you say those two girls were?" asked Kit.

"They told me they was college girls goin' to school over in Laramie. They'd gone for a bike ride in the foothills. They got lost and then the one, her name was Lisa, got a flat tire. That's when I found them."

"What happened then?" asked Kit.

"I led them back to my cart and then over to my cabin. I let them spend the night out of the storm. They slept on the floor of the cabin. In the mornin', I fixed the flat on their bike and led them down to the trail to the Nordstrom's Ranch and the county road. They thanked me and that's the last I ever heard of 'em," said Ted.

"When they were in your cabin, did they mention the letters you had framed on the wall?" asked Kit.

"Come to think of it, they did. The one gal, her name was Rose, she said she was studyin' art and she knew all about old Charlie Russell," said Ted.

"Can you describe these two girls?" asked Kit.

"Lisa had dark hair, and Rose was a blonde," said Ted. "Rose wore her hair in long pigtails. Looked kinda strange. They were both kind of tall and thin. They was nice girls. Both of them were real polite."

"Did either of them tell you their last names?" asked Kit.

"I don't believe they ever mentioned their last names. Their first names was good enough for me," said Ted.

"Did they say anything else about themselves?" asked Kit.

"Lisa did say she was studyin' psychology or sociology or some kind of-ology," said Ted. "I think they said they was both in their second year at Laramie."

"Anything else you can remember?" asked Kit.

"I think that's all she wrote," said Ted.

CHAPTER SEVENTEEN

Kit and Swifty had gone outside the cabin after Eleanor asked for time to change the dressings on some large cuts on Ted's body that had not yet healed.

"That was hard to hear," said Swifty.

"I'll never understand thinking it's OK to beat an old man, toss him off a cliff, and leave him for dead," responded Kit.

"Same guys who bullied you in high school," said Swifty.

"I don't recall anyone bullying me in high school," said Kit.

"Really!" said Swifty. "How did you manage that? I thought every guy had some shit head picking on him when he was growin' up."

"Not me," said Kit. "I was shy and just kind of stayed invisible through most of high school."

"Sort of like you are now," said Swifty with a wide grin on his face.

"Loser," said Kit.

"What happened to the shy, invisible guy you were just describing," said Swifty, with an exaggerated look of surprise on his face.

"He died when I came to Wyoming," said Kit. "Wyoming changed me from a boy to a man."

"Amen to that," said Swifty. "Wyoming's got no use for weak sisters and slackers."

"What should we do about Ted?" said Kit.

"He seems to be in pretty good hands. I say we find out what, if anything, Eleanor needs and go get it and bring it back to her. We can check in on her and Ted in a few days. When Ted's good to travel, we get him back to his cabin," said Swifty.

"We'd be smart to take him in to Laramie and have a real doctor take a look at him," said Kit.

"We also need to take him over to see Deputy Parcell and have him tell the cops what happened," said Swifty.

"We did promise Deputy Parcell we'd let him know all we found out and right now, that's quite a bit," said Kit.

Swifty was about to respond when he was interrupted by Eleanor coming out of the cabin and onto the porch.

"How's Ted doin'?" asked Kit.

"He's fast asleep. He's plumb worn out from all the excitement of meetin' you boys and tellin' his story about what happened. I think talking about them three galoots got his blood up and he's not in great shape to be getting' pissed off," replied Eleanor.

"We can't thank you enough for taking such good care of Ted," said Kit.

"You did an amazing job, Eleanor," echoed Swifty.

"I just did what I thought was right," said Eleanor.

"You did more than that," said Kit. "You saved a good man's life. Ted's going to be forever in your debt."

"So is his granddaughter," added Swifty.

"Ain't nobody in my debt," said Eleanor. "I live my life my way and all I ask is to be left alone."

"Couldn't have said it better myself," said Kit. "You are a woman to admire, Eleanor."

"Are you boys gonna take Ted away?" asked Eleanor, with a little tremble in her voice.

"We were just talking about that," said Kit.

"We decided that the best thing for Ted was to leave him here in your care," added Swifty.

"We'll be back in a few days to check up on Ted," said Kit. "In the meantime, is there anything you need and I mean anything? We'll be happy to go get it and bring it back to you."

Eleanor thought for a minute, and then said, "I got a few items I could use. I'll go in and make a list for you boys."

While she was back inside the cabin, Swifty spoke. "What are we gonna do about them three scumbags?"

"We're going to give all the information we have to Deputy Parcell," replied Kit.

"I expect that," said Swifty. "What I'm talkin' about is what we do when we get our hands on them," said Swifty grimly.

"If we're the ones who find the three dirt bags, I'm sure we'll come up with something appropriate," replied Kit just as grimly.

"This could give the word appropriate a whole new meanin'," said Swifty.

"It certainly could," replied Kit.

When Eleanor appeared with her list, Kit and Swifty said their good-byes and made their way down the lane to their horses.

The ride back to Ted's cabin was much faster this time. After a stop at Ted's spring to water the horses, the two horsemen headed for the Nordstrom Ranch. When they reached the ranch, Kit and Swifty stopped at the ranch house to let Nels know they had found Ted. Both men looked around for Boonie before they dismounted. The dog was nowhere to be seen.

When they knocked on the front door, they were surprised to be met at the front door by a tall, middle-aged, attractive blonde woman.

"You two must be Kit and Swifty, the boys from Kemmerer," said Betty with a smile on her face. "Welcome to our house. Please come in."

Kit and Swifty removed their cowboy hats and followed Betty into the kitchen, where she directed them to sit at the round table. Betty expertly produced two hot cups of coffee and a plate of rusks. She placed a small pitcher of cream and a bowl of sugar in front of Kit.

Both men looked at her in amazement. She recognized the look and laughed out loud.

"You're wondering how I knew how each of you took your coffee," Betty said. "Nels told me. We Swedes are big on coffee, and we try to remember how each of our guests take theirs. I knew which one of you was Kit and which was Swifty by Nels' descriptions."

"Speaking of Nels," said Kit, "Is he around?"

"He and one of the hands are out fixin' fence. I don't expect him until supper time," replied Betty.

"Could you give him a message for us?" asked Kit.

"Certainly," replied Betty.

"Please tell him we found old Ted Kelly alive, but in pretty bad shape. He got beat up and left for dead by some robbers and an old lady named Eleanor found him and cared for him," said Kit.

"Did you say Eleanor?" asked Betty.

"The one and the same," said Swifty.

"You know Eleanor?" asked Kit.

"I know who she is. She asked us for permission to use our lanes to get down from the foothills to the county road. She's been around here for years. I believe she has a mule and a two-wheeled cart. I've seen her leading the mule past the ranch on many occasions," said Betty.

"Well, it turns out she was a nurse in the army," said Swifty.

"Lucky for old Ted," added Kit.

"So, she nursed this old Ted back to health?" asked Betty.

"Ted had a broken leg and arm, as well as a lot of cuts and bruises," responded Kit.

"Do we need to get him to a doctor?" asked Betty.

"He seems to be on the mend, ma'am," replied Swifty. "We decided to leave him in Eleanor's care for now."

"That's probably a good idea," said Betty. "Does Eleanor need any help or any medical supplies?"

"We have every reason to believe Eleanor doesn't need any help and doesn't want any help," said Kit with a grin.

"She did give us a short list of stuff she does need," said Swifty.

"If you'll trust me with the list, I'll be glad to get all the items and then have Nels take it up to her," said Betty. "Where does she live?"

"It's a little complicated," said Kit, "but I think I can draw a map that Nels could follow."

"Please do," said Betty. "Let me get you a pen and paper." With that she rose from her chair and quickly produced a pen and paper for Kit.

Kit took a few minutes to draw his map and he made a few notes at the bottom of the paper. Then he wrote down the longitude and latitude for the cabin he had stored on his GPS. "I think this will do," said Kit. "Does Nels have a GPS?"

"He certainly does," said Betty.

"If he uses these coordinates, he should have no trouble finding Eleanor's cabin," said Kit

"I'll be sure to give him the information," said Betty.

"Thanks for the coffee, Mrs. Nordstrom," said Kit. "We need to get going. We've got to get our horses back to Woods Landing and then drive in to Laramie to the Sheriff's office, so we can report this."

"I understand," said Betty. "But in the future, please call me Betty. Mrs. Nordstrom sounds so old."

"Betty, it is," said Kit. He and Swifty shook hands with Betty and soon were back in the saddle, riding back to Woods Landing.

The ride back to their cabin was quiet except for the sound of the horses' hooves hitting the blacktop. The only traffic they encountered was an old Ford pick-up truck that slowed as it headed toward them and came to a stop in front of them.

The truck door opened and out stepped Shorty. "Howdy boys," he said.

Kit and Swifty reined in their horses and returned Shorty's greeting. "Howdy, Shorty," said Kit and Swifty, almost in unison.

"You boys have any luck finding that old timer?" asked Shorty.

"We did," said Kit. "We found him up in the foothills. He'd been hurt and got taken in by Eleanor, the old cart lady."

"I ain't surprised," replied Shorty. "I always thought that old bat was some kind of a witch. I made sure to stay clear of her."

"She ain't no witch, Shorty," said Swifty. "She was a nurse in the army and she was a great help to old Ted. I don't think he would have survived without her help."

"Well, I'll be damned," said Shorty. "She saved the old boy's life. Ain't that something. Who woulda guessed it."

"Life's full of surprises," said Kit with a grin.

"Well, I don't want to be holding you boys up," said Shorty as he climbed back into the old Ford. "See you boys at breakfast." Shorty engaged the clutch, the old Ford truck lurched forward, and Shorty was soon out of sight.

Kit looked over at Swifty's agitated face. "I know, we're burnin' daylight. Let's ride," he said.

The two men put their spurs to their mounts and were soon trotting down the road. They rode into the parking area around the cabins and brought their horses to a halt at the corral. They unsaddled their horses, and Kit took the tack over to the truck where he hung it over the side of the bed. Swifty led the horses into the corral and watered and fed them.

After storing their guns and gear in their truck, they headed for the café. They walked in the bar and found it empty except for Bess, who was behind the bar, washing glassware.

Bess looked up and said, "You boys are either late for lunch or early for dinner. Which is it?" she asked as she held up two separate menus, one in each hand.

"Surprise us," said Swifty as he and Kit headed for the dining room. The room was deserted and they had their pick of tables. They seated themselves and Bess quickly appeared with two glasses of ice water and two sets of menus for each of them.

"How about a cheeseburger with everything and onion rings and a cold beer?" said Kit.

"Same thing for me," echoed Swifty.

"You got it," said Bess. "I'll be right back with the beers now." She disappeared back into the bar.

"There goes a woman who actually understands men," said Swifty.

"What you mean is there goes a woman bartender who has seen a ton of men and has figured out what they want," said Kit.

"Either way, it works for me," said Swifty.

Bess appeared with their cold beers and just as quickly she disappeared.

"Here's to a successful hunt," said Swifty as he raised his glass.

Kit raised his glass and touched Swifty's with a soft clink. "But this hunt isn't over. Not by a long shot," he said.

"What've you got planned now?" asked Swifty.

"We finish this meal, and we drive to Laramie and give everything we've got to Deputy Parcell," replied Kit.

"Works for me," said Swifty.

Bess soon arrived with their meals. Both men were famished and they wolfed down their burgers and onion rings. While they were eating, Bess brought them a second round of beers.

"I told you that woman understood men. She brought us a second round of beers without us ordering them," said Swifty.

"I think that means she deserves a generous tip," said Kit.

"As long as you're payin' for the meal, give her a big tip, tenderfoot," said Swifty.

"What a surprise," said Kit with a smirk on his face.

CHAPTER EIGHTEEN

Half an hour later they were driving east toward Laramie. Kit found a parking spot near the Sheriff's office, and he and Swifty made their way inside to the receptionist's desk.

"We'd like to see Deputy Parcell," said Kit. "Is he in?"

"Let me check," said the receptionist. She got on her phone and punched some buttons. She replaced the phone and said, "He'll be with you in a few minutes. Have a seat over in the reception area." She pointed to a semi-circle of chairs near the front of the office.

"Thank you, ma'am," said Kit and he and Swifty went over to the area and each took a seat. Kit picked up a magazine from the small table in front of them. Swifty slid back in his chair, pulled his cowboy hat down over his eyes, and immediately went to sleep.

Ten minutes later, Deputy Parcell strode into the front of the office. Kit rose from his chair, punching Swifty in the arm as he did so. Swifty snorted and then came awake and rose from his chair as well.

Deputy Parcell strode over to the two men and shook their hands. "Good to see you boys again," he said. "Have you got anything interesting for me?"

"We've got a good story and some pictures," said Kit.

"Sounds like a good start to me," said Parcell. "Let's go to the conference room, and you can fill me in on what's goin' on with the missing Mr. Kelly."

Parcell led them to a small conference room. The table and chairs were made of industrial steel and painted institutional grey. Once they were seated, Kit took out his folder with the pictures they had obtained at the lodge.

Kit told their story to a very interested Deputy Parcell and used pictures to help illustrate what he was telling the Deputy.

"Holy shit," said Parcell. "So, the old guy is still alive after the three thieves tried to kill him by throwing him off a cliff. That's almost unbelievable. Can I see the pictures of the truck and trailer in the parking lot? I want to see if we can make out the license plates and find out who they belong to."

Kit handed the photos to Parcell, who excused himself and left the conference room.

"I'll bet you five bucks them plates were stolen," said Swifty.

"How do you know that?" asked Kit.

"Because this whole deal reeks of being planned by someone a lot smarter than those three mouth breathers who robbed Ted. Someone got the location of the cabin and the existence of the framed Russell letters from one of those two gals who stayed overnight. Then someone arranged for the three assholes to take ATVs equipped with cargo boxes out to the cabin and rob Ted. Ted had seen their faces, so they took him out to beat and kill him. Anybody that smart doesn't let the getaway vehicles have their picture taken, unless the vehicles are stolen," said Swifty.

"You could be right," said Kit. "Although sending the one dip wad out to try to shoot us doesn't seem very smart."

"My guess is the same someone heard about us investigating Ted's disappearance and then sent one of his boys to check up on us and the dirt bag got concerned and decided to take us out on his own," said Swifty.

"It didn't work out so well for him," responded Kit.

"If you were a better shot, that dirt bag would be dead and we'd know who he was," snorted Swifty.

"He was on the high ground and behind good cover. I was lucky to get a shot at him," said Kit.

"Excuses, excuses," said Swifty.

Kit knew Swifty was just pulling his chain, and he just smiled at his partner.

The door to the conference room opened and Deputy Parcell entered. He had the photos in his hand as he sat down.

"Well boys, it turns out that the truck and trailer in these photos were stolen in Cheyenne. They were both found burned up in a gully outside of Tie Siding about a month ago," said Parcell.

"I told you so," said Swifty with a knowing look.

"Did you find anything else on the photos?" asked Kit.

"Yes, we did," said Parcell. "The photos of the men were not very helpful, but we got a good view of the ATVs they used. We enlarged and enhanced the photos and all three ATVs have custom paint jobs."

Deputy Parcell produced the enhanced photos. "If you look carefully, you can see flames painted on one, lightning bolts on another and arrows on the third. Someone painted those on, and only a custom paint shop could do that."

"Can you trace the paint jobs?" asked Kit.

"We're sure gonna try," said Parcell. "I'm gonna send in a stenographer, and I want you to give her your story so I can get it printed up and in the file. We're also gonna contact all the hospitals, clinics and doctors in the area to make sure no one with a wound like one a gunshot could cause has been treated. I need those coordinates for Eleanor's cabin. I'll send out a deputy and an EMT to check on Mr. Kelly and get his statement. I've got your cell phone numbers, and I'll call you and let you know what we find. I really want to nail these guys."

"So do we," said Kit. "If we can be of any help, just let us know."

"You two have been a big help already. You just sit tight and let us do our jobs. With any luck, we'll find these three bozos," said the Deputy.

Almost an hour later Kit and Swifty were done reciting their story to the Sheriff's stenographer, and they were walking back to their truck.

"So, how do you feel about sitting tight?" asked Swifty.

"It doesn't feel right to me," replied Kit.

"It doesn't suit me either," said Swifty. "What can we do without gettin' in trouble with the Sheriff's office?"

"It occurs to me we might just wander over to the university and see if we have any luck finding an art student named Rose," said Kit

"Why her?" asked Swifty.

"She was the art student who stayed with Ted. She knew who Russell was and she knew about the Russell letters," said Kit. "She's the most likely person to remember them and mention all she saw to someone who's also in the art business."

"I'm sure you just forgot in all the excitement and everything, but it seems to me that in all that information you gave to the Sheriff's stenographer, you somehow managed to omit the part about the two girls staying in Ted's cabin, including their names and the fact that one of them was an art student," said Swifty.

"It must have slipped my mind," replied Kit.

"That's a load of crap if I ever heard one," snorted Swifty. "Let's ride."

Kit drove the truck over to the university, stopping at an information booth. Kit asked the young woman in the booth questions. She answered his questions and handed him several brochures, including a map of the campus. Kit thanked her and returned to the truck.

Kit laid the map out on the dash of the truck. He located the art building and then located where they were on the map. He folded the map and handed it to Swifty.

"What is it?" asked Swifty.

"We're about four blocks from the art building. Let's drive over there and stake it out," said Kit.

"Stake it out?" said Swifty. "You mean sit in our truck and watch all the hot coeds walk by. Count me in!"

Kit just shook his head, put the truck in gear, and drove away from the information booth.

Kit made his way through campus, using the map and his truck navigation system to find the art department building. He was able to find a parking spot about two blocks from the building. He and Swifty walked to a spot across the street from the entrance to the art building and quickly found a bench. The bench was occupied by a couple of nerdy guys who were engrossed in their electronic tablets. One hard look from Swifty was all it took for them to change their minds and decide to head out for other parts.

After about twenty minutes of staking out the building and watching the university students pass by, Swifty was sound asleep.

Kit sat on the bench and kept watch on the passing students for over an hour. He also watched for anyone entering or exiting the art building. He saw no sign of a tall, blonde coed with her hair in pigtails. As a matter of fact, he saw no coeds, regardless of the color of their hair, with pigtails.

Kit nudged Swifty awake with his elbow.

"What's up?" snorted a bewildered Swifty.

"I'm going to take a look inside the building," replied Kit. "You stay awake and keep a look out for Rose."

"How the hell do I look for someone I have no idea of what she looks like?" complained Swifty.

"You look for a tall blonde with her hair in pigtails," said Kit. "From what I've seen in the past hour, pigtails must not be in style here in Laramie."

"Whatever," responded Swifty.

Kit walked slowly up to the entrance of the art building. In most universities in the United States, a man like Kit dressed in denims, a cowboy hat, and cowboy boots would stick out like a sore thumb. At the University of Wyoming, he blended in with the students.

Kit entered the old stone building and was soon in a large foyer. Large double doors at the end of the foyer led further into the building. Kit paused in the foyer to look around. There were several bulletin boards on the walls. Each board was labeled and most were used for announcements. One board was for general use, and there were all kinds of notices for everything from books for sale, job openings, parties, requests for roommates, and students looking for rides. Most of the notices had tabs with phone numbers on the bottom, this allowed students to tear off a tab with a phone number and the notice remained in place.

Looking at the notices, Kit had an idea. He left the art building and walked over to where Swifty was trying to stay awake on the bench.

"Let's go," said Kit.

"So soon?" said Swifty. "I was just starting to enjoy the scenery."

"Let's go, now" said Kit in a disgusted voice.

"OK, OK, hold your horses," said Swifty as he struggled to his feet.

They walked back to the truck. After they slid into the truck, Kit started the engine and quickly pulled out his iPhone. He spent a few minutes tapping the keys and then he said, "706 Cottonwood Street" out loud.

Swifty looked at Kit like he was losing his marbles. "What the hell is at 706 Cottonwood Street?" he asked.

"A copy and print shop," replied Kit.

"I don't need anything copied or printed," said Swifty.

"Yes, we do," said Kit, and he pulled the truck out of the parking space and headed for the print shop.

The trip took about fifteen minutes. When they arrived at the print shop, Kit parked the truck. "Stay with the truck," said Kit. "I'll be right back."

"No problem," said Swifty as he leaned back and dropped his cowboy hat over his eyes.

Kit just shook his head. He exited the truck and entered the print shop. He explained to the clerk at the counter what he wanted. The clerk handed him a form and a pen and asked him to fill it out the way he wanted the print job done. Kit took just a few minutes to fill out the form and passed it back to the clerk.

"How long will this take?" asked Kit.

"I'll have this done in less than ten minutes," said the clerk.

"Thanks," said Kit. "I'll wait."

Kit took a seat on a chair by the front of the shop. He took out his iPhone and saw he had five bars. He punched in a number and waited while the phone was ringing. He knew this was a long shot, but it was worth a try.

"Is this a call from the dead," said Shirley.

"I'm not dead, but I know I should have called sooner," said an apologetic Kit.

"You're damn right you should have called sooner," said Shirley. "I've been worried sick about you. Where are you?"

"I'm in Laramie," replied Kit.

"What the heck are you doing in Laramie?" asked Shirley.

"Trying to wrap up some loose ends on the Ted Kelly case," said Kit.

"Did you find him?" asked Shirley.

"We did, and the old buzzard is alive and sorta well," said Kit.

"Sorta well?" asked Shirley.

"Some jerks robbed him and threw him off a cliff and left him for dead," replied Kit. "He broke a leg and arm and cracked some ribs."

"Good God, how did he survive?" asked Shirley.

"He's a tough old bird and an old gal who used to be a nurse in the army found him and nursed him back to health," answered Kit.

"Lucky for him," said Shirley.

"It certainly was," said Kit.

"Now that you found him, are you headed back to Kemmerer?" asked Shirley.

"We're sorta helping out the Sheriff's office on finding the dirt bags who tried to kill him," said Kit. "They robbed him of those Russell letters, and Swifty and I are trying to help recover them."

"Good for you," said Shirley.

"Thanks," said Kit.

"You need to keep me informed," said Shirley. "Otherwise I find myself worrying about you."

"There's no service to speak of where we've been staying," replied Kit.

"Text me, you dummy. It can get through when voice service won't," said an exasperated Shirley.

"I'll do that," said Kit.

"I miss you, Cowboy," said Shirley.

"I miss you too," replied Kit.

"I've got to go," said Shirley, "You caught me in a rare free moment. I appreciate the call, Cowboy."

"I'll do better on letting you know what's going on," said Kit.

"You better. Goodbye, Cowboy," said Shirley and she broke the connection.

"You about done?" asked the clerk, who was behind the counter holding a flat cardboard box.

"Yep," said Kit. "How much do I owe you?" he asked as he got out of his chair.

"That'll be $12.55 with the tax," said the clerk.

Three minutes later, Kit was back at the truck with his box. Swifty was sound asleep inside the truck. He woke up when Kit opened the driver's side door.

"Did you get somethin' for me to eat?" said Swifty as he looked at the flat box in Kit's hand.

"Nope, I didn't," said Kit. "But, that's a damn good idea."

"Happy to be of service," said a smiling Swifty.

Kit just shook his head and started the truck.

CHAPTER NINETEEN

Kit drove until he came to a pancake house restaurant. He pulled into the parking lot, and he and Swifty were quickly seated in a booth looking at menus.

The waitress arrived and the men gave her their orders. Both ordered eggs, sausage, hash browns and pancakes along with orange juice and coffee.

"What's in the box?" asked Swifty.

Kit took a sample the clerk had given him out of his pocket and handed it to Swifty.

The printed page was a notice like the one's Kit had seen on the bulletin board in the art building. Basically, the notice read as follows:

"Looking for a female art student, blonde with pigtails and the first name Rose. Information needed about contact with a Ted Kelly at his cabin in the foothills near Woods Landing, Wyoming. Please call the number below."

At the bottom of the notice were tabs with Kit's cell phone number printed on them.

"Clever idea," said Swifty. "Think it'll work?"

"I have no idea, but right now it's better than nothing," said Kit.

"One thing concerns me," said Swifty.

"What's that?" said Kit.

"What if Rose ain't her real name. What if she gave old Ted a phony name?" said Swifty.

"Why would she do that?" asked Kit.

"Why was she ridin' a mountain bike late in the day durin' a thunder storm?" asked Swifty.

"I don't get it," said Kit.

"I'm not surprised," said Swifty. "Sometimes your lack of knowledge about women amazes me."

"You got a better idea?" asked Kit.

"Nope," said Swifty. "So, what do we do now?"

"We head back to Woods Landing and get a good night's rest and wait to hear from the sheriff," said Kit.

"Sounds like a stupid plan to me," said Swifty.

"What's your plan?" asked Kit.

"Go back to Woods Landing, get a good night's sleep, and then we go huntin' for the three dirt bags who tried to kill old Ted," said Swifty.

The two men walked to the truck and climbed inside. Kit started the truck and turned to face Swifty.

"How about we decide what to do in the morning after we've had breakfast," said Kit.

"Works for me," said Swifty and he slipped his cowboy hat over his eyes and leaned back in his seat. Minutes later, Swifty was fast asleep and snoring loudly.

In less than an hour Kit pulled up in front of their cabin. Both men went to the corral and fed and watered their horses. When they were finished, they returned to the cabin. Both men washed up at the sink in the cabin. Swifty took a nap, while Kit studied his maps and sat on his bed and tried to think about the three thieves who tried to kill old Ted.

"There can't be that many guys like the ones Ted described in Laramie," he thought. "But maybe they aren't from Laramie. Maybe they're from Rawlins or Casper or Cheyenne or God knows where?"

Kit put down his maps and joined Swifty in a short nap. Kit was awakened by the sound of a duck quacking. He looked around and then realized it was the signal from his iPad that he had received a text. He retrieved his iPad and retrieved the message screen. The text message was from Shirley.

"BE CAREFUL AND DON'T GET HURT. I'M NOT THERE TO PATCH YOU UP."

Kit grinned and punched the keys for a return text. "Thanks, Mom."

Kit looked at his watch. It was almost six o'clock. He rolled out of bed and went to the bathroom and splashed cold water on his face. He dried himself off and combed his hair. When he emerged from the bathroom, he yelled at Swifty. "Rise and shine, Swifty. Time to hit the chow line."

Swifty was instantly up, awake, and ready to go. They headed to the café and were soon seated in the dining room.

The young waitress they had seen before took their orders, and they each enjoyed a drink of bourbon on the rocks while they waited for their meals.

"Did you give Tang a call to let her know we found her grandfather?" asked Swifty.

"Deputy Parcell told me he'd make the call since Tang had filed a missing person report with the Sheriff's office. Better him than me," said Kit.

"Amen to that," said Swifty as he took another swig of his drink. "I think old Tang would be a handful for any man."

"Do I detect some interest in Tang on your part?" said Kit slyly.

"Me? Good God no. I may be a little crazy, but I'm not stupid or suicidal," responded Swifty.

187

"I thought you liked your women a little wild," said Kit.

"I like them a little wild, but not a lot crazy," said Swifty. "That woman is the kind who gets a man and then is determined to change him even if it kills him."

"You could be right," said Kit as he stifled a laugh.

Further discussion was interrupted when the waitress delivered their meals. Both men dug in like they hadn't eaten in days. When they finished their meals, Kit paid the check including a generous tip for the waitress and they retired back to their cabin. Within minutes, the cabin was filled with two separate sets of snoring.

Dawn found both men up and about and after feeding and watering the horses, they entered the café. Tess was behind the bar, and she gave them a welcoming wave of her hand.

Shorty, Hoppy, and Cal were already at the bar, their breakfasts already half consumed. "You boys want the usual?" asked Tess.

"Absolutely," said Swifty. Kit just grinned and nodded his agreement to Tess. They joined the three old time ranchers at the bar.

"How goes the search?" asked Hoppy.

"You mean Shorty didn't tell you?" replied Kit.

"Shorty don't tell me crap," said Hoppy. "If he did, I wouldn't listen anyhow."

Shorty just glared at Hoppy, but he didn't stop eating his breakfast.

"What's goin' on?" asked Cal.

"We found old Ted," said Kit. "He got robbed by three scumbags. They beat him up and threw him off a cliff and left him for dead. Old Eleanor found him, took him home, and nursed him back to health. He had a broken arm and leg and some cracked ribs along with a lot of cuts and bruises."

"What kind of piss poor excuse for a human being would do that to a harmless old man?" fumed Hoppy.

"The kind we ought to string up," said Cal.

"Right after we brand and castrate the bastards," added Shorty.

"Did you find them three scumbags?" asked Hoppy.

"No, we didn't find them. One of them shot at us from up on a bluff, but Kit winged him and he ran," said Swifty.

"Do we need to organize a posse?" asked Shorty.

"No, we ain't doin' nothin' like that," said Swifty. "We turned over everything we had to the Sheriff's office in Laramie. The law will take care of them boys."

"Our job was to find old Ted and we did," said Kit. "Our job here is finished."

"Does that mean you'll be leaving Woods Landing?" asked Hoppy.

"It does, but not until we take a stab at trying to recover the Russell letters those thieves stole from old Ted," said Kit.

"Just how are you gonna do that?" asked Shorty.

"We left a notice in the art building at the university in Laramie saying we're looking for this Rose, the art student who stopped at Ted's cabin. We think she told someone about the letters and if we can find her, we can find out who she told. That very well might lead us to the brains behind this theft," said Kit.

"Makes sense to me," said Hoppy. "How does she get in touch with you?"

"I left my cell phone number on the notice. The problem is I can't get any service on my phone here," said Kit.

"Well, we know how to fix that," said Hoppy.

"What do you mean?" asked Kit.

"The café has internet service, and they got a booster for their cell phones," said Hoppy. "Ask Tess and I bet she'll get you fixed up."

Kit turned to Tess. "Is that true?" he asked.

"I can give you a guest access code, and you should have five bars of service here," said a smiling Tess.

"How soon can we do this?" asked Kit.

"Right now works for me," said Tess.

She gave Kit the guest access code for the café's booster and within a few minutes, Kit's cell phone was registering five bars of service.

"Thank you, Tess. I really appreciate this," said Kit.

"No problem, Kit. You and Swifty have become good customers. I'm happy to help you."

Kit checked his phone. He had received several calls, but none from Rose the art student. Kit shut off his phone, just as Tess came out of the kitchen with breakfast for him and Swifty.

Kit and Swifty finished their breakfasts and stayed to talk with the three old ranchers and drink a last cup of hot coffee. They were about to leave when Kit's cell phone rang. Kit quickly answered, but whoever was calling, promptly hung up without saying a word.

"Wrong number?" asked Hoppy.

"I'm not sure," said Kit.

"Check and see who it was from," said Tess, who had been listening in from behind the bar.

Kit checked his phone and the caller had a Wyoming area code of 319. "Looks like it was a Wyoming number," he said.

"Call it back and see what happens," said Tess, who obviously had more experience with cell phones than any of the five men in her bar.

Kit called the number and put the phone on speaker so everyone in the bar could hear. The phone rang three times and then a woman's voice said, "Hello?"

"Is this Rose?" asked Kit.

The woman on the phone said, "Oh God," and hung up.

Kit stood there looking at his phone. "Crap, I wonder if that was Rose," he said.

"You can use a reverse directory and find out who it was," said Tess.

"How do I do that?" said Kit.

Tess took the phone from Kit and after a couple of minutes, she wrote something down on a pad of paper she had on the bar. She looked at what she had written and shook her head. "I don't think this is gonna be a lot of help," Tess said.

"Why? What does it say?" asked Kit.

"I have a name and address, but I think the phone may be in a family plan that includes this Rose gal, because the address is in Riverton, Wyoming," said Tess.

"Of course, a cell phone address is going to be where the bill gets sent," said Kit.

The three old ranchers remained silent. Understanding cell phones to them was like understanding flying to the moon.

Tess tore the paper from the pad and gave it to Kit. "Maybe you can still use this," she said.

Kit looked at the name and address on the paper. He read T.M. Wilson, 229 Elk Drive, Riverton, WY.

"Hell, her last name could be different than Wilson," said Swifty.

"You could be right, but it may be worth a shot to get a list of students at the University of Wyoming and see if there is a Rose Wilson," said Kit.

"What then?" said Swifty. "She may have called you, but she left no message and when you called her, she didn't seem any too damn anxious to talk to you. How do we know it isn't a prank call? Anybody who read that notice could have called just for kicks. We got no way of knowing if that call was from this Rose gal."

"You could be right, Swifty. I'm not sure who called me. I still think it's worth a shot to try to talk to whoever called. If it is this Rose, she talked to someone about those Russell letters, and that's got to be the link to whoever planned this whole deal," said Kit.

"Let's drive to Laramie and call her from there," said Swifty. "If she agrees to talk to us, we can get to her right away."

"That's not a bad idea, Swifty," said Kit. "Does this booster thing work on my phone when I'm in my cabin?" Kit asked Tess.

"It's supposed to work up to five hundred feet from the café," Tess replied.

"Good," said Kit. "Thanks, Tess."

Swifty swallowed the last of his coffee. "I'm ready when you are," he said to Kit.

"Let's stop at the cabin, and then we'll head out," said Kit.

Both men said their good-byes to Tess and the three old ranchers and were quickly out the door of the café.

Fifteen minutes later, Kit and Swifty were in the truck heading east to Laramie. Kit was driving and Swifty was slumped in the passenger seat with his cowboy hat pulled down over his eyes.

CHAPTER TWENTY

Thirty-five minutes later they were pulling into Laramie. When they got near the university, Kit pulled into a nearby parking lot and stopped the truck. He pulled out the map of the university and checked for the registrar's office. Once he had it located, he put the address into the truck's navigation system and when the system was ready, he left the parking lot and followed the system's directions.

Ten minutes later they drove by the registrar's office and began looking for a parking place. That took another ten minutes. Parking in a university, even the University of Wyoming, was always a problem. Parking spaces were rarer than hen's teeth. Finally, Kit saw a pickup truck pulling out of a space, and he quickly filled the space with his truck.

"I'll go on and you stay with the truck," Kit said to a still slumped down Swifty.

"Umpfg," was Swifty's muffled reply.

Kit just shook his head as he got out of the truck and began walking back to the registrar's office. The office was three blocks away, and as Kit walked, he passed groups of students who were chatting with each other or talking on their cell phones. Kit was invisible to them.

Kit entered the front door of the registrar's office and after a stop at the receptionist's desk, he found himself standing in front of a desk manned by a middle-aged woman with short greying hair. She eyed him suspiciously. She looked at Kit, as though she was sure he was guilty of something. The sign on her desk said Assistant Registrar.

"May I help you?" said the woman with a complete lack of sincerity in her voice.

"Yes, ma'am," said Kit. "I'm trying to locate a student."

"What's this student's name?" she asked.

"I believe her name is Rose Wilson. She's an art student," said Kit, trying to be helpful.

"I see," said the woman. "Are you a relative of the student?"

"No, ma'am," said Kit. "I'm trying to locate her to ask her some questions about a missing old man."

"If you are not a relative, I'm afraid I can't help you, sir," said the woman. "We have privacy laws in this state, and it's my job to see they are followed."

"Ma'am, I only want to ask her some questions because I know she talked to this missing gentleman," said Kit.

"That's not my concern. I can't help you. Good day, sir," said the woman, and she looked down at her desk.

Kit started to say something, and then he saw it would be a waste of time. This woman didn't want to help him and nothing he could say would change her mind.

"Thank you, ma'am," said Kit. "You have a nice day." Then he turned and walked out the door and headed back to the truck.

As Kit walked back to the truck, he reflected on the woman's obvious rudeness. Then he realized that was pointless and tried to think of what else he could do to locate the elusive Rose Wilson. He pulled out his cell phone and tried the phone number that had called his phone back in Woods Landing. The phone rang and rang and finally went to an institutional message for voice mail. Kit shut the phone off and returned it to his pocket.

When Kit opened the truck door, Swifty lifted his cowboy hat and stared at his partner. "Any luck?" he asked.

"Nope. I tried and I got squat. The lady quoted privacy laws and shut me down," said Kit.

"Want to try it my way?" asked Swifty.

"Not if it involves breaking the law and getting us tossed in the clink," said Kit.

"Why would you think I would break the law?" said Swifty with a phony look of hurt feelings on his face.

"I can give you a list," said Kit.

"OK, OK, so maybe I have stretched the law a time or two," said Swifty. "This is perfectly legit and above the law. I swear."

"Let's hear it," said Kit.

"Let me drive," said Swifty.

"Why?" asked Kit.

"You'll see. Trust me," said Swifty.

"I'm sure I'm going to regret this," said Kit as he got out of the driver's seat and walked around the truck to the passenger seat. Swifty slid over to the driver's seat and started the truck up.

Swifty drove through the campus for about five minutes when he slowed down and pulled over and parked by a coffee shop.

After parking the truck, Swifty got out and entered the coffee shop. The place was full of students. Every table was filled with students using their laptops and tablets or talking on their cell phones. There was a line of students waiting to give the baristas their order. Swifty got into one of the lines behind three coeds and struck up a conversation with them. When he got to the front of the line, he ordered a plain

195

coffee and then struck up another conversation with five guys standing near the door of the coffee house.

After about fifteen minutes, Swifty emerged from the coffee shop with his coffee cup in hand and slid into the driver's seat of the truck.

"What was that all about," said Kit. "You go into a coffee shop and get coffee for yourself? What am I, an Uber driver?"

"That my friend, was a masterful job of intelligence gathering," said a smug Swifty.

"How so?" asked Kit.

"I learned the names of what are probably the three best campus bars in Laramie," said Swifty.

"Why's that important?" asked Kit.

"Because the three dirt bag thieves we're looking for are the right age to hang out at a campus bar for recreation, and to try to pick up coeds," said Swifty.

"I hate to say this, but that actually makes good sense," said Kit.

"You ain't the only guy with brains, tenderfoot," said Swifty.

"So, what are the names of these bars?" asked Kit.

"I wrote them down on this napkin," said Swifty.

"You have a napkin?" said Kit. "Wonders will never cease."

"Kiss my ass," said Swifty.

Kit took the napkin from Swifty and entered the first address in the truck's navigation system. The system quickly led them to a bar on the edge of campus. Swifty slowed down to get a good look at the bar and the adjoining parking lot and then continued driving by it.

"Aren't we stopping to check it out?" asked Kit.

"You never spent much time in bars as a youngster, did you?" asked Swifty.

"No, why do you ask?" said Kit.

"Campus bars don't come to life until it gets dark. The only dudes in a campus bar at this time of day are majoring in pickled livers," replied Swifty.

"So, what do we do now?" said Kit.

"We could take in a movie or visit the local library," said Swifty sarcastically.

"We could go back to the coffee shop," said Kit.

"Why would we do that?" asked Swifty.

"We could stake it out and I could use their free wi-fi to fire up my laptop and see if I can find a way to get a list of art majors at the university," said Kit.

"Who am I to refuse to sit and spend an afternoon watching coeds come and go," said a suddenly smiling Swifty.

Swifty drove back to the coffee shop and was able to get a parking spot across the street from the shop. Swifty shut off the truck and settled back in his seat, while Kit opened his lap top. After acquiring the wi-fi signal from the coffee shop, Kit began to search on the internet.

The two men sat in the truck for almost two hours, but they saw no blonde coeds with pigtails and Kit was unsuccessful in trying to get a list of art majors. Their stake-out was interrupted only by Swifty making a trip into the coffee house to use the bathroom.

"Man, you got weak kidneys," said Kit.

"I do not. It was that damn coffee I had," said a defiant Swifty.

"Unless you have some other brilliant idea, I vote we head back to Woods Landing and get some supper and then return to look in those bars after it gets dark," said Kit.

"Sounds like a plan to me," said Swifty.

Swifty started the truck and they were soon heading west to Woods Landing. After they arrived they fed and watered the horses and headed for the café.

They entered the café and were greeted by Bess behind the bar. They walked into the dining room and were soon being served their dinner. Kit had a pasta dish and Swifty stuck with the steak dinner special.

When their meal was finished, the two men sat at the table and relaxed as they each worked on finishing up the beer in front of them.

"Since you're the expert on campus bars, how do you want to play it tonight?" asked Kit

"We go in dressed like we are as cowboys and we get a couple of beers and we find a table that's out of the way. Then we watch and listen. We wait at least an hour and then we do a little minglin' and we try to strike up a few conversations," said Swifty.

"Why wait for an hour?" asked Kit.

"'Cause no one is half loaded in the first hour", said Swifty. "Folks get a lot friendlier in a bar after they've had a few."

Kit nodded his understanding and leaned back in his chair. "I worry when things you say start to make sense," he said. "If we start now we should hit the first bar at about the right time."

"Let's ride," said Swifty.

Kit paid the bill and the two men were soon in their truck headed for Laramie. The road was almost deserted and they were parked in the lot behind the bar in forty minutes.

The bar was rapidly filling up and the crowd was almost all college aged. There were about three guys to every girl, but Kit thought that was about the same ratio he remembered when he was in college.

The music was loud and so was the noise made by the crowd. Smoke began to waft through the air and Kit was sure he smelled the distinct aroma of marijuana. He and Swifty sat at a table located at the back of the bar. Even so, they were able to get a good view of most of the room. Kit and Swifty acted disinterested, but they keep carefully scanning the room, looking for a tall, blond coed with pigtails.

A harried waitress came to their table and asked if they wanted another round of beers. Swifty told her he did, and when she returned with the beers, he gave her a five-dollar tip. She took the tip and gave Swifty a grateful smile.

"I think old Swifty could score with that waitress," he said.

"We're here to find an art student named Rose," said an irritated Kit.

"I'm just sayin,'" said an amused Swifty.

"Quit sayin' and keep looking," retorted Kit.

A tall blonde coed entered the bar with several of her friends. A closer look saw she had short hair and no pig tails. Kit kept looking. After a little more than an hour had passed, Swifty rose from his chair and moved to the bar.

Swifty motioned to the bartender to get his attention, and then ordered another round of beers. While he waited, he struck up a conversation with the two college boys sitting at the bar. He kept talking even after the bartender delivered his beers. Finally, Swifty picked up his beers and said good-bye to the students. He carefully made his way through the crowded bar until he arrived back at the table where Kit waited.

"Any luck?" asked Kit.

"Sort of," replied Swifty. "Them two boys are regulars at this bar and we talked about the Cowboy's football team and how they're doin' this year. They're playin' real well and doin' much better than them boys thought they would."

"Thanks for the college football update," said Kit. "What about Rose?"

"I asked them if they knew a blonde art student named Rose, but I drew a blank," said Swifty.

"A blank?" asked Kit.

"Them two boys didn't know her, and they been hanging out at this bar for two years. That tells me Rose has probably never been in this bar and we could sit here till hell freezes over and probably never see her in this place," said Swifty. "We need to move to another bar."

"Here's to you," said Kit, raising his glass of beer.

"Here's to me," said Swifty and he clinked his beer glass against Kit's. Both men drained their beers and left the glasses on the table and made their way to the bar's exit.

Once in the bar's parking lot, the two men checked their surroundings and then made their way to the truck. Swifty started the truck, while Kit gave the navigation system the address of the second campus bar from Swifty's napkin.

Soon the system was ready, and Swifty followed the system's instructions as they pulled out of the bar's parking lot. It took Swifty about ten minutes to drive to the next bar. This one had no parking lot, so they had to drive around for a while, looking for a place to park.

Kit and Swifty checked their surroundings before they exited the truck. Satisfied that things were normal, both men got out and headed for the bar about two blocks down the street. The sidewalk was deserted and the main light for their walk in the dark came from the big neon signs on the outside walls of the bar.

Swifty held the door to the bar open and said, "Age before beauty."

"Cram it," replied Kit as he walked into the bar with Swifty close behind him.

The bar was jammed with college-aged young men and women. The noise was even louder than the last bar. A combination of loud music and lots of college kids trying to hear and be heard was overwhelming. The interior of the bar was hot from so many bodies pressed into such a small space and the air was smoky.

Swifty returned from the bar with two beers and he and Kit leaned against a back wall of the bar. They drank their beers and each man appeared disinterested in their surroundings, but they were carefully scanning the bar. After about ten minutes, Kit and Swifty looked at each other and shook their heads slightly from side to side. Neither man had seen anyone who resembled Rose. After almost half an hour, a small table opened near them. Swifty and Kit moved quickly over to claim the table. Once seated, they returned to their surveillance of the bar. Another half an hour passed and Swifty arose and made his way through the crowded room to the bar. Once there he signaled the bartender. It took a while, but she finally saw Swifty and moved over to him. He ordered two beers and while he waited, he struck up a conversation with three coeds who were standing by the bar.

Kit watched from his table across the crowded room. The bartender arrived with the beers and Swifty paid her, but ignored the beers on the bar and kept talking to the coeds. Swifty was paying attention to a short, well-built coed with short dark hair. She was laughing at everything Swifty said and paying rapt attention to him.

"Crap, Swifty," thought Kit. "This isn't the time to try to carve another notch on your damn bedpost."

Finally, Swifty broke away from the three coeds and made his way through the bar crowd as the short, dark haired coed looked longingly at him.

Swifty reached their table, handed Kit one of the beers and sat down.

"I thought we were here to find Rose, not to add to your harem," said Kit.

"Hey, I was just gettin' acquainted with some of the local wildlife," said a smiling Swifty.

"How the hell does that help us find Rose?" asked Kit.

"Well, to start with, I asked them gals if they had ever seen our gal Rose, and they hadn't. They said they come to this bar pretty often, so I don't think we're in the right place," said Swifty.

"Judging from those two yahoos heading our way, I'd say you were right about us not being in the right place," said Kit as he stared over Swifty's head at two young toughs headed to their table. The two men were a little old for college students. Kit judged them to be in their late twenties. They were dressed in t-shirts and baggy shorts with tennis shoes. Their arms were well-tattooed, and their t-shirts were about a size too small so they could show off their well-developed chests.

"Say nothing," whispered Swifty. "Let me handle this."

When the two men reached the table where Kit and Swifty were sitting, they got very close to the back of Swifty's chair and the taller of the two spoke.

"I think it's high time you two dicks left," he said.

Swifty turned in his seat and faced the man. "I'm right comfortable right where I am," he said with a smile on his face.

"You two ain't from around here, and you got no business in this bar," said the tall one in a menacing voice.

"Has this got somethin' to do with that little dark haired gal up at the bar?" asked Swifty.

"Don't you be bringing Katy up in this," said the tall man.

"Son," said Swifty, "I'm about to do you a tremendous favor."

"What do you mean," said the tall man.

"I'm gonna save you a trip to the hospital and an increase in your health insurance premium," said Swifty.

"What?" said the tall man, looking confused.

Faster than either of the two men could imagine, Swifty spun out of the chair. As he rose to his feet, Swifty grabbed the man's right arm and quickly snapped it up behind the man's back, forcing his face down on the surface of the table.

"Now," said Swifty. "I'm gonna let you go and if you're half as smart as I think you are, you and your friend are gonna walk away and go back up to the bar and have a beer and enjoy your good fortune. You savvy?"

The man moaned from the pain of having his arm almost broken, and he nodded his head up and down to let Swifty know he understood. Swifty released the man and he and his friend fled back to the bar, the tall man rubbing his arm as he walked. The entire incident happened so fast and was over so quickly that almost no one in the bar had noticed.

"Are you done now?" said Kit as he sat drinking the last of his beer.

"I think that's all the fun for tonight," said Swifty.

"I think it's time to head for the barn and return to fight another day," said Kit.

"Sounds like a plan to me," said Swifty. He finished his beer and followed Kit out of the bar and back to their parked truck. Half an hour later they were back in Woods Landing.

CHAPTER TWENTY-ONE

Kit pulled the truck in front of their cabin and woke Swifty.

"We're home," said Kit.

"It's about time," said Swifty. "Did you ever get the damn truck out of first gear?"

Kit just shook his head. They left the truck and walked to the cabin.

Before they got to the first step of the cabin's porch, Swifty turned his head to the left.

"There's a light on the cabin next to us," he said.

"Thelma and Louise must have rented it to someone," responded Kit.

Swifty kept looking, straining his eyes to adjust to the darkness. "I think I see the back end of a Jeep parked on the other side of that cabin."

"I'll make a note of that," said Kit sarcastically.

Kit opened the door to their cabin and Swifty stepped inside. Kit followed and he flipped on the light switch, illuminating the inside of the cabin. Swifty headed for his bed, but Kit came to a rock-still halt.

"What the hell is going on?" said Kit.

"What the hell are you mumbling about?" said Swifty.

"My stuff," said a confused Kit.

"What about your stuff?" asked Swifty.

"All my stuff is gone," said Kit. "My clothes, my ditty bag, my duffel. It's all gone. Where the hell did it go?"

"It's all in a safe place," said a female voice behind them.

Both men whirled around and standing in the doorway to their cabin was Shirley. She was leaning on the doorway with a huge smile on her face.

"Shirley!" said a surprised Kit. "What're you doing here? What's going on?"

"Relax, Cowboy," said Shirley. "I've been working overtime to get more equivalent time off. You'd be surprised to know it's only a little over a two-hour drive from Boulder to Woods Landing."

"You took my stuff?" said a still confused Kit.

"I rented the cabin next to you and took your stuff over there. I thought you might be more comfortable there with me than here with old Swifty," said Shirley.

"I resent that, but I can't say I disagree with it," said a grinning Swifty.

"You rented the cabin next to us?" said a still confused Kit.

"You seem a little slow on the uptake tonight, Cowboy. Why don't you follow me next door, and I'll try to help you understand just what's going on here," said Shirley.

Kit's mind finally clicked into gear, and he found himself following Shirley out the door of his cabin. She was dressed in tight jeans and a form fitting top and cowboy boots. Her blonde hair was in a pony-tail.

Minutes after Kit followed Shirley into her cabin, the lights in the cabin were turned out.

Dawn of the next day found Kit and Shirley knocking on the door of Swifty's cabin.

"We're burning daylight, Swifty," said Kit. "Let's head over for breakfast."

The response from inside the cabin was a series of moans and curses. Five minutes later, Swifty appeared at the door of the cabin.

The three of them walked over to the café.

"The sign on the café says it's not open," said Shirley.

"You can't believe everything you read," said Kit.

"The sign also says they're open for lunch and dinner, but it doesn't mention breakfast," said Shirley.

"They're not open for breakfast," said Kit.

"Then why don't we go somewhere else where we can get breakfast?" asked Shirley.

"Just play along with us, and it'll all work out," said Kit.

Kit opened the door and let Shirley and Swifty enter the café. The three of them were greeted by Tess from behind the bar. The three old ranchers sat frozen at the bar, staring at Shirley.

"I'll have the usual," said Kit.

"I'll have the same," said Swifty.

Shirley looked confused. "May I see a menu, ma'am?" she asked Tess.

"There ain't no menu 'cause we don't serve breakfast. We got eggs, bacon, sausage, hash browns, and pancakes," replied Tess.

After a little bartering, Shirley settled for an order of scrambled eggs, toast, and a side of fruit as well as orange juice and coffee.

Kit, Swifty, and Shirley joined the three old ranchers at the bar. Kit introduced Shirley to Hoppy, Shorty, and Cal. All three of the old ranchers shook hands with Shirley, never taking their eyes off her.

Mugs of hot coffee appeared in front of Shirley, Kit, and Swifty. A small pitcher of cream and a bowl of sugar were placed in front of Kit.

"She knows you take cream and sugar with your coffee?" said an incredulous Shirley.

"She is very observant," said Kit.

"So, what brings you to Woods Landing, Miss Shirley?" asked Hoppy.

"I got tired of waiting for my boy-friend to call or text me, so I thought I'd drive up and remind him of what he was missing," said a smiling Shirley.

Kit found himself blushing, despite his efforts to avoid it.

"Well, it looks pretty obvious who your boyfriend is," said Hoppy as he grinned at Kit.

"Man, Kit, I though you was smarter than that," said Shorty. "Miss Shirley is the prettiest filly I seen in quite a spell."

"I gotta agree with Shorty," chimed in Cal.

"What my less than articulate friends are sayin' is we're right proud to meet you, Miss Shirley," said Hoppy.

"Thank you, gentlemen," said Shirley. "You are all very kind."

The conversation was interrupted by Tess bringing breakfast for Kit, Shirley, and Swifty.

"Eat it while it's hot," said Shorty. "Don't let us bother you none while you have your breakfast. We already had ours."

Tess refilled mugs of coffee for the three old ranchers. They thanked Tess, and she retreated behind the bar.

After Shirley had finished her scrambled eggs and was working on her fruit bowl, Shirley looked at Kit.

"Have you boys made any progress?" she asked

"Not very much, I'm afraid," said Kit. "We've been trying to find the girl named Rose who was at old Ted's cabin, but we're not having much luck."

"Where have you looked?" asked Shirley.

Kit related to Shirley their efforts of the previous day and their trip to the two bars that evening, along with their unceremonious exit after Swifty's antics.

Shirley looked at Swifty. "So, you couldn't resist the chance to put those two drugstore cowboys in their place," she said.

"I viewed it more as a public service," said an unrepentant Swifty.

"I'm sure you did," said Shirley. "So, what have you two got planned for today?"

"I thought we might get back in touch with Deputy Parcell at the Sheriff's office," said Kit. "We haven't heard anything from him and maybe he has a lead on who owns those custom painted ATVs."

"If he does, why do you think he might share it with you?" asked Shirley.

"What do you mean?" asked Swifty.

"What I mean is this deputy is real law enforcement. You two are not. He's not going to be happy if he finds out you boys are conducting your own private investigation of the theft of those Russell letters. He might even charge you with something," said Shirley.

"Charge us?" said Swifty. "We're the good guys. We got every right to snoop around on our own. Hell, we probably made more progress on the thefts than he has."

"It won't matter to him," said Shirley. "You two are probably nothing more than would-be vigilantes to him. He did tell you to sit tight, did he not?"

"He did," said Kit.

"Well, I might be mistaken, but from what you've told me you two have been up to, I don't think it meets the definition of sitting tight," said Shirley.

"So, what do you suggest we do?" asked Kit.

"I think this would be a lovely time for you to take me to Laramie and show me the sights. While we're there, you might give the deputy a call and ask for an update," said Shirley.

"How is that different from what I just said?" asked a confused Kit.

"It isn't," said Shirley. "It just sounds good when I suggest it and even better when I'm involved in the search."

"Whoa, wait just a minute," said Swifty. "We're a two-man team. We're not a two-guys and a gal team."

"Really," said Shirley. "It seems to me that a woman could go in places and get different answers than you two could. With all the obvious snooping around you two have been doing, chances are these thieves are now aware of you. They've never seen or heard of me."

"The lady has a point," said Kit.

"All right," said a reluctant Swifty. "She can come along."

"I'm glad that's settled," said Shirley. She turned to face Tess behind the bar. "Tess," she said. "Could I possibly get a coffee to go?"

"Coming right up," said Tess.

Minutes later the three of them were walking out of the café.

"I didn't even know you could get a coffee to go," muttered Swifty.

"You'll get over it, Swifty," said Shirley.

CHAPTER TWENTY-TWO

Kit fed and watered the horses, and Swifty checked and loaded gear on the truck. Fifteen minutes later they and Shirley were seated in the truck as Kit drove it east toward Laramie.

Kit pulled into the parking lot next to the Sheriff's office and parked the truck. "You two stay in the truck. I'll go in and see if Deputy Parcell is available and if I can get an update," said Kit.

Kit got out of the truck and made his way into the Sheriff's office. He stopped at the receptionist's desk and asked for Parcell. After the receptionist made a phone call, she told Kit to have a seat and said Deputy Parcell would be out soon.

Kit took a seat in the reception area and waited. Five minutes later, Deputy Parcell entered the room and came up to Kit and shook hands.

"Good to see you, Mr. Andrews," said the deputy.

"Please call me Kit. Calling me Mr. Andrews makes me feel like an old man," said Kit.

"Kit it is," said the deputy. "Let's go to the conference room where we can talk in private."

Kit followed Deputy Parcell back to the conference room. The deputy opened the door for Kit to enter and followed him in the room, shutting the door behind him.

"I suppose you're here to get some kind of an update on the Ted Kelly case," said Parcell.

"I'd certainly appreciate anything you can tell me," said Kit.

"We were able to get a deputy and an EMT out to Eleanor's cabin. The EMT checked on Mr. Kelly and he seems to be doing pretty well, considering what happened to him. Eleanor did a good job of tending to his injuries. She must have been one hell of a nurse in the army," said Parcell.

"Of that I have no doubt," said Kit with a smile.

"The deputy took a statement from Mr. Kelly and it pretty well matches up with the story you told me, with one exception," said Parcell.

"What was that?" asked Kit, knowing well what the answer was.

"He mentioned the two college girls who sought shelter in his cabin during a thunderstorm a month or so prior to the arrival of the three thieves at his cabin," said Parcell.

"Oh, yeah," said Kit. "I guess in all the excitement I forgot about them."

"We tried to run them down, but we had no last names and Mr. Kelly never asked for any. He mentioned that one of the girls was named Rose and she was an art student. He wasn't sure what the other girl's major was. Anyway, this Rose showed interest and knowledge of the Russell framed letters he had on the walls of his cabin that were stolen. We got the university to give us a roster of all the art majors at the university, but there was no one named Rose listed," said the deputy.

"Really," said Kit. "I wonder why, if she was an art student."

"There are several possible reasons," said the deputy. One is that maybe she is only getting a minor in art. Another is that she may only be a part-time student or she may currently be unenrolled. Lots of students stay out for a semester or so to work because they have run out of money," said Parcell.

"So, Rose has turned out to be a dead end?" asked Kit.

"I'm afraid so," said the deputy.

"That's disappointing," said Kit.

"It certainly is," said Parcell. "We also contacted all the body shops in the area, and we drew a blank on finding a shop that might have painted those symbols on the ATVs the three thieves were riding."

"None of them did the work?" asked Kit.

"None of them," answered the deputy. "We asked each shop if they knew of any freelancers or small, private shops that might do that kind of work, but we came up with zero leads."

"So, where does that leave the investigation?" asked Kit.

"We're pretty much back to square one," said the deputy. "Thanks to you, Mr. Kelly has been found, and he is recovering from his injuries. We have squat on the three thieves who tried to kill him, and we have no leads on the Russell letters they stole. We've put out inquiries to all the western art galleries in Wyoming and the surrounding states, but nothing has turned up so far."

"That's disappointing," said Kit.

"Very disappointing," said Parcell. "We still think the thieves are going to try to sell the paintings and when they do, we will have a chance to nail them. The problem is so much stuff gets sold on the internet making the market place for the letters world-wide, not just in our back yard. Plus, we know the description of only one of the letters. Mr. Kelly could only really describe the one he called the Night Hawk letter."

"I appreciate you sharing this with me, Deputy Parcell," said Kit. "I'm just sorry you've been hitting so many dead ends."

"It's been frustrating, but I believe we'll get a break," said Parcell. "From everything I've learned, these three dudes do not sound like rocket scientists. Most thieves are dumb and eventually they screw up and we catch them."

"Good luck with your investigation, Deputy," said Kit. "I hope you catch these guys and get old Ted's letters back. They mean a lot to him."

"We can use all the luck we can get, Kit. Are you going back to Kemmerer?" asked the deputy.

"I think we may stick around for a while," said Kit. "We're staying out at a rented cabin in Woods Landing, and it's not a bad place to relax," said Kit.

"I'm sure Woods Landing is plenty quiet," said the deputy with a laugh.

Kit walked out of the Sheriff's office and returned to the truck where Swifty and Shirley were impatiently waiting.

"Well, what did you learn from the deputy?" asked Swifty.

Kit related everything the deputy had told him to Swifty and Shirley.

"So, no luck on the custom paint job or on finding Rose enrolled as an art major at the university?" asked Swifty.

"None, zero, zip, nada," said Kit.

"No one has called your phone since that one call?" asked Shirley.

"Let me check my phone," said Kit. He opened his phone and searched it for any recent calls he might have missed or any voice mails. "I got nothing on my phone."

"Well, we do have a fairly good description of Rose, if that is her real name," said Swifty.

"What good does that do us?" asked Kit.

214

"We still have one bar to check out," said Swifty.

"Why? Isn't that a waste of time?" asked Shirley.

"Guys are still guys and if Rose, or whatever her name is, is normal, she's been in one of the local bars and guys would remember a tall blonde with pigtails even if her name was Brunhilda," said Swifty.

"He has a point," said Shirley.

"He always has a point when it comes to women and bars," said Kit.

"So, what do we do while we wait for it to get dark?" asked Swifty.

"I have no idea," said Kit.

"I do," said Shirley.

"What?" asked Kit.

"We shop," said Shirley.

"Oh, God, not shopping," moaned Swifty.

"I can drop you boys off somewhere entertaining while I shop," said Shirley. "You know, like the library."

"A fate worse than death," said Swifty. "What the hell would I do at the library."

"I meant that library," said Shirley as she pointed at a small bar across the street from the Sheriff's office. A sign over the door of the bar read, "The Library."

"Works for me," said Swifty.

"I'll come and get you when I've finished looking around," said Shirley.

"Do we have a choice?" asked Kit.

"No, you don't, Cowboy," said Shirley.

Kit turned to get support from Swifty, but he was already out of the truck and walking toward the bar.

Kit got out of the truck and followed his best friend across the street. By the time Kit caught up with Swifty, Shirley was driving the truck down the street.

CHAPTER TWENTY-THREE

At the same time, Shirley was driving away from Kit and Swifty, Sid Wooly was back in the deserted barn yard of his uncle's run-down farm just outside of Laramie.

He was on his knees, working on his custom ATV, his toolbox at his side. Sid was working on a particularly stubborn bolt. He was a strong man, but as he pulled hard on the wrench, his upper right arm bulged with the effort, causing the tattoo of a skull and crossbones to seemingly grow larger.

"Shit," said Sid, as his wrench slipped and he banged his knuckles on the unyielding steel of the ATV's engine. Disgusted, Sid threw the wrench down on the barren ground and got to his feet. He made his way to an old battered chair located under the shade of a large cottonwood tree. He flopped down on the chair and stared at the skinned knuckles on his right hand.

He reached down with his left hand and opened the small cooler located next to the chair, getting out a cold can of beer. Sid turned in the chair and stuck his injured right hand down into the ice in the cooler. The cold ice made his knuckles feel better.

Sid withdrew his hand and opened the can of beer. He took a long drink and sighed and sat back in the old chair. He took another drink and paused to look around him. The old farm house was in ruins, but a small barn was in decent shape. His uncle rented out the farm land, but let Sid live there for free. Sid had bought an old hard sided camper and parked it behind the ruined farm house. The camper had been his home for the past two years.

He used the barn as a workshop. Sid was handy with machines and small engines and he had held several jobs at repair shops in the Laramie area, but he never lasted long at any one place. Sid had a lot of bad habits. He liked dope, booze, and he was a thief. None of those things helped to guarantee lengthy employment at any one place.

Sid took another swig of beer. He was sick of the farm, sick of living in a dingy, cramped camper, and sick of Laramie in general. He had decided that if he could get enough cash together he would head for California and a fresh start. The thought of sunny California, the beautiful babes in bikinis on the ocean beaches, and the laid-back lifestyle made him smile.

He had a tin box buried in a corner of the old barn containing a little more than twelve hundred dollars. That wasn't nearly enough for what Sid had in mind. He took another swig of beer. Now he was close, very close, to getting enough cash to get the hell out of Wyoming.

Sid had been surprised when one of his buddies had called him and said he knew someone who was looking for a guy like Sid for a less than legal job that would pay very well. Sid was interested and his buddy gave him a phone number. Sid did think it was odd his buddy said he needed to call within forty-eight hours or the number would no longer be any good. He had never heard of that before.

He had called and got a recording that told him to leave his name and number. Sid had nothing to lose, so he did. Six hours later he got a call from someone using a device that disguised their voice. The voice sounded like Darth Vader in that Star Wars movie, but Sid listened. The voice gave him very explicit instructions and after hearing them, Sid agreed to take the job.

The job had turned out to be easier than Sid had thought. He was given general directions and after a couple of hours of riding his ATV in the foothills, he managed to locate the cabin he was told to find. He used the GPS device he had been sent to pinpoint the location, and then he returned with the two Collins brothers on their ATVs. They had rousted the old man and beat him up. Then they removed the Russell letters from the walls and packed them in the cargo boxes on the ATVs. Sid and Nate took Ted for a walk and threw him off a cliff and left him to die. The old guy had to be eighty. Sid didn't think he'd last more than a few hours. Then he and Nate Collins had returned to the old dude's cabin where Ned waited for them with the loaded ATVs.

Sid had received directions to go to a hardware store in Laramie. The boxes had been paid for and were being held in Sid's name. Inside the cargo boxes was packing material. There were six framed letters and Sid was to get $10,000.00 for each framed letter safely delivered. Sid had promised $10,000.00 to the Collins brothers to split between themselves and would keep the remaining $50,000.00 for himself. He and the Collins brothers would get their money when the framed letters were sold. The voice had told him that might take as long as a month.

He and the Collins brothers had stolen a truck and trailer in Cheyenne and used them to transport their ATVs to the lodge. Then they took the truck and trailer out in the boondocks and burned them. Sid had thought that was a waste of possible money, but the voice had insisted.

Sid and the Collins brothers had delivered the cargo boxes to a storage unit in Laramie. He had received the entrance code, location, unit number and key to the padlock in the mail. The padded envelope had no return address, but Sid had noticed the postmark was from Cheyenne.

Then the voice had called Sid and told him about a possible problem. It seemed two cowboys were investigating the old dude's disappearance and the voice wanted Sid to have someone check on the cowboys and report back if they were making any progress.

Sid thought he was playing it smart and sent Ned, who was the dumber of the two Collins brothers. Unfortunately, Ned had gotten carried away and took potshots at the cowboys. They had shot back. Now Ned had his arm in a sling after Sid had an old buddy who flunked out of med school patch up the bullet wound. The voice had been very unhappy about that turn of events.

Sid couldn't believe how stupid Ned had turned out to be. Getting shot had served him right. Dumb bastard.

Sid drank the last of the beer and tossed the empty can over his shoulder and behind the chair. He was about to get out of the old chair and give the bolt on the ATV engine another try, when his cell-phone chirped. He pulled the cell phone out of his shirt pocket and looked at it. He didn't recognize the calling number, but he answered it anyway.

Sid said, "Hello." Then he heard the voice on the phone. "Yes, I can hear you fine," said Sid. The voice then gave Sid another set of instructions.

"What's in it for me?" asked Sid.

The voice responded.

"Another ten thousand for me?" asked Sid.

Again, the voice responded.

"How much for the Collins brothers?" asked Sid.

The voice paused and then responded to Sid's question.

"OK," said Sid. "Please repeat the timing again. I want to make sure I got it right."

Sid listened for another two minutes, and then the connection was broken.

"Ten thousand for me and four thousand for the Collins brothers," thought Sid. "And if I dispose of the Collins brothers, I get to keep their four thousand as well. I like the sound of that."

Sid dialed a number on his cell phone, ignoring his ATV and the wrench lying in the dirt of the old barn yard.

CHAPTER TWENTY-FOUR

Kit and Swifty quickly discovered that the Library Bar had a pool table. They were on their tenth game of eight-ball when Shirley entered the bar.

She had no trouble locating Kit and Swifty, since they were the only customers in the bar.

"I hate to break up your game, boys, but I think it's time you two took me out for dinner," said Shirley.

"You finished shopping?" asked Kit.

"Spoken just like a man," said Shirley. "A woman's shopping is never done. You would do well to remember that, Cowboy."

Kit and Swifty slipped their pool cues into a wall rack and followed Shirley out of the bar and into the fading light of a late afternoon.

With Kit at the wheel of the truck, the trio located a steak house, and Kit pulled the truck into the restaurant's parking lot. They piled out of the truck and were soon seated in the dining room.

After the waitress brought them glasses of ice water and departed with their dinner orders, Kit looked over at Shirley.

"What did you shop for?" asked Kit.

"None of your business, Cowboy," said Shirley. "When you're paying for what I'm buying you can ask, but not until then."

"A little touchy tonight?" asked Swifty.

"Did I ask you two what you did while I was gone?" said Shirley.

"Nope," said Swifty.

"Well, there you go," said Shirley.

Kit looked down at his plate in an attempt to hide the big grin on his face.

"So, where is this bar we're checking out tonight?" asked Shirley.

"It's located just east of the campus," said Kit.

"What's the plan for this evening?" asked Shirley.

"We go into the bar, find us an out of the way table, have a couple of beers, and watch the crowd," said Swifty.

"That's it? That's your big plan?" asked Shirley.

"We wait about an hour for folks to get a couple drinks in them, then we do a little minglin' and chat with a few folks and see if we get any leads on Rose," said Swifty.

"So, do I just sit at the table and look blonde and dumb, or do I get to participate?" asked Shirley.

"Ah, I'm not sure," said Swifty. "Just how do you see yourself participatin'?"

"I've had my share of mingling at a bar," said Shirley. "As a matter of fact, I can't recall the last time I had to pay for a drink in a bar."

"I don't doubt that one bit," said Swifty. "I woulda been one of the guys buying you drinks."

Shirley laughed. Kit just shook his head.

"OK, all three of us try to work the room and see what we can come up with," said Swifty.

"Try to stay away from the hot women, Swifty," said Shirley. "We don't want to have a repeat of your last outing and wind up getting tossed out of the bar."

Swifty just shrugged his shoulders. Shirley took that for some form of acceptance of her suggestion.

After they finished their meals and Kit paid the bill, they got in the truck and drove to the bar. Kit found a parking place in the bar's parking lot. They entered the bar. The place was about half full and Kit led them over to a table in the back corner of the bar.

They ordered beers from the waitress and watched as the bar began to fill up. Twenty minutes later, the bar was full, the music was loud and it was hard to hear yourself think. Kit, Swifty, and Shirley acted like they were chatting among themselves, but all three of them were subtly scanning the room, looking for a tall, blonde girl with pig tails.

During the next hour, each of the trio took turns going to the bar and ordering beers rather than waiting for a waitress to come to their table. During each trip to the bar, they struck up conversations with other customers standing near the bar. When each of them returned to their table with beers, they shared what they had learned, if anything.

Kit looked at his watch. "We've been here for almost two hours, and it looks like we've struck out again."

"Speak for yourself, Cowboy," said Shirley. "I've had at least six offers to buy me a drink and two guys have given me their business cards."

"Very funny," said Kit. "I find it hard to believe we have polled the three most popular campus bars and no one has seen or heard of Rose."

"Maybe she don't drink," said Swifty.

"Even if she didn't drink, she would hang out in a bar just to socialize. She could be drinking Dr. Pepper all night. The guys wouldn't mind," said Shirley.

"Which brings us back to where the hell is she?" said Kit.

225

Just then Kit's cell phone rang. He looked at the phone and didn't recognize the number on the screen. Kit answered with a slightly questioning "Hello."

He paused for a second and looked around in frustration. "Just a minute," he said. "It's really loud in this bar. Let me go outside where I can hear you," said Kit.

Kit rose from his seat and quickly headed for the door to the bar. He opened the door and disappeared through it.

"What the hell was that?" said Swifty.

"I think he couldn't hear the caller in here. It's really loud," said Shirley. "He'll be back soon."

Swifty nodded and took a swig of his beer. Shirley kept her gaze on the door, watching for Kit's return.

After about ten minutes, Kit appeared in the doorway of the bar. He waited for two guys who were coming out of the bar, and then he stepped inside, making his way over to their table and sat down.

"So, was it a robo call, or one of those guys trying to sell you penis enlargement pills?" said a grinning Swifty.

Kit looked at Swifty with disgust in his eyes and Shirley kicked him in the leg under the table.

"No on both counts," said Kit.

"So, who was it?" asked Swifty.

"A girl who claimed to be Rose," said Kit with a smug look on his face.

"You're kidding," said Shirley.

"No, I'm not kidding," said Kit. "Let's get out of here, and I'll fill you in on what she had to say."

Five minutes later, the trio was back in the truck with Kit at the wheel.

"OK, tell us what happened," said Swifty.

"This girl said her name was Rose and wanted to know if I was the person who put the notice up on the board in the art building. I told her I was," said Kit.

"I asked her if she was the same Rose who had stayed at old Ted's cabin during a thunderstorm and she said she was," said Kit.

"I tried to get her to talk, but she said she wasn't in a good place and told me where we could meet and she would answer all the questions she could. I made her repeat her instructions, and then she hung up," said Kit.

"She said to meet her in the parking lot behind the ag building at four-thirty tomorrow afternoon," said Kit.

"Tomorrow is Sunday," said Shirley.

"Why wait till tomorrow?" asked Swifty. "What's wrong with tonight?"

"Hey, I just told you what I heard. I wasn't exactly in charge of the situation. She sounded really skittish on the phone. Like she was afraid of something," said Kit.

"You got that map of the campus?" asked Swifty.

"Yeah," said Kit. "I put it in the truck console." Kit opened the console and pulled out the map of the campus. Kit turned on the overhead light in the truck and opened the map. It took a minute for him to find the ag building Rose had mentioned.

"There it is," said Shirley, pointing to a spot on the map.

"Man, that is way out on the edge of the campus," said Swifty. "There's no houses or anything around three sides of that parking lot. Just open ground and sagebrush."

"What do you think?" asked Shirley.

"Looks a lot like a trap to me," said Swifty.

Kit started the truck and put it in gear. After checking the area around him, Kit pulled out of the bar's parking lot.

"Where are we going?" asked Shirley.

227

"I think there's no time like the present to go take a close look at the location of tomorrow's meeting place," said Kit.

"Good idea," said Swifty.

Fifteen minutes later they were pulling around the side of the ag building and into a large parking lot. There were only a few light poles in the lot and the lack of illumination made the place look quite gloomy.

"This looks like a bad place for a friendly meeting and a good place for an ambush," said Swifty.

Kit stopped the truck and left the motor running. After a thorough scan of the area around the truck, Kit put the truck in gear and slowly began to drive around the perimeter of the parking lot.

The map had been mostly correct. To the rear and both sides of the lot there was no development of any kind, residential or commercial. Just rolling land dotted with sagebrush. The lot was behind the ag building and shielded from view of the roads and buildings located beyond the ag building. There were no vehicles parked in the lot. The building was dark. Even the lights on both sides of the rear entrance of the building were dark.

"I can feel the hair on the back of my neck rising," said Swifty, "and that's never a good sign."

"This place does look spooky," said Shirley.

"I wonder why she picked this spot to meet us?" said Kit.

"At least the meeting is in the afternoon, not the middle of the night," said Shirley.

"Four thirty in the afternoon isn't the middle of the day," said Kit. "It's likely just starting to get close to dusk at that time."

"I can't figure why she chose this place," said Swifty. "If she's scared of something or someone, you'd think she'd pick some place real public and full of people in the middle of the day."

"Maybe she doesn't want anyone to see her talking to us," offered Shirley.

"She could have met us in the post office or the library or some building on campus," said Kit.

"Hey," said Swifty, "It is what it is. This is the place and tomorrow is the day and four-thirty is the time. Let's use it and plan for it."

"Swifty's right," said Kit. "Let's head back to Woods Landing and do a little pre-meeting planning."

"Sounds good to me," said Shirley.

Swifty said nothing. He slid down in his seat and pulled his cowboy hat down over his eyes.

Kit drove back to Woods Landing in silence.

CHAPTER TWENTY-FIVE

Kit pulled into the parking area in front of the cabins at Woods Landing. As they exited the parked truck, Kit took Shirley by the arm. "We'll take care of the horses and meet you in your cabin. Does that work for you?" he asked.

"I'll see you there," said Shirley and she headed for her cabin.

Kit and Swifty fed and watered the horses. Kit stopped at Swifty's cabin to get his laptop and then the two of them walked over to Shirley's cabin. When they stepped up on her porch, Kit could see her yellow and black Jeep Wrangler parked next to the building.

Both men stepped into the cabin and found Shirley sitting in a chair at a small, round table. Kit and Swifty each pulled up a chair and joined her.

Kit opened the campus map and spread it out on the table. Then he opened his laptop and turned it on.

Kit took a pen out of his shirt pocket and used it to point out the ag building and the parking lot behind the building. "Like we just saw, there's nothing behind the ag building but the parking lot and a ton of sagebrush," said Kit.

"That must be one of the most isolated spots on campus," said Shirley.

231

"It's definitely isolated, and the only way in or out is by the road in front of the ag building," said Kit. "What do you see, Swifty?"

"I don't like much of anything I'm seein' on this here map," said Swifty.

"I don't either," said Kit. "But, this is the hand we've been dealt and we need to figure out how to use it to our best advantage."

"I agree," said Swifty.

"So, what's the best way to play this?" asked Kit.

Swifty continued to study the map before answering Kit's question. Finally, he spoke. "I think I need to get there on foot, about one-thirty tomorrow afternoon. I'll find a decent hide in the brush either behind or to the side of the parking lot. I'll try to find the highest ground I can. We can use the little encrypted radios to communicate," said Swifty.

Shirley looked puzzled. Kit turned to her and said, "Swifty goes in early and sets up where he can see everything and cover me in case something goes wrong. We can talk and hear each other, but no one else can listen in."

"What could go wrong?" asked a now worried Shirley.

"This could be an ambush. Bad people could try to kill Kit," said Swifty.

"Oh, my God," said a horrified Shirley.

"Don't worry, Shirley," said Kit. "Swifty's job is to see nothing like that happens. If it should be a trap or an ambush, we'll turn the tables on the bad guys."

"So, what do we do tomorrow?" asked Shirley.

"You don't do anything," said Kit. "Swifty sets up an over watch position. I drive the truck near the front of the ag building and leave it there. Then I walk around to the back of the building to the parking lot and wait for Rose to show up."

"What about me? What do I do?" asked Shirley.

"You stay lying down on the back seat of the truck and wait until this thing is over," said Kit.

"That's it? I just lay on the back seat of the truck until it's over? What if something happens? What if I see more vehicles or guys with guns?" said Shirley

"If anything like that happens, you call 911 and get help here as fast as you can," said Kit. "Under no circumstances are you to get out of the truck or do anything that might place you in danger. Do you understand me, Shirley?" said Kit.

"I understand," said Shirley, "but I don't like it."

"Duly noted," said Kit.

"What about weapons and gear," asked Swifty.

"I'll have the radio, my Kimber pistol, and a boot knife," said Kit.

"I'll have my radio, my .308 sniper rifle, my pistol, and my boot knife," said Swifty.

"What about me," said Shirley. "Don't I get a gun?"

"You get a radio," said Kit. "That way you can hear what's going on. If you hear something bad, you call 911 and get the cavalry here as fast as possible."

"So, no gun?" asked Shirley.

"No gun," said Kit. "You stay low and out of sight. I don't want anyone to know you're within ten miles of the ag building."

"I don't like it," said Shirley.

"I'm sorry you don't like it," said Kit, "but we're trained for these kinds of situations and you aren't. I can't risk you getting hurt."

"That's the nicest thing you've said to me all day," said Shirley. She got out of her chair and put her arms around Kit and kissed him.

"I'm outta here," said Swifty as he covered his eyes with his hands with a show of great exaggeration.

"See you in the morning at breakfast," yelled Kit at Swifty's rapidly disappearing back.

"Yeah, right," said Swifty and was out the door of the cabin.

"Whatever will be we do now?" asked Shirley with a smile on her face.

"I'm sure you'll think of something," said Kit.

"You can count on that," said Shirley as she moved to the door of the cabin and locked it.

CHAPTER TWENTY-SIX

Just after sunrise Kit, Swifty, and Shirley entered the door to the café. Hoppy, Cal, and Shorty were already having their breakfast at the bar and chatting with Tess.

"You're up early on a Sunday morning," said Hoppy to the trio.

"Early bird gets the worm," said Swifty with a smirk on his face.

"Ignore old grumpy," said Shirley brightly. "He's not a morning person."

"You'd think normal people would sleep in on Sunday morning," said Swifty. "It's a day of rest."

"No rest for the wicked," countered Shirley.

Tess took this moment to interrupt the morning banter. "What'll it be this morning?" she said.

"The usual," said Kit.

"Me too," said Swifty.

"Likewise," added Shirley.

"Got it," said Tess and she disappeared into the kitchen.

"So, what are you folks up to this fine Sunday morning?" asked Hoppy.

"Any news of them three scoundrels who robbed poor old Mr. Kelly?" added Shorty.

"After we have another of Tess's wonderful breakfasts, we're headed into Laramie," said Kit.

"We just might have a lead on this Rose gal who stayed overnight at old Ted's cabin during a thunderstorm," added Swifty.

"But no new leads on the three thieves?" asked Shorty.

"Nothing new on the three bad dudes," said Kit. "We keep shooting blanks in trying to find them."

"Maybe they ain't from around here," offered Cal. "Maybe they was imported from somewhere else."

"Anything is possible," said Kit. "The Sheriff's office isn't having any better luck than we are. It seems like those three thieves just vanished into thin air."

"Like one of them vampires," said Shorty.

"There ain't no such thing as a vampire, Shorty," said Hoppy. "You gotta quit watching them late night movies. It's affecting what little brain you got left."

"I aint so sure," said Shorty.

"Have you even seen a vampire?" asked Hoppy.

"Just 'cause you can't see them, don't mean they ain't real," retorted Shorty.

"You're hopeless," said Hoppy. "Next time I git to the store, I'm gonna buy you some garlic so you kin make a necklace to wear around your neck."

"Why would I do that?" asked Shorty.

"You watch all that vampire crap and you don't know about garlic protecting you from vampires?" asked Hoppy. "You're unbelievable."

Shorty just drank his coffee and rolled his eyes.

Tess arrived with plates of breakfast for Kit, Shorty, and Shirley. She also brought a small bowl of fruit and a glass of orange juice for Shirley.

"Thank you, Tess," said Shirley.

"You're welcome, honey," replied Tess. "It's refreshing to have a female voice in here with all these galoots."

"Now we're galoots?" said Hoppy.

"If the cowboy boot fits, wear it," retorted Tess from her station behind the bar.

Swifty broke out in laughter and soon everyone, including Hoppy, joined in.

After breakfast, Kit and Swifty tended to the horses and then met in Shirley's cabin. The three of them sat around the little round table. Kit had a pen and a note pad.

"Swifty is going to slip into position around one o'clock this afternoon," said Kit. "Do you have everything you need, Swifty?"

"I have all my gear and I'll be wearing a full Ghillie suit. It would be helpful if I could borrow Shirley's Jeep. I could drive it in and park it a few blocks away and then take my time getting into position. I'll call you on your cell phone to let you know when and where I'm in position," said Swifty.

"Any objections?" asked Kit.

"None," said Shirley and she handed her car keys over to Swifty.

Kit proceeded to write notes on his note pad.

"What are you writing?" asked Shirley.

"I'm making an outline," said Kit.

"You're making an outline for today?" said Shirley incredulously.

"What's wrong with that?" asked Kit in a puzzled voice.

"You can't ever find the time to write me a letter, but you're writing an outline for this trip to talk to this Rose girl?" said Shirley in a voice that kept growing louder.

"Oops," said Swifty in a low voice.

Kit was totally confused until finally his brain clicked in on the fact that Shirley didn't like his priorities when it came to writing things down.

"I'm sorry about not writing you, Shirley. I just have trouble thinking of things to say to you. I don't have that trouble when I'm with you," he said. "If I've upset you, I'm truly sorry."

Shirley had folded her arms in front of her. Her body language was quite clear. She was pissed.

"Can we get over the hurt feelings stuff," said Swifty. "This is why you never take women on a mission of any kind. Too much touchy-feely stuff. We've got a mission here to find out how the damn robbers found out about the Russell letters and who this Rose gal told about them so we can get the letters back. We need to focus here."

"I hate to admit it, but Swifty's right," said Shirley. "I'm sorry I got upset, Kit."

"I'm sorry I was insensitive enough to get you upset, but I agree. We need to find out who Rose talked to," said Kit.

Kit pulled out the campus map and laid it down on the table. Using his pen, he pointed to the area behind and on the sides of the ag building parking lot.

"Swifty takes your Jeep and parks it a few blocks away from the ag building. He gears up around one o'clock and makes his way to the best high ground spot he can find to give him the best view of the parking lot. When he is in position, he calls me on my cell phone and lets me know when he is in position, and where he is," said Kit.

"Shirley and I travel in the truck and we arrive here about 3:30 P.M.," said Kit as he used his pen to point to a spot about four blocks from the ag building. "We wait to hear from Swifty on the cell phone."

"Swifty will phone me his positon when he has set up an over watch on the parking lot. When Rose, or anyone else shows up, Swifty will use our encrypted radios to let us know and give us the details."

"Why not just use the cell phone?" asked Shirley.

"Because there's a chance that Rose won't be alone. This could be a trap. If it is, the thieves might be sophisticated enough to have devices to listen in on any local cell phone calls. There is almost no chance they could hear our radio transmissions," replied Kit.

"Then what?" asked Shirley.

"You and I sit tight. At about 4:15 P.M., I leave the truck and walk to the ag building and then around it to the parking lot in back," said Kit.

"What about me?" asked Shirley.

"I want you to stay with the truck. If we need you, we'll call you on the radio. Otherwise, you stay put until you hear from us to do otherwise. Do you understand?" asked Kit.

"This is bullshit," said Shirley. "Why can't I come along. If you're going to talk to this Rose, you might have better luck if I was the one talking to her. Woman to woman is a lot more likely to get good answers from her."

"You're not to leave the truck. The potential for this deal to turn dangerous is too great. I want you to stay with the truck. I don't want anything to happen to you. Swifty and I are trained and experienced for this kind of deal. You are not," said an exasperated Kit.

"This isn't fair. It's just because I'm a woman," said Shirley.

"No, it's not fair," said Kit.

"Then why do I have to stay in the truck?" pleaded Shirley.

"You have to stay in the truck because I love you," said Kit.

"What did you say?" asked Shirley.

239

"I said you have to stay in the truck because I love you," said Kit.

"Oh," said Shirley, and then she was suddenly speechless.

"Sorry to interrupt this episode of Days of Our Lives," said Swifty, "but what do we do if it turns nasty and it is a trap?"

"You cover me and radio Shirley to dial 911 and call in the cavalry," said Kit.

"It'll be a pleasure," said a smiling Swifty. "Do I get to shoot them?"

"Only if there is no other choice. If it is a trap, we want these dudes alive, not shot all to pieces," said Kit.

"Roger that," said Swifty.

Shirley couldn't seem to find her voice, even if she could have thought of something to say.

While Kit and Swifty went out to see to the horses, Shirley recovered from her surprise and rummaged through some of the purchases she had made in Laramie. She gathered a few together and placed them in one shopping bag which she then set by the door.

Using Shirley's keys, Swifty started her Jeep and drove it over to his cabin. After packing weapons and gear in the Jeep, he drove the it over and parked it next to the truck.

Kit went through the storage area in the truck and pulled out the weapons and gear he needed. He took out three small radios and put fresh batteries in them. Then he made sure his cell phone was fully charged. Finally, he began checking his weapons and making sure he had sufficient ammunition magazines and insured they were properly loaded.

Shirley came out of the cabin carrying her shopping bag, and while Kit was busy checking his weapons, she placed her shopping bag on the back seat. Then she went to the back of the truck where Kit was checking his gear.

"Where do you keep all your weapons?" asked Shirley.

Kit showed her the two weapons lockers that were bolted to the bed of the pickup truck. The lockers had digital combination locks. Shirley watched as Kit punched in a code and opened the lock to one of the lockers. Kit opened the locker and showed Shirley the contents.

"This locker contains our long guns," said Kit. "There are rifles and shotguns in this one. I keep the pistols and other gear in the other locker."

"I don't see any ammunition," said Shirley.

"I keep the ammo in those plastic dry boxes you see next to the lockers. The boxes are labeled with the type and caliber of ammo in them."

"You don't keep them locked up like the guns?" asked Shirley.

"No, it's hard to shoot the ammo without the guns. Keeping them separate is like having them locked up," said a smiling Kit.

"Which gun do I get to use?" asked Shirley.

"You don't. I thought I made that clear earlier. I don't want you anywhere near that parking lot," said Kit.

"Did you mean what you said?" asked a suddenly quiet Shirley.

"What did I say?" asked a puzzled Kit.

"You men are all alike. Smart about some things, and dumber than a box of rocks about others," said Shirley.

"I don't understand," said a confused Kit.

"I'm talking about what you said about me," said Shirley. "Don't you remember anything?"

"Yes," said Kit. "I do remember. I know I've never said it before, but it's how I feel. And I never felt it stronger than I did today."

"Kit Andrews, you are one of the most exasperating and clueless men I have ever met, but I love you, too."

Kit smiled and pulled Shirley to him. He looked into her beautiful blue eyes and bent down to kiss her. Shirley slipped her arms behind his head and pulled him in close. When they broke apart from their kiss, they continued to hold each other.

"I love you, Shirley," said Kit.

"I love you, Kit," said Shirley.

"Get a room, you two," shouted an embarrassed Swifty. "We got work to do. Save it for later."

Kit and Shirley separated and then went over the final inspection of weapons, ammo, and gear. When Kit and Swifty were satisfied they had everything they might need, and every item was in good working order, they packed everything up in the Jeep and the truck.

"I aint sure about you two, but I'm gonna take a nap. Wake me when it's time for lunch," said Swifty.

With that announcement, Swifty headed back to his cabin.

"A little nap sounds good to me," said a smiling Shirley. She reached out and grabbed Kit's hand and started to lead him to their cabin. "Let's go take a nap, Cowboy."

Kit offered no resistance to her leading him and followed dutifully along.

Kit was up and ready at a little after eleven A.M. Shirley joined him, and they stopped at Swifty's cabin to get him up and moving. By eleven thirty they were sitting in the café dining room having lunch.

After the waitress left with their orders, Kit looked up at Swifty and Shirley. "Are there any last-minute questions?" he said.

"I got one," said Shirley.

"Fire away," said Kit.

"If there is a girl who shows up in the parking lot, how do we know she really is Rose?" asked Shirley.

"Good question," said Kit. "Next question."

"What the heck do you mean, next question," asked Shirley.

"What he means is he ain't got no idea how we can know if the gal is really Rose," said Swifty.

"Which is why Swifty will spend part of his time today between one o'clock and four o'clock setting up a remote video camera on a tripod so we can film whoever is in the lot and what happens," said Kit.

"A camera?" said Shirley.

"Our insurance company loves it when we have video proof of what happens. It really helps solve lots of liability issues," said a smiling Swifty.

"Which is another reason why there will be no shooting unless it's absolutely necessary," said Kit.

"What do you think will happen this afternoon?" asked Shirley.

At that moment, the waitress appeared with their lunch orders, and her question hung in the air until the waitress had left.

"We don't know," said Kit. "It may be that this is not some sort of trap. Rose may show up as she promised and we'll find out who she told about seeing the framed Russell letters in old Ted Kelly's cabin."

"Or, she could be in on it and whoever is in charge is setting up a trap so they can get rid of us to stop us from blowing up their little plan," said Swifty.

"Or, Rose could be dead and this is an imposter being used to lure us into a trap to get rid of us," added Kit.

"In a situation like this, you must remember the first rule of combat," said Swifty.

"What rule is that?" asked Shirley.

"When the first shot is fired the plan usually goes to hell," said Swifty.

"He's talking about the fog of war concept," said Kit.

"What is that?" asked Shirley.

"Once the shooting starts and bullets are flying all around, no one has a clear picture of what is really going on," said Kit.

"It's hard to see much with your head in the dirt," added Swifty.

"This all sounds so dark and grim," said Shirley.

"It is dark and grim," said Kit. "There are a lot of bad things and bad people in the world."

"All it takes for evil to succeed is for good men to do nothing," said Swifty. "We're the good guys. We bring light to the fight and we light the bad guy's asses on fire."

"You two have to promise me you'll be careful," said a suddenly teary-eyed Shirley. "Please promise me."

"We'll be very careful, Shirley," said Kit. "Both Swifty and I plan on living to a ripe old age," said Kit.

"I plan on dying in a whorehouse, after the fact, and before I've paid the bill," said a grinning Swifty.

"Oh, God, that's disgusting," said Shirley.

"It's who I am," said Swifty.

"Unfortunately, he's telling you the truth," said Kit.

Once their meals were finished and Kit paid the bill, the trio left the café and headed to their vehicles. Swifty led the way in the Jeep, followed by Kit and Shirley in the truck.

They drove the speed limit all the way to Laramie. Neither Kit nor Shirley spoke a word during the entire trip.

After then entered Laramie, both vehicles stopped at a gas station, and they filled the tanks of the Jeep and the truck. Kit and Swifty shook hands when they had finished filling the gas tanks of the two vehicles.

"See you at 4:30, Swifty," said Kit.

"If I don't see you before then," replied Swifty.

"Good hunting," said Kit.

"Same to you," said Swifty.

Swifty left the gas station first and headed in the direction of the ag building. Kit stayed on the main highway leading into downtown Laramie.

The countdown had begun.

CHAPTER TWENTY-SEVEN

Sid sat on the step of his camper. He was sharpening a Bowie knife he usually wore in a leather sheath on his belt.

He had received a call from the voice yesterday. The voice had been very explicit and had made Sid repeat each and every instruction he had been given on the phone.

Sid looked over at the old barn. His ATV was safely stored in the barn, and the door was closed so no one could accidently look in and see it.

He went over the instructions in his mind and mentally checked off each item or task he was responsible for. Then Sid picked up every item he had stacked at his feet and checked it until he was sure he had everything he was going to need.

He heard a vehicle approaching on the road in front of the old farm house, but it passed on by without even slowing down.

He looked at his watch. "Those damn stupid, lazy Collins brothers are already fifteen minutes late," he thought to himself. "They're about as dependable as a used rubber."

Ten minutes later he heard another vehicle approaching and this time the vehicle was slowing down. When it reached the driveway in front of the old farm house, the vehicle turned in and drove slowly around the old farm house and stopped in the farm yard about twenty yards from Sid's trailer.

Sid studied the vehicle. It was an old Volkswagen camper van. The kind you saw in movies when it was full of hippies and painted in psychedelic colors. This one was a plain faded green and white combination paint job with a little rust tossed in around the wheel wells for good measure.

The driver's door on the van opened and Nate Collins stepped out. Sid rose from his seat on the camper step and sheathed his knife.

"You're late," said Sid.

"We had a little trouble with the girl," said Nate. "She got real skittish on us, and we had to tie her up and gag her."

"You didn't hit her or hurt her, did you, Nate?" asked Sid.

"Ned kinda smacked her when she started yelling and trying to get away, but he didn't hurt her none. Anyway, she ain't bleedin'," said Nate.

"And where is Ned and our precious cargo?" said Sid.

At that moment, the back door of the van came open and down stepped Ned, his left arm in a sling. "I could use a little help here," said Ned.

Sid and Nate walked over to the rear of the van and looked inside. There on the debris strewn and none-too-clean floor was a tall, young girl, tied and gagged. She was blonde and her hair was in pig tails.

Sid took a careful look at the bound blonde, and he could see no visible marks and no trace of blood on her.

"Do we take her out of the van?" asked Nate.

"It won't do no harm," said Sid. "Are her legs tied?" he asked.

"Yep, they are," said Nate.

"You two help her over to that stump over there and have her sit on it," said Sid.

Nate did most of the helping, as Ned was practically a one-armed man with his left arm in a sling. They got the girl over to the stump and made her sit. Nate took great pains to explain to the girl what would happen to her if she tried to get away. When he asked if she understood, she fearfully nodded her head up down that she did.

"So, this is the famous missing Rose," said Sid.

"Hell, she was never missin'," said Ned. "She's been working as a waitress over at the Elk Mountain Lodge. The owner's got some cabins there and Rose here got to stay in one as part of her job. I knowed where she was all along. I don't see what the big deal about her bein' missin' was."

"Well, nobody else knew where to find her, including the cops and those two cowboy investigators. I had no idea who she was until I got instructions to get her and then bring her to this meetin' in Laramie at 4:30 today," said Sid.

"So, when do we head for Laramie?" asked Ned.

"We don't want to get there too soon," said Sid. "I got orders to bring her to the parking lot behind the ag building on the campus just about 4:30 P.M."

"So, what do we do in the meantime?" asked Nate.

"I got some cold beer over in the cooler by the camper," replied Sid. "You boys help yourself."

The three men walked over to the camper. Sid sat on the camper step, and the two Collins brothers sat on the ground next to the cooler.

Soon all three men were drinking cold beer and pretty soon Nate cleared his throat.

"Just exactly what are we expected to do on this here assignment?" Nate asked.

Sid looked at the Collins brothers. Nate was a little smarter than Ned, but neither brother was in danger of breaking the IQ level of 100. The two brothers had been helpful in carrying out the robbery at old man Kelly's cabin, but then Ned couldn't handle a simple assignment of watching the two cowboy investigators to see if they had found anything. He had gotten stupid and excited and tried to shoot at them. The result was he was the one getting shot, and Sid had to use an old friend of his who flunked out of medical school to patch Ned up. "Dumb bastard," thought Sid.

After looking both brothers in the eye to make sure he had their attention, Sid began to explain the assignment to them.

"We drive this old VW van you stole in Cheyenne over to Laramie," said Sid. "You did rub mud over the license plates, didn't you, Nate?"

"I shore did," said Nate. "You can't read them numbers unless you was to wash the dirt off."

"Good," said Sid. "When we get to Laramie we stop about five blocks from the ag building and wait for a phone call. That will be our signal to untie the girl and drive to the parking lot. You two will stay in the back of the van. The girl will drive the van to the lot and I will be in the passenger seat. When we get there, we sit and wait."

"Wait for what?" asked Nate.

"We wait for those two cowboy investigators to show up. They're expectin' to meet with this girl Rose and nobody else. We wait for them to approach the van. When they do, I'll pull the girl over to the passenger seat and both of us will exit the van on the passenger side, away and out of view of the two cowboys. Do you follow me, so far?" asked Sid.

Both Collins brothers nodded their heads that they understood.

"When I get out of the van with the girl, I'll drag her around to the back of the van where they can see me. I'll have a knife to the girl's throat, and I'll tell them to drop their weapons and step back or I'll kill the girl."

"Man, that sounds hot," said an excited Ned.

Nate just looked at his brother like he was an idiot.

"When they are disarmed, I'll have them step back and you two will come out from the back of the van. You'll both have your pistols out and while one of you covers the cowboys, the other will pick up their weapons," said Sid.

"Who gets to pick up their weapons?" said a still excited Ned.

Sid rolled his eyes. "Nate covers them and you pick up their weapons," said Sid in a disgusted voice.

"Then what?" asked Ned.

"This ain't a damn movie, Ned," said his brother Nate.

"I know, I know, I just wanna get even with them cowboys for shooting me in the arm," said Ned.

"Then I call this number and the person runnin' this whole she-bang will show up and take it from there," said Sid.

"What do yah mean, take it from there?" asked Ned.

"I mean our boss, who I ain't never met nor seen, has a plan and our job then is just to take orders until this whole deal is over," said Sid.

"Man, I hope I get to shoot them two bastards who shot me," said Ned.

"I'd be happy to spend a little time with little blondie," said a grinning Nate.

"Whatever is gonna happen is not up to us," said Sid. "We just do what we're told. Do you two understand that?"

Both brothers nodded their heads that they understood. Sid was obviously disgusted with them. "It's sure damn hard to get good help these days," he thought. Sid was only interested in the money. He didn't give a rat's ass about some skinny blonde girl or what happened to the two cowboys. If things worked out right, he would dispose of the two Collins brothers as well as the girl and the cowboys. More money for him and no witnesses to come back and haunt him.

"Do you boys have your weapons?" asked Sid.

Nate produced a Glock 17 pistol and Ned pulled out an old Colt Diamondback pistol.

"Let's spend a few minutes to clean our guns and make sure they are in good working order and loaded," said Sid.

Sid went into his camper and returned with a large box of gun cleaning tools and materials. Soon all three men were cleaning their pistols, while the blonde girl named Rose looked on in horror.

After the three men had finished cleaning and loading their pistols, they drank a couple more beers from Sid's cooler and waited until it was time to leave for Laramie.

At about 3:30 P.M. Sid stood up, and Nate and Ned loaded Rose into the back of the old VW van. Sid started the engine and drove the van out of the old barn yard.

CHAPTER TWENTY-EIGHT

Swifty had parked Shirley's Jeep on a residential side street where it blended in with several other vehicles. Swifty exited the Jeep and pulled on his tactical back pack. Then he pulled out his drag bag and slipped the bag's sling over his shoulder. He walked about two blocks before passing the last house on the street. He had seen no one during his walk. He walked another block on the vacant street and then slipped over into a vacant lot and made his way through the open field toward the ag building parking lot.

When he was out of sight of any buildings, Swifty went to his knees and unslung his drag bag. He took out a Ghillie suit and pulled it on. The suit made his body resemble a small mound of grasses and weeds. Swifty painted his face with cammo paint so his skin would not reflect. Then he slid to his belly and began crawling through the tall grass and sagebrush populating the large field, pulling the drag bag on a rope tied to his leg behind him.

Swifty moved slowly and carefully as he sought to remain unseen by anyone who happened to be looking that way. He chose his path based on avoiding brushing against tall grasses so they wouldn't wave in the air as he passed and give notice to his location. He would crawl for ten minutes and then he would pause. During his pause, he would listen carefully, sniff the air, and look carefully at his surroundings.

After an hour and a half had passed, he stopped and slowly and carefully rose to his knees. Swifty pulled out a small, armored pair of binoculars and carefully scanned his surroundings for 360 degrees. He could see no one, and there were no vehicles in the parking lot of the ag building. Swifty took a compass reading and lowered himself back to his belly.

He followed the new compass heading he had set and crawled for another half an hour. Then he repeated the process of slowly rising to his knees and using his binoculars. After scanning his surroundings, he smiled. He was almost in position to set up the camera. He had located a small hump in the surrounding fields. Right in front of the hump and between it and the ag building parking lot was a large sagebrush plant.

He crawled for another ten minutes and reached the back side of the hump. He carefully and slowly crawled up on the hump. Once he was behind the sagebrush plant, he rolled to his side and pulled the drag bag up next to him.

Swifty opened the drag bag and pulled out the camera and tripod. He set up the tripod and then adjusted the height before placing the camera on top. He adjusted the camera power to on and set it to motion activated. Then he placed it on top of the tripod and adjusted it to focus on the ag building parking lot.

Swifty slid back away from the camera for a few feet and stopped. He rose to his knees and after scanning his surroundings, he looked over the top of the camera. Swifty grinned. The position was perfect. Any activity in the parking lot would trigger the motion detector in the camera and it would start recording.

Swifty took out his GPS and made a waypoint for the exact location of the camera. Then he sent the coordinates of the camera location over his phone with an e-mail to the computer in their office in Kemmerer. Satisfied with his work, Swifty put away the GPS and his phone and crawled his way backward off the mound.

Once off the mound, Swifty again slowly rose to his knees and used his binoculars to scan his surroundings. He again saw no one, and there were still no vehicles in the parking lot. He noted his final destination in the field, and took a compass setting. He lowered himself to his belly and began crawling in the direction of the new compass setting.

He again fell into the same pattern. Crawl for about ten minutes, and then check his surroundings. He kept this up until he reached his new destination, a spot about seventy-five yards from the back side of the ag building parking lot.

Once Swifty had reached his new destination, he again rose to his knees and used his binoculars to check his surroundings. He still had seen no one and the parking lot remained empty of any vehicles. He pulled the bag up next to him and opened it. He removed his .308 caliber sniper rifle and proceeded to assemble it, checking each piece as he snapped it together. Then he loaded the rifle and placed two extra magazines of ammo in his vest.

He placed the rifle next to him, and then pulled out his .45 caliber semi-automatic Kimber pistol and slid it into a pocket on his right hip. He took out a boot knife which he slid into his boot. Then he pulled out a second .45 caliber Kimber pistol with a shorter barrel. He slipped the second pistol into a built-in holster located behind his back.

Swifty pulled out a tiny five-shot .22 magnum caliber pistol and secured it inside the left sleeve of his Ghillie suit. Finally, he took a folding hunting grade slingshot and slid it inside his chest. He added a handful of marble sized ball bearings to a pocket on the suit. Satisfied with his preparations, Swifty closed the drag bag and slid it to his left. Then he crawled forward about three feet until he was behind a sizeable sagebrush bush. Once there, he made himself comfortable. After Swifty was satisfied with his sight picture, he set up his rifle and used the scope to scan the parking lot.

He still saw no one moving around and the parking lot was still empty. Swifty wiggled his body around until he had the best and most comfortable firing positon he could create. When he was done, he glanced at his watch and then pulled out his phone. He checked to see the phone was fully charged and on. Then he placed it on the ground in front of him. Swifty pulled out the small encrypted radio, turned it on, and placed it next to the phone in front of him. His preparations complete, Swifty settled in to wait. Like all trained snipers, Swifty had a great deal of patience.

CHAPTER TWENTY-NINE

Kit stopped at a drive-through coffee shop and purchased hot coffee for himself and Shirley. He parked on the street near the coffee shop, and he and Shirley sipped their coffee and waited.

Kit kept glancing at the clock on the dash of the truck. Kit did not have Swifty's patience and the minutes seemed to be crawling slowly by. He and Shirley waited in silence. Shirley had placed her hand on top of his and he had instantly put his hand around hers.

"Waiting is hard," said Shirley.

"It's really hard for me," said Kit. "I believe in good preparation, but then it's like when I played football."

"How's that?" asked Shirley.

"You're lined up for the kick-off and you've spent a week getting prepared for this game. Your stomach is full of butterflies and nervous energy. The whistle blows and the kicker starts forward. You move with him. Then he kicks the ball and you're racing downfield as fast as you can run. You feel somehow detached from the earth and floating in the air as you run. The butterflies are now dominating your senses. Then you hit someone downfield and suddenly everything is fine. The butterflies are gone and the nerves are suddenly vaporized. You're ready to play," said Kit.

"I got goosebumps just listening to you," said a smiling Shirley. "I wish I had known you back then."

Kit laughed. "No, you wouldn't," he said. "Back then I was shy and awkward, and I would never have had the nerve to even talk to a gorgeous creature like you."

"Keep talking," said Shirley. "For a shy, awkward guy, you're doing pretty well." Her eyes were shining as she looked at Kit. "I love you, Kit. Please be careful today. It couldn't stand to have something happen to you."

Kit leaned over and kissed Shirley. "I love you, Shirley. Believe me when I tell you that heaven and earth couldn't stop me from coming back to you. Some punks and their boss aren't much more than a speedbump in the road to me."

Kit and Shirley hugged and then just held each other in silence. Finally, the clock on the dash of the truck flashed four o'clock. Kit started the truck and pulled out of their parking spot. He drove through very light traffic in Laramie. He slowed the truck when they reached a spot about three blocks from the ag building.

Kit pulled the truck into an empty faculty parking lot and parked the truck. Kit and Shirley got out of the truck and they moved to the rear of the truck where Kit opened the weapons locker as Shirley watched. Kit slipped on a gun belt and holster. Then he pulled out his new Smith and Wesson 1911 Performance Center .45 caliber semi-automatic pistol. He loaded a magazine of .45 caliber bullets into the pistol and slid it into the holster on his right hip.

Kit added a small .45 caliber pistol from Springfield Arms and slipped it into a spot between his belt and his back. He picked up two more magazines for the Smith and Wesson, carefully loading each magazine. Kit snapped each magazine against his hand to make sure all the rounds were seated. When he was satisfied, he slipped them into his vest pocket.

Kit pulled out a boot knife and slid the dagger-like knife into his right boot. He checked his phone to make sure it was on and fully charged. After satisfying himself, he turned the phone on and placed it in his shirt pocket. Finally, he checked the batteries on the small radio and after turning it on, he attached the clip on his radio to the right front pocket of his jeans.

After Kit did a mental checklist of his gear, he turned to Shirley. "I want you to stay in the truck. You are to lay down in the back seat and keep both your phone and radio on," he said.

"Why do I have to lay down in the back seat?" asked Shirley.

"I don't want any of the bad guys driving by and noticing you. I don't want them to see anyone just sitting in their vehicle. You can bet that would make them suspicious and could screw up our plan," said Kit.

"I thought you were just going to meet this Rose girl and get her story about who she told about the letters at Mr. Kelly's cabin?" said Shirley.

"She may be there, she may not," said Kit. "This sounds and smells like a trap, and I'm not taking any chances. I need you here to call for the cavalry if we get in any trouble."

"How will I know if you're in trouble?' asked Shirley.

"Swifty and I will leave our radios on and with your radio also on, you'll be able to hear everything we hear. If we run into trouble, I'll make sure you can hear me as well as whoever we might run into," said Kit.

"O.K.," said Shirley. "I understand."

Kit leaned down and kissed Shirley. She grabbed the back of his head and pulled him into her. They held each other for almost a full minute. Then Kit broke the hug.

"Wish me luck," said Kit.

"I wish you all the luck in the world. If something happens to you, I'll kill you," said Shirley.

"You'll probably have to wait in line," said a smiling Kit.

Kit started to walk away, and then he stopped and turned around to face Shirley.

"I love you, Shirley. I'll be back."

Shirley tried to speak, but found her throat had closed and left her speechless.

Kit turned and walked away toward the ag building and whatever waited for him there.

After a brisk walk, Kit reached the front of the ag building. He kept his head on a swivel, as he was constantly checking his surroundings.

He stopped in front of the ag building and stood still. He listened, sniffed the air, and kept scanning all around him. He could sense nothing that indicated any danger to him. Kit started walking again and moved down the left side of the building along the driveway leading to the parking lot in the rear.

When Kit reached the edge of the building, he stopped. He slowly made his way forward to the very edge and then slowly peered around the wall. He could see nothing. There were no vehicles in the parking lot.

Suddenly his radio chirped. Kit grabbed it and hit the receive button.

"Howdy there, tenderfoot, how was the walk? You look plumb tuckered out," said Swifty, his voice enhanced electronically over the radio.

"Howdy yourself, Swifty. Do we have any visitors?" asked Kit.

"Nope. Quiet as a grave, if you'll excuse my sense of humor," replied Swifty.

"Where are you?" asked Kit, who was scanning the field behind the parking lot.

"I'm about 75 yards behind the parking lot, right behind a good-sized sagebrush," said Swifty.

"Is the camera set?"

"Does a bear shit in the woods?" replied Swifty.

"Where is it?" asked Kit.

"The camera is to your left, about thirty-five yards from the edge of the parking lot. It's hidden behind some sagebrush. You won't be able to see it until you're on top of it," said Swifty.

"Roger that," said Kit. "I'm going to wait in the stairwell leading down to the basement."

"Good choice," said Swifty.

"Good hunting," said Kit.

"You too, tenderfoot," replied Swifty.

CHAPTER THIRTY

Sid had driven the old VW van through Laramie without any incidents. He reached his checkpoint about four fifteen. He pulled the van over and parked. He was nervous and he was sure the Collins boys had a case of nerves themselves.

Sid checked his gun and looked over at the young blonde girl. She was securely tied and appeared to be frozen with fear. Sid didn't feel sorry for her. The girl was here in this situation because she got involved in something she shouldn't have. Now she was paying the price. Too bad for her.

He looked up at the rear-view mirror to check on the Collins brothers in the rear of the van. Nate looked pale and nervous. The moron Ned was just sitting there grinning like an idiot. Sid would be glad to be rid of them both.

Sid started to think about what he was going to do with the money when all this was over. He'd always wanted to go to California. Now he had the money and he found himself imagining what it would be like to be on the beach of the Pacific Ocean with all those bikini-clad honeys running around.

Sid's thoughts were suddenly interrupted by the ring tone on his phone. He grabbed the cell phone and looked at the screen. He didn't recognize the number. It had to be the voice. He hit the answer button with his thumb.

"Hello," said Sid.

"Are you in position?" asked the electronically masked voice.

"I am."

"Do you have the girl?"

"She's tied up and sitting in the passenger seat of the van," said Sid.

"Why isn't she in the driver's seat as we discussed?" asked the voice.

"It's too awkward for me to climb over her and then haul her out the passenger door. This way works much easier," said Sid.

"Well, OK then," said the voice. "Proceed to the parking lot. Once there, make the two cowboys show themselves. When they do, exit the van with the girl and hold the knife to her throat so they can see you clearly. Do you understand?"

"I understand," replied Sid.

"Then tell them to drop their weapons and step away from them. Make sure they are at least ten yards away from their weapons. They have a history of being tricky," said the voice.

"I'll make sure it's ten yards," said Sid, thinking this was a little silly.

"Then have the two brothers hold guns on them and have the dumb one pick up their weapons."

"Will do," said Sid, who was getting a little impatient with all this trauma drama.

"When you have achieved this, call me on the same number you see on your phone. Do you understand?" asked the voice.

"I understand. I'll call you when we have them disarmed," said Sid.

The voice disconnected the phone.

Sid put his phone in his pocket and turned to face the rear of the van. "We're headed in. Get ready," said Sid.

Sid started the van and began making his way to the ag building. A few minutes later found Sid in front of the building. He pulled the van into the driveway and slowly drove past the ag building to the parking lot behind it.

Sid entered the parking lot and stopped the van. He looked around, and he could see nothing. The parking lot was completely empty.

Sid pulled the van forward until he was parallel to the middle of the building. He brought the van to a stop and cut the engine. He still saw nothing. Maybe the cowboys weren't going to show. Maybe something had gone wrong. Sid's instincts told him to go, but he calmed himself. The voice's plan was a good one. All he had to do was follow orders and he would soon have his money and be on his way to sunny California.

Sid kept alert, but he remained motionless in the driver's seat of the van. He placed one hand on his Bowie knife and he waited.

CHAPTER THIRTY-ONE

Kit watched as the old VW van pulled slowly into the parking lot. He could see someone had put mud over the license plates to make them unreadable. This had to be it.

He decided to make the driver nervous, and he waited in the darkness of the basement stairwell of the ag building. He glanced at his watch. He waited a full five minutes. Five minutes when you are waiting feels like a lifetime.

Then Kit stepped out of the stairwell and walked in front of the van. The shadows from the ag building were long enough Kit could not make out the driver. He walked past the van and when he was about ten yards from the driver's side of the van, he halted. Kit stood and waited.

"Next move is up to you boys," thought Kit.

The driver's side door of the old VW van began to open.

Kit's right hand fell to his side, so it rested on the butt of his pistol.

A tall dark haired man, dressed in a black t-shirt and worn jeans was visible behind the now open door. He was wearing a red bandanna over his lower face, much like the outlaws in the old west had done to hide their identities. He was leaning into the cab of the old van. He seemed to be struggling with something. Finally, the man straightened up just as he successfully drug a tall, thin young blonde out of the cab and pulled her up so she was standing in front of him. Kit saw the young blonde had her hair in pigtails.

The tall man emerged from behind the door of the old van. He held the young blonde in front of him. Kit could now see the blonde had her hands tied behind her back. The tall man was holding a large Bowie knife to her throat.

"Which one of them cowboys are you?" asked the tall man. Kit could see the tattoo of a skull and crossbones on the man's upper arm.

"I'm Kit Andrews of Rocky Mountain Searchers out of Kemmerer," said Kit as though he was addressing a client instead of a crook with a knife to the throat of an innocent young woman.

"Where's your partner?" asked the tall man as he began to scan the area behind Kit as though he was searching for something.

"He's back in Woods Landing," said Kit. "I put up the notice, and I was the one this young lady called to set up this meeting," said Kit.

"Well, partner, that's just your bad luck," said the tall man. "Blondie here didn't call nobody. You got called by someone else."

"Who called me?" asked Kit.

"It don't look to me like you're in any positon to be askin' me questions, cowboy. I want you to unholster your weapon. Use your left hand to pull the gun out."

Kit reached across his body with his left hand and pulled his gun out of the holster.

"Now toss that gun out in front of you at least five yards," said the tall man. "And do it slowly. No funny business or I'll slit this chippy's throat."

Kit tossed his pistol about five yards in front of him with his left hand. The pistol hit the parking lot, bounded once, and slid to a stop about six yards in front of Kit.

"He's disarmed boys," said tall man.

The two Collins brothers burst out of the back of the van with pistols in their hands. Nate took up a positon about fifteen yards from Kit and held his gun on him. Ned moved slowly forward toward Kit's gun. Ned never took his eyes off Kit.

Kit noticed that Nate had his back to the rear of the parking lot and to Swifty's positon. He also noticed the tall man had taken out a cell phone and was making a call, while still holding the Bowie knife against the blonde girl's throat.

"So, what is it that you three boys want?" said Kit. "You got the Russell letters and you got me and the girl. Just what's your game?"

"I told you to keep your mouth shut. I'll be askin' the questions here," said the tall man as he put his cell phone away.

"Who did you call?" asked Kit.

"None of your damn business, asshole," snarled Ned as he picked up Kit's pistol and stepped back a couple of yards to Kit's left.

"Naw," said the tall man. "The cowboys got a right to know what's in store for him. My boss will be here soon and then you can ask all the questions you want." He then put away his Bowie knife and proceeded to tie up the blonde girl's legs to make her immobile.

"Were you the one who shot me?" demanded Ned.

"If you were the dumb shit who tried to bushwhack us by the ravine, then, yes, I'm the one who shot you," said Kit in a calm voice. "Looks like I should have aimed a little more to the right."

"Can I shoot him now?" pleaded Ned.

"Nobody's shootin' anyone till my boss gets here and tells us what to do," replied the tall man.

Kit glanced down at his side to check that his radio was still on. The tiny red light on top meant the radio was powered up and anything he said was being broadcast to Swifty and Shirley.

"Can I at least punch the bastard in the nuts?" asked Ned.

"That's what he wants, you moron," said the tall man. "You get close to him and he'll find a way to get his hands on you. I've heard of these two cowboys. You need to keep your distance. Both of them are dangerous."

"He don't look too dangerous to me," sneered Nate. "He looks pretty tame right now." Ned laughed at his brother's remark.

"So, where's this boss of yours?" asked Kit.

"My boss will be here soon enough. You'll likely be sorry when the time comes," said the tall man.

The group then stood in the parking lot, frozen in their respective positons. The tall man had shoved the bound young woman into the back of the van and closed the van door.

Then a low sound broke the silence. The sound got louder and louder and finally Kit recognized it. The sound was a motorcycle engine and it was getting closer. Judging from the amount of noise it was making, Kit was pretty sure it was a Harley. A minute later the motorcycle with a helmeted, leather clad rider rode around the side of the ag building and into the parking lot.

The Harley came to a stop behind the VW van and the rider dismounted and parked the bike. Kit could see the black helmet had a smoked full face shield so the rider looked like a giant bug. The rider's face was hidden behind the helmet shield.

The rider was short and slim. When the rider walked over next to the tall man, he towered at least six inches over the rider, even with the rider's helmet.

"Where's the girl?" said the rider in a very female voice.

The tall man appeared to be startled. Kit realized the tall man had no idea his boss was a woman.

"She's tied up in the back of the van," said the tall man.

The woman turned and looked at Kit. "Where's the other cowboy?" she asked.

"He came alone. The other cowboy is back at Woods Landing," said the tall man.

"How do you know that?" asked the woman.

"He told me," said the tall man.

"And you believed him," said the woman incredulously. "Jesus Christ! For all we know the other one is sitting out there somewhere with us in his gun sights," she screamed at the tall man.

"What do you want me to do?" asked an obviously confused tall man.

"Kill the cowboy and the girl and take them out in the desert. Strip off all their clothes and bury them where they can't be found," said the obviously upset woman.

"Naked?" said the surprised tall man.

"That's what happens when you have no clothes on. It also means there is no way of identifying the bodies if they're accidently found, you idiot," shouted the woman.

"You heard the lady," said the tall man as he stepped to the rear of the van to get the girl out.

Both the Collins boys stepped further away from Kit and began to raise their pistols.

A shot rang out and a large red hole appeared in Ned's uninjured right arm and the impact spun him around.

Nate looked at his brother in shock and a second shot rang out and then he looked on in disbelief as his right arm was almost separated from his shoulder. His gun dropped to the parking lot and blood spurted out of the large wound. Nate stood for a second in shock and then fell to the parking lot.

Kit dropped to the ground and pulled out the pistol he had in his back holster as he fell. He could see the tall man still had his hand on the back-door handle of the van as he looked on in total surprise. He seemed frozen and unable to move.

The woman reacted instantly. She jumped on the Harley and kicked it into life and then did a quick turn and roared out of the parking lot.

"Shit," said Kit. "The woman is getting away on her motorcycle."

A third shot from Swifty was a little to the right and it went through the saddlebag on the right side of the Harley. The bullet passed through and did nothing to impair the woman's flight from the parking lot.

"Drop your weapon, or I'll shoot you in the balls," said Kit from his prone positon on the parking lot. The tall man tossed his pistol out in front of him and raised his hands.

"Please don't shoot me, please don't shoot me," begged the tall man.

"Get down on the ground with your hands over your head," said Kit as he began to rise from his prone positon on the parking lot.

"Swifty, we got a problem," said Kit into the radio.

"I saw her fly out of the parking lot," said Swifty. "I took a shot, but I was a little low and to the right."

"I'll take the van and try to run her down," said Kit. "You get over here and take charge of these three buttheads and the girl. Then call 911 and get the cops over here to secure things."

"Will do," said Swifty. "Good hunting."

"I'll need some luck," said Kit. "We know it's a woman, but we don't know who and neither do these three idiots she hired."

Kit ran to the van as Swifty emerged from behind the sagebrush in the field behind the parking lot. Swifty kept the tall man and the wounded Collins brothers covered as he advanced.

Kit pulled the blonde girl out of the van and laid her on the ground. He ran to the driver's side of the van and jumped in. Luckily the keys were in the ignition. He started the van, and he flew out of the parking lot. He had his windows down and before he got all the way down the ag building driveway, he heard a loud boom. It was the unmistakable sound of a shotgun.

"Shit, what's happened now?" thought Kit.

Then he heard a second boom and the noise of a crash and then the sound of metal scraping against concrete. Kit floored the van and shot out from the driveway. He drove down the road and after he had gone no more than a block, he braked the van to a sudden stop.

There on the side of the street was the wreckage of the Harley. Kit could see the skid marks left by the bike on the road. The Harley's tires were shredded. He could see the leather clad rider lying on the road about fifteen yards from the bike. Her helmet was still on.

Standing over the fallen rider was a surprising sight. Shirley stood over the rider. She was holding a Remington 870 Defender shotgun in her hands. The barrel of the shotgun was still emitting some smoke.

Kit shut the engine off and jumped out of the truck. When he got to Shirley she seemed in shock. Kit kneeled down next to the motionless rider and checked her pulse. She was still breathing. He quickly checked her for weapons.

She had none. He got to his feet and touched Shirley on the arm. When she saw it was Kit, she dropped the shotgun and let him take her in his arms. He could feel she was trembling. He held her like he had never held her before.

Slowly, her trembling slowed and finally came to a stop. She looked up at Kit. She was crying and her face was stained with her tears.

"Oh, my God, Kit," she said.

Kit put a finger to her mouth. "It's OK, Shirley. Relax. Everything is going to be fine," said Kit.

He put his arm around Shirley and helped her walk over to the side of the road. He took her to a grassy area and had her sit down. Then he ran to the van and came back with a bottle of water he had seen. He opened the bottle and raised it to her lips. Shirley took a drink, paused and then took another drink. Then she pushed the bottle away. Kit continued to hold her tightly with his right arm.

"Are you all right?" asked Kit.

"I'm fine," said Shirley, "but I think I killed that poor woman." Then she began to cry again.

Kit reached into his back pocket and took out a blue bandanna. He took it and slowly and gently wiped the tears off Shirley's face. Then he handed it to her. She took it and finished the job he had started.

Kit reached out and touched Shirley's face softly with his fingers. "She's alive. You didn't kill anyone," he said.

Shirley continued to cry, but now more slowly and softly.

"What happened?" asked Kit. Shirley looked up at him and started to speak, when they heard a low moan. Both of them looked to the source of the sound and watched as the leather clad woman began to move her body.

"You stay right here, Shirley," said Kit. "I think it's time we found out just who was behind this whole mess."

274

Kit leaned in and kissed Shirley on the cheek. She smiled and lifted her face to him. Kit kissed her on the mouth, and she responded.

"I love you, Shirley," said Kit. "Please don't worry about a thing. It looks like the woman is very much alive so you didn't kill anyone."

With that, Kit kissed Shirley again and then he rose to his feet and walked over to the now struggling figure on the road.

Kit stopped in his tracks when he heard the sirens. They were close and getting closer. In a minute, he saw at least two patrol cars racing toward the ag building from the opposite direction. Swifty had called 911, and the cavalry had arrived.

As Kit got near the leather clad figure on the ground, his radio crackled. It was Swifty.

"Cops are here. Where the hell are you, tenderfoot and did the bitch get away?"

"Bitch is secure," said Kit. "Send some of the cops to 1711 Aspen Drive," he said as he read the house number off the home in front of him.

The woman on the ground moaned, louder this time. Kit looked down at her. It appeared the leather outfit, boots, and helmet had done a good job of protecting her from her lengthy skid on the concrete surface of the road.

The woman on the ground became aware of Kit's presence and turned her head to face him.

"It appears you had a little accident," said Kit with a smile.

"Fuck you," snarled the woman.

"I don't think you're my type," said Kit.

"Asshole," said the woman.

"It's a point of view shared by others," said Kit. "Let's see who you really are."

Kit leaned down and unsnapped her helmet and gently removed it, exposing her face for the first time.

"Well, I'll be damned," said Kit. He recognized the woman as the lady from the registrar's office who had been so rude to him when he had gone there to request a list of the art majors at the university.

Kit kneeled down next to the woman. "You know, they say what goes around, comes around," said Kit. "It looks like you could be the poster child for that saying."

"Fuck you," said the woman.

"I got it the first time," said Kit.

Seconds later two more patrol cars screeched to a halt by Kit and the woman. One was the University police and the other was a Laramie Police Department cruiser. The cops ran up to Kit, who had his hands in the air.

Four hours later, Kit, Swifty, and Shirley were walking out of the Laramie Police Department headquarters building. They had spent a lot of time answering questions. The police had initially treated them like suspects in a crime. Then Kit suggested they get in touch with Deputy Parcell. After he arrived, things calmed down and the tide shifted. Plus, the footage from the camera and the audio from the radio fully supported their story. Swifty had attached a small recording device to the radios and he could play back everything that was said.

Kit got a blanket out of the truck and put it around Shirley as he tucked her into the passenger seat of the truck. Satisfied with his work, he slipped into the driver's seat and drove out of the police parking lot. Swifty followed in Shirley's yellow and black Jeep. Half an hour later they were parking in front of their cabins at Woods Landing.

Swifty took care of the horses while Kit carried an exhausted and emotionally drained Shirley into their cabin. Kit undressed Shirley, got her dressed in her pajamas and put her in bed. Kit slipped quietly out of the cabin and took a seat on the steps of the front porch.

He was soon joined by Swifty, who thoughtfully had brought along a bottle of Eagle Rare bourbon and two paper cups.

Swifty opened the bottle and poured each cup about half full.

"To Shirley," said Swifty, and he and Kit tapped their paper cups and took a long swig of good whiskey.

The two men sat in silence for a few moments. Then Swifty produced two excellent cigars from his shirt pocket. He lit his first and then lit Kit's. They each drew deeply on the cigars and then expelled the smoke, watching as it dissipated in the evening air.

"What the hell happened with Shirley?" asked Swifty.

Kit looked over at his best friend. He had listened carefully to everything that had been said at the police station and then pieced together what he heard from the Laramie cops and Deputy Parcell. He still wasn't sure he had the whole story, but was sure he had the most important parts.

"Shirley heard what we were saying on the radio," said Kit. "She heard when the gal on the motorcycle took off and was getting away."

"I guessed that, but what did she do?" asked Swifty.

"She'd been watching me when I opened the gun locker and she memorized the combination. She ran to the back of the truck and opened the gun locker. She took out the 870, checked to see it was loaded, and ran down to the end of the block."

Kit paused to take a draw on his cigar. Then he resumed.

"She got to the end of the block and went to one knee and waited. She knew the motorcycle rider would have to come through that intersection, and she was right."

"When the motorcycle entered the intersection, Shirley shot out the front tire from a distance of about fifteen yards. Then she shot out the rear tire. The bike went out of control and over on its side and slid. The rider got thrown off and she slid as well. Shirley ran over to the rider and that's when I showed up.

"You must have been quite a sight," said Swifty with a grin. "A full-blown Wyoming cowboy drivin' a damn hippie VW van."

"I grabbed what was available," said Kit.

Swifty just laughed.

Chapter Thirty-Two

The next morning, Kit opened the door to the cabin while balancing a tray full of breakfast. He entered the cabin to find Shirley sitting up in bed.

"Good morning, sunshine," said Kit with a smile on his face. "How are we feeling this morning?"

Shirley jumped out of bed and ran across the room to Kit. Kit saw her coming and quickly put the tray on the small table. Shirley practically jumped into his arms and began peppering his mouth, face, and eyes with kisses.

Kit offered no resistance and when Shirley had covered every available space with kisses, she leaned back and looked Kit in the eye.

"The next time I insist on you taking me along on one of these dangerous missions, your job is to lock me in a room until I come to my senses," she said.

"Duly noted," said Kit.

Shirley released Kit and stepped back from him. "Oh, God, I must look a mess. I need a shower. Just put that breakfast tray on the table and I'll be right out," she said.

Twenty minutes later a cleaner, and happier Shirley emerged from the bathroom. She ignored Kit and pulled out a chair and began shoveling the now somewhat cold breakfast into her mouth.

"I'm sorry, is the food is little cold?" said Kit.

"The food is fine. I was famished," said Shirley. She paused in her eating binge and looked across the table at Kit. "What happened yesterday wasn't a dream, was it?" she asked.

"No, Shirley," said Kit. "It wasn't a dream. You handled yourself like a pro. I'm very proud of you. Without you that bitch might have gotten away, and we had no idea who she was."

"I'm glad she didn't get away, but I never want to do anything like that again. I'm a nurse. My job is savings lives, not shooting at people," she said.

"I don't think shooting at tires qualifies as manslaughter," said a smiling Kit.

"Maybe not, but I'm done going on missions with you and Swifty. Never again," said Shirley.

"You have no idea how happy that makes me," said a smiling Kit.

Shirley finished her breakfast and pushed her plate away. She took a sip of lukewarm coffee and grimaced. "What are you up to, today?" she asked

"You, me, and Swifty are going to take a little trip to Laramie to have a sit-down with Deputy Parcell and get the final story on what really happened," said Kit.

"Then we'll be done with this whole mess?" asked Shirley.

"Then we'll be done," said Kit.

"Good, because I have to be back to work tomorrow at six A.M.," said Shirley.

"Already?" said Kit.

"It's not my fault you spent my free time chasing after bad guys and bad gals," said Shirley.

Kit just sat back and smiled. Shirley left to freshen up. A half hour later, Shirley reappeared out of the bathroom. She looked sensational in a pair of tight jeans, a light blue top, and cowboy boots. Her hair was no longer in a pony-tail and fell down on her shoulders. She looked terrific to Kit.

They left the cabin and found Swifty asleep on his bed in his cabin. He jumped up and joined them as they drove to Laramie in the truck.

They hadn't driven more than four miles before Swifty was sound asleep in the back seat.

"How does he do that?" asked Shirley.

"You mean Swifty?" replied Kit.

"Yes, Swifty. How does he just fall asleep anywhere?" asked Shirley.

"He learned it in the army," said Kit. "I've learned he can sleep in any positon, anyplace, any time of day or night, and in any weather. When he gets the chance, he catches some sleep. The amazing thing is when he wakes up, he's not groggy or confused. He always wakes up ready to go."

"I tried to do that in nursing school," said Shirley. "Sometimes it worked and sometimes it didn't."

"I think Swifty's just a natural," said Kit with a smile on his face.

Shirley smiled back at him and leaned her head on Kit's shoulder as he drove.

Soon, Kit was pulling into the parking lot of the Sheriff's office. As soon as he stopped the truck and shut off the engine, Swifty was awake and sliding out of the back seat. Kit just looked at Shirley. They both smiled.

Ten minutes later they were seated in the small conference room they had been in before. Deputy Parcell sat down across from them with a large file folder in his hand.

"I suppose you folks would like to know what's been happening in the investigation since yesterday?" asked Parcell with a grin on his face.

"Yes, we certainly would," said Kit.

"Basically, the story line runs this way," said Parcell. "Bernice Sandoval, the assistant registrar of the university, was trying to help a part-time, some-time art student named Rose Wilson. Rose is one of those dreamer types of creative people who sort of drifts in and out of the academic world. She's been attending a class here and a class there for over three years."

"Rose was trying to get into a class for which she did not have the necessary prerequisites. She was trying to convince Ms. Sandoval she had experience in art even though she didn't have the required courses. She told Sandoval about her stay at Mr. Kelly's cabin and seeing the original Russell letters framed on Mr. Kelly's walls. Ms. Sandoval encouraged Rose to talk about the letters. Rose went so far as to show Ms. Sandoval the approximate location of Kelly's cabin, which she said was above the Nordstrom Ranch on the Big Laramie River."

"So, that's how she got the location of the cabin," said Swifty.

"We think so," said Parcell. "Then Ms. Sandoval used some help from a friend in the geography department to help her pinpoint the location."

"Was the friend involved in the heist?" asked Kit.

"No," said the deputy. "Her friend had no idea why Ms. Sandoval was looking for the location of the cabin. Sandoval found out about Sid Wooly through a friend and managed to contact him anonymously. She kept it that way and gave directions to him by phone. She also used a voice modifier to disguise her voice on the phone. I listened to it, and it makes you sound like Darth Vader."

"Who the hell is Darth Vader?" asked Swifty.

"You'll have to excuse Swifty," said Kit. "He doesn't get out much."

Parcell laughed. Swifty shot Kit a dirty look.

"Why did she set up the trap for us?" asked Kit. "She already had the letters?"

"She had planned to just lie low and hang on to the letters for a few months to allow things to die down. Then she planned to use an intermediary to sell the letters directly to hard core Russell collectors. When she found out about you and Swifty investigating the disappearance of Mr. Kelly, and then your discovery of the theft, she got frightened. She decided you two and Rose had to disappear. She even offered Sid more money to get rid of the Collins brothers after you were disposed of," said Parcell.

"What's happened to the Russell letters?" asked Kit.

"Sandoval had them hidden in a rented storage unit in Cheyenne," said the deputy. "She got careless and rented it in her own name. In addition, she kept the paperwork on the lease which we found."

"Do you have the letters?" asked Kit.

"The Russell letters are stored safe and sound in our locked evidence room," said the deputy.

"Would it be possible for us to see the letters?" asked Kit. "We went through a lot to try to get them back to old Ted, and I'd kind of like to see what they look like."

"I don't see why not," said the deputy. "I'll have an evidence room clerk bring them here to the conference room. It'll be a lot easier to see them here."

"That would be great," said Kit.

The deputy left the room and while he was gone, a female deputy brought a pot of coffee, three cups and some creamer and sugar to the conference room. Kit, Swifty, and Shirley all took a cup. They were sipping on their coffee when the deputy reappeared in front of a uniformed clerk who was pushing a four-wheeled cart.

The clerk wore white linen gloves and carefully laid each of the six framed Russell letters out on the conference room table.

"This is amazing," said Kit. "All of these letters are addressed to Ted's father. The handwriting and the grammar are terrible, but the messages are heartwarming."

"The water color pictures and scenes drawn on the tops, bottoms, and margins of the letters are simply awesome," said Shirley. "The man was an amazing talent."

"I think this letter is the one old Ted is most proud of," said Swifty. He pointed to a letter with the scene of a mounted night hawk cowboy dressed in a yellow slicker. The night hawk was riding guard on a herd of cow ponies during a thunderstorm. The letter referred to Russell's time with Ted's father as night hawks.

"This is the letter old Ted called the Night Hawk Letter," said Kit.

"It's beautiful," said Shirley.

Swifty just looked at the letter and smiled.

After the clerk had returned the letters to the evidence room, Kit, Swifty, and Shirley said their good-byes to Deputy Parcell and thanked him for all his help.

"I'm the one who should be thankin' you folks," said the deputy. "You helped solve a tough case. Without your help, Ms. Sandoval might just have gotten away with this."

"We owed it to old Ted to get his letters back," said Kit. "Those letters were written to his dad and they belong in the Kelly family."

All of them shook hands and Kit, Swifty, and Shirley were back in the truck. "Where to?" asked Kit.

Swifty started to say something, but he was interrupted by Shirley.

"Back to the cabins," said Shirley in a determined voice.

"You need time to pack?" asked Kit.

"That and other important things," said a smiling Shirley.

Kit wisely shut his mouth and headed back to Woods Landing.

Swifty showed his wisdom by keeping quiet in the back seat of the truck.

CHAPTER THIRTY-THREE

TEN MONTHS LATER

Kit and Swifty drove down from Kemmerer to Woods Landing. They had accepted an invitation from Ted Kelly to a party at the Woods Landing café. Shirley had been invited as well, but she was unable to get off work at the hospital.

When they arrived, they exited the truck and Swifty paused to check himself out in the side mirror of the truck. Kit looked at his friend with a knowing glance. The two cowboys were dressed in new jeans, denim shirts, polished cowboy boots, and Stetson cream-colored cowboy hats.

Kit led the way into the café door. Tess waved to them from the bar and they continued into the dining room. They no sooner walked into the room when they were greeted warmly by none other than Ted Kelly. Ted was clean shaven and his hair was fashionably cut. He wore new bib overalls and a new blue denim shirt. Ted vigorously shook their hands. Old Ted had recovered well from his injuries and standing at his side was a woman that Kit did not recognize at first. Then he realized he was looking at a cleaned up and well-dressed Eleanor. She had a grin on her face, and she gave Kit and Swifty each a big hug.

There was quite a crowd. The party-goers included Deputy Parcell, several officers from the Laramie Police Department, Hoppy Cassidy, Cal Biggs, Shorty Dawson, and Jenna Richards and her husband. Other guests included old Randy Scott, Priscilla and Ned Snyder along with Trace Bitters. Nels and Betty Nordstrom were there along with Thelma and Louise from the general store.

Tess and her daughter Bess were busy providing drinks from the bar and a big table was set out, groaning under the weight of a huge display of food provided in buffet style.

After about half an hour, Mustang Kelly, dressed in a sleek green dress set off with a string of pearls around her neck, walked up to a small podium and asked everyone to take a seat. When all were seated, Tang addressed the crowd.

Tang welcomed everyone and thanked them for coming. Then she got to the reason for the party.

"My grandfather has lived much of the last thirty years of his life as a recluse. He had little use for people and went out of his way to avoid them. That included his family. When he moved up to the foothills above the Big Laramie River, he fully intended to live the rest of his life alone."

"What happened to him a year ago taught him that he was wrong. He learned that a man in Wyoming is never alone. He has his friends, his neighbors, and his family. People in Wyoming help each other in good times and bad. My grandfather is usually a man of few words, but he has some things he wishes to say to all of you."

Tang then motioned to her grandfather and he joined her at the podium.

Old Ted Kelly looked out over the people gathered in the room. Then he slowly spoke. It was obvious that public speaking was not his thing, but he had things he needed to say.

"I'd like to thank all of you folks for your help and support. I'm damn proud to call you friends and neighbors."

Ted paused. "I'd especially like to thank a certain lady who stopped to care for a man she'd never met and succeeded in nursing me back to health." Ted pointed to Eleanor, and she blushed as the crowd clapped to show their approval.

"I had them Russell letters set up on easels at the back of the room, so you folks could get a look at them," said Ted. "I've decided to sell one of them to help me get by in my old age. I'm donating four of the letters to the University of Wyoming historical museum. I want folks in Wyoming to always be able to see some of the works of one of the greatest western artists to ever live."

This announcement got another round of applause. Ted beamed. "I'm keeping the one letter I call The Night Hawk as I always felt the figure in the drawing was my daddy. This letter will stay in my family."

Ted paused to wipe away a tear which had mysteriously appeared on his cheek.

"I doubt I'd be here today if not for the efforts of two men who I'd never met before," said Ted. "I'd like Kit Andrews and Swifty Olson to please come up here."

Kit and Swifty looked at each other in surprise, and then they rose to their feet and made their way to stand next to Ted at the podium.

"I know I can never repay you two for what you did for me, but I do have a little surprise for you," said a smiling Ted. With that he motioned to the back of the crowd.

From the back of the crowd came Ted's granddaughter, Mustang Kelly. Her bright red hair seemed to shine in the lights of the dining room.

Tang came up to the front of the room. A waiter burdened with some objects followed her. When she reached the front of the room, she stood next to her grandfather.

"It is my distinct honor to present a gift of appreciation from my grandfather to Kit and Swifty," said Tang.

Tang retrieved two framed prints of the Russell letter her grandfather referred to as the Night Hawk Letter. She handed one to Swifty and gave him a hug. Then she turned to Kit and handed him the other print. Tang gave Kit a hug and then she kissed him hard on the lips. Before she released her hug, she whispered in his ear. "I just thought I'd give you a sample of what you're missing," she said.

When Tang stepped away from Kit, the crowd was applauding and Kit's face was bright red.

"Actually, I have something to present to Ms. Kelly," said Kit. With that, he reached inside his jacket and pulled out the addressed and stamped red envelope containing the birthday card he had found in Ted's cabin. Kit handed the card to a very surprised Tang. She proceeded to give him another hug and another hard kiss on the lips. The crowd laughed and applauded again.

After the party had wound down, Tang came up to Kit when she saw he and Swifty were preparing to leave.

"Please send me your bill, tenderfoot," she said.

"I'll mail it to you," said Kit.

"I plan on showing up in Kemmerer to pay it in person," said Tang, with a smirk on her face. "Who knows, there might even be a little bonus for you."

Swifty was doubled over laughing at the embarrassed look on his partner's face.

"I'm sorry, Tang," said Kit. "I'll be glad to see you, but I've already got a girlfriend."

"We'll see about that," said a smiling Tang.

Kit and Swifty quickly exited the café and were soon driving well above the speed limit in the direction of Kemmerer, Wyoming.

THE END

ACKNOWLEDGMENTS

Woods Landing, Wyoming is a real place. This story, all the characters, and the locations are all creations of my imagination.

I got the idea of for *The Night Hawk* after attending an exhibit of Charles Russell's work at the Longmont Museum. I had seen examples of his illustrated letters in the Buffalo Bill Museum in Cody, Wyoming, and in the Charles Russell Museum in Great Falls, Montana. A book by Russell's wife contains many of his illustrated letters, and I was struck by the letter with a water color illustration of a mounted night hawk dressed in a yellow slicker.

This is my sixth novel, and the fifth in my series about Kit Andrews and Swifty Olson. I hope you have enjoyed reading it as much as I have in writing it.

Please feel free to let me know what you thought about the book and contact me at rwcallis@aol.com. Praise and criticism are equally welcome.

My thanks to my patient and loving wife, Nancy, who serves as proofreader, critic, and my main support team. I also received help from Mary Marlin, Kerry Wong, and my son, Steve Tibaldo. The three of them read segments of the book as it was written, and offered suggestions and their impressions. I listened to all of them and utilized many. I also received a tremendous amount of help from an old high school classmate, Shirley Nordstrom Roth. Shirley offered to help proofread the manuscript as it was written. She did a great job and proposed changes and suggestions, all of which I listened to. All of these folks were extremely helpful in getting this book written.

You write because you enjoy writing. I enjoy creating a story about something real and historic and then letting my imagination take over. When people read my books, and enjoy them, it gives me a tremendous sense of satisfaction. Thank you for being one of my readers. Kit and Swifty live only in my imagination. When I think about them, they come to life. What could be more fun than that?

Previous novels by Robert W. Callis:

1. Kemmerer
2. Hanging Rock
3. Buckskin Crossing
4. Ghosts of Skeleton Canyon
5. The Horse Holder

I am currently working on novel number seven. This untitled novel is a story about Kit and his sudden discovery of an old family secret, set in the Big Horn Mountains of Wyoming.

Printed in the United States
by Baker & Taylor Publisher Services

Printed in the United States
By Bookmasters